Be Her

Emma Ellis

This book is written in British English

This is a dark novel. Readers should be aware that it contains references to drug use including spiking, violence, sexual misconduct, and murder.

Chapter One

Layla

I jolt in my chair as Katarina walks through the apartment. She isn't due back for hours. I should have some time to myself without worrying about what Katarina's going to say or do, but instead of relaxing, my muscles stiffen and the ache in my neck returns.

She holds her hands out in front of her, parading them through to the kitchen sink without so much of a word as an explanation. I stare at her, though this is nothing new. She's used to having everyone's attention. But my look is not one of admiration and awe. My eyes are wide with dread at the blood coating her hands. It has dried, but under the dim kitchen light it's clear her palms are caked with thick deposits crusting around her knuckles. As red as her nail polish.

My eyebrows arch as she turns on the faucet, leaving a crimson smudge on the tap. I stand to help, silently passing her the soap, its floral scent not enough to overpower the coppery tang, and my stomach rumbles. It's primal, the scent of blood and my churning stomach. It could go either way: hunger or nausea.

My stomach would also growl all those years ago during biology lessons at school, and I'm still riddled with the same shame. My cheeks would flush as the other kids stared, like it made me some cavewoman. With my scruffy hair, I probably looked like one. One more reason the kids were mean. One more memory I have to shut away and forget.

Katarina holds up her hands to inspect them, clean now, so I pass her a towel. It's dark brown, though it shouldn't stain if there is any residue. I push the thought aside, then get to work cleaning the taps. I'm always cleaning up after Katarina. It is becoming a habit for both of us.

'Are you going to explain?' I summon the courage to ask as I wonder if I really want to know.

Katarina passes me back the damp towel. 'I'd rather show you,' she says with a glint in her eye, then licks her bottom lip. 'Come on, Layla. You'll be pleased this time.'

I look at Katarina's face, familiar yet alien. Whatever she's been up to hasn't so much as smudged her makeup. Not even a hair is out of place. Her clothes are clean, though it isn't like the blood would show on her lacy black top. It's too cold outside for such attire, but Katarina never feels the cold. It's like she's made of ice.

The glint in her eyes sparkles like a black diamond, darker than they have ever been. She was everything I wanted to be once. Now she is everything I fear.

I look away. I've been sucked into her misdeeds before, so I shake my head and try to think of other things instead. I used to be able to distract myself so easily. When did it become impossible to lose focus? I am not the same person I once was. She has changed me. Bit by bit, she is eroding away who I am, who I once was. Has that been her plan all along?

I glance around the kitchen and force my mind to go to the leftovers in the fridge, the bottle of wine that needs finishing, the late hour, my plans for an early morning run tomorrow, and the work I have to catch up on. Remedying all those things will please me. Tasks give me fulfilment, some sense of relaxation or purpose. Dealing with the aftermath of whatever Katarina has been up to will most likely not.

Katarina's pillowy lips curl up into a smile, so smug and so certain this time, more so than last time. And the time before.

My breath shortens as my mind turns over one question: *What the hell has she done now?*

Chapter Two

Two months earlier

Layla

Video game development was never where I wanted to end up. I had brighter prospects once, but I guess the universe has other plans. Brains aren't enough. Big jobs require women to have the Three Big Cs, the recruitment consultant told me: charisma, confidence, and contacts. If I had those, I'd have called him a big C and found a decent job without his help.

Sitting at my desk, mousy brown hair falling unstyled over my shoulders, shielding my profile from view, I gnaw at the skin around my fingernails on one hand and type code with the other. The rigid plastic seat digs into my sit bones and offers no back support. You'd think such a rich company could spring for padded seats, but our comfort is way down their priority list.

Every few seconds, I glance down at my IMAtech. The Internal Metadata App shows the graph climbing as I bank my productive seconds at twork. I pause to sip some water from my bottle, but as soon as my typing halts, the computer informs the app and it flashes orange. The graph halts its climb, then flashes red as it descends. Three productive seconds that drink cost me. Not so bad.

'Psst!' Joel's whispering is unnecessary. No one is listening, no one can afford the distraction.

'What?'

'I'm over a hundred minutes down and it's only Wednesday.'

I don't look up and don't look surprised. Because I'm not. If my colleague spent as much time working as he does moaning about work, he wouldn't be so behind. 'Best get back to it then,' I say.

'It's bollocks.'

'Yep,' I say, still not looking up. 'Yes, it is.'

He huffs, then sinks back in his chair and groans. 'I tried typing nonsense for a while yesterday.'

I stop to look around the partition wall at him. He has his bottom lip out like a sulking child, the food stains down his shirt only adding to the image. 'You know that doesn't work. It monitors productive seconds, not wasted seconds.'

'I know. I just—'

I turn back to my screen and the endless monotony. Humouring Joel's nonsense is only wasting more time. If everyone grumbles as much as him, the country would be stuck in the stock market crash forever instead of clawing its way back out.

I leave my fingernails alone for a moment to rub my eyes, one at a time, so I can keep the other eye on my screen. The office lights are too bright, but they're supposed to aid productivity and stave off any tiredness. At least that's what we were told the day the wattage was hiked up. Though a quick glance around the office at rows of desks tended to by yawning faces disproves that theory. The sun beams in through the glass wall at the entrance to the office, bright enough to induce a migraine if facing the wrong way. Yet the glaring light offers no extra warmth as the air con constantly blasts out. Funny that they think to keep the staff awake, they have to make us as cold as a corpse.

On the wall at the front of the office, the collective IMAtech seconds are displayed. Four thousand seconds down so far this week. I'm breaking even on my target, but I'll be punished the same with my bonus being docked. Like the staff are a swarm of locusts rather than individual people.

The office is quiet enough besides the percussion of keyboards tapping that serve as a tenacious metronome, stretching out for hours each day. I hear that sound in my sleep. It's a constant tinnitus reminding me of the tedium that is always to come.

Despite the quietness, a thicker silence descends as the footsteps approach. Six of them walk in unison towards the boardroom. The clip-clop of well-heeled shoes makes every one of my hairs stand on end. The board members who run the company are like hornets to the honeybees. They can pile on the heat and devour each of us if they want.

'Keep up the good work, guys,' Adam Ward says. *The patronising arse.* 'Keep banking those seconds.'

I don't need to look up to know who spoke. Adam Ward's voice is unmistakable. How had Joel described it once? Like a weasel choking on cat shit. I grit my teeth and crack my knuckles, then continue to type, the tension in my hands slowing me slightly. Four seconds are knocked off my IMAtech tally.

I dare the briefest glance up when they're in line with my desk, and ball my fists. Another few seconds lost, but right now I don't care. It's an impulse, for I hate them more than anything.

Peter Ward, the company owner, complete with his silver-streaked hair and donning his standard pinstripe suit that would have looked better a few decades ago, leads the pack. One of the wealthiest men in Britain and too tight to update his wardrobe. His support of the Clarity Directive shows his attitudes towards women are even more ancient than his taste in clothes, like he's hoping for some renaissance of the 1950s. A hundred years have passed since then, yet it's like he and other wealthy men arrived in this decade through some time warp, bringing their ideals with them. *No means no, but otherwise, it's yes,* was the slogan that got the Directive passed. As catchy as it is moral.

His aftershave is strong and has the notes only men of a certain age would consider wearing. Woodsy and spicy. A cocktail of testosterone-fuelled ego. I fight the need to gag as he walks past.

His son, Adam, holds his chin higher than the rest, looking down on what will one day all be his, even though he's never lifted a finger to achieve anything. No chance he has an IMAtech chip under his skin. He probably even gets a full eight-hours sleep a night. From what I've read about him, his duties consist of rinsing the company's finances to fund his habits and rehab, as well as condescending speeches that he obviously thinks are motivating. The sight of him only adds to my nausea.

They don't acknowledge me or notice my glance. I've spoken to all of them at some point, but they would likely have forgotten me by now. I've one of those faces, and one of those personalities. Easily dismissed, I've not a single memorable feature. Average height, build, the sort of smile that has never lit up a room. I'm of as much interest to them as the chair I sit on.

Adam Ward commended me for my work once, as if he really knew anything about me. It was just buzzwords, the same crap he says to everyone. Every time he feels the desire to speak to the lesser people, he comes out with some sanctimonious bullshit, the sort of stuff they print on canvas for gaudy living rooms and stitch into sofa cushions. Antonia, my line manager, greets them as they walk past, her face reddened with fluster and her voice at least an octave higher than usual. Antonia looks like the sort to have such cushions. I'd bet half a day's seconds Antonia has *Live, Laugh, Love* embroidered onto a dishcloth.

'You've turned a corner. Well done,' Adam Ward said once. Whatever.

Problem is, if you turn too many corners, you end up back where you started.

The six of them walk up the stairs to the office on the first floor, its glass wall giving the board members a towering view down on me and the minions below. The Powerhouse of Productivity, they call the office floor, capital Ps clearly accented, ever since IMAtech was forced upon us and no one got so much as a toilet break without it counting against us. Every employee has their app on display always, ticking away the day's work seconds, the app deciding if each second is useful enough to be counted. To make everyone more efficient, they say. To remind everyone of their own demise, I think. Life is short enough, and internment comes in many guises. Life in one prison, death delivers another. That is what IMAtech means to me.

Not seconds banked, but seconds wasted.

The CEOs all believe in the product, touting it as a game-changer for the workforce. It's going to bring the corporate world into the twenty-first century, they said when they injected the chip under the staff's skin.

Why wouldn't they believe in it? No one has died yet.

Well, no one important enough.

Chapter Three

Layla

My Greenwich flat is small for one person, let alone two. But any place to live in London is too expensive for one wage alone, unless that one wage is board-level or comes with some inherited wealth. A woman trying to rent alone invites questions: Daddy's money, or is she boosting her income through less scrupulous methods? I'd raised many eyebrows when I took on this lease, and if they made such assumptions, then fine. A need for a roof is a more pressing need than that of my reputation. London is a big enough city. Gossip doesn't stain one woman for long.

I arrive home exhausted, note the grimy scent of dirty dishes coming from the kitchen and kick off my functional flat shoes, putting them neatly next to Katarina's heels that lay on their sides. When I was showing potential housemates around, the other people all wore their shoes through the house. Katarina took hers off at the door. Polite, I thought. House-trained. Funny that Katarina's shoes being left so untidily at the door are now one of the things that annoy me the most.

Me and Katarina hadn't crossed paths in nearly fifteen years before she showed up to view the spare room, yet I recognised her instantly. How could I not? Everyone at school knew who she was. She stands out everywhere she goes. Katarina knew exactly who I was too, which was surprising, since I was never popular enough for her to notice when we were at school. But then she came into my home, and asked me how I'd been all these years, and for the first time in my life, I felt seen.

I walk through to the kitchen and flick the lights on since I'm home so late and it's dark outside. I side-step through the kitchen to keep my back to the pile of dishes I can't face yet. Just two weeks ago, I was in the staffroom at work and one of the board members, Diego Smith, came in and nodded at the dirty dishes there and told me to get on with it. 'The men are all too busy,' he said.

I should have thrown one of the soiled plates at his plasticky face. Instead, I did the dishes and lost seven minutes off my IMAtech total. The sight of more dirty dishes now makes me regret not carving lines into his Botox-smoothed skin.

My back is starting to resemble a weeping willow tree, permanently hunched over from long days at my computer with no break. I stretch out my neck, then my eyes widen at the new fridge–freezer. Brand new. I've been nagging the lettings agency for weeks about the old one being broken, and they'd been fobbing me off with every excuse under the sun as to why they hadn't replaced it. I open the freezer door and am greeted by a blast of cold air. For the first time in ages, I am able to take some ice from the freezer. I sit at the table, holding the ice, cooling my knuckles in an attempt to take the day's strain away.

Katarina emerges from her bedroom, dressed in a little black dress with lace around the neckline. My poorly-fitted trouser suit must make me look like a pile of laundry next to her. Katarina always says I can borrow her clothes, but that isn't who I am. I'd feel like some imposter wearing such items with more skin on show than fabric, with more curves accentuated than concealed.

'How are you liking the new freezer?' she asks.

'I'm amazed they sorted it finally.'

'Yeah,' she says, taking her hair out of rollers. 'I called them yesterday, and they sorted it today.'

'What! Seriously?' My voice squeaks with surprise, though it shouldn't. Katarina gets what she wants, always. 'They've been dodging replacing it for ages.' I should have written a list for her to complain about: the sporadic hot water; the cupboards that need the hinges tightening; the windows that don't close properly.

Katarina's smile looks more than a little smug. 'What can I say? I speak their language. You look like shit, by the way,' she says after the briefest glance my way.

'Thanks,' I say with a tut. As if I need reminding.

'Let me guess, those pricks came into the office again?'

'The board members? Yep.'

'And they still don't have to wear that torture device?' Katarina points to the red bump on my collarbone where the IMAtech chip was injected.

'Nope. Special addition just for us minions.'

Katarina sits and runs her fingers through her hair to separate the curls. They fall in a way that defies gravity. 'They're arseholes. Especially the top brass. You should just punch his face in.' She says this so nonchalantly, it's as if she's giving cooking instructions rather than suggesting assault.

'The CEO of Ward Innovation Technologies? One of the richest men in the country. My employer. Yeah, why don't I just punch his face in.' I say the last bit with a lilt to highlight the ridiculousness of it.

'I would,' Katarina says.

'No shit.'

I dump the half-melted ice in the sink, wincing at the sight of the dirty dishes, then open the fridge. There isn't much to eat, even less to eat it off. Some cheese and leftover pasta. Katarina has cleared out the food and not replaced anything. Again.

'One stock market crash and now rich people think they can get away with anything.' Katarina holds up a compact and applies what looks like a third coat of mascara.

'That's because they can.' I sit back down with a thump and pick at the leftovers. I'm not as hungry as I thought I was, or perhaps the food is not appetising enough.

Peter Ward is credited as being a man of the people, of saying out loud what everyone else is thinking. The anti-woke brigade made their mark last year when *#behave* was trending for months, and anyone who spoke against the status quo was silenced into oblivion.

'The economic crash last year,' Peter Ward said during a live TV interview one morning—just before the last elections and it was clear who Peter Ward was backing. 'We all know what caused that, and it takes a brave man to stand up and say it.'

I was watching this broadcast while drinking my morning coffee. My pyjamas are still stained from where I spat it out.

'Quotas. That was the issue. Equality. This idea that generations of evolution should be undone because those lower down the evolutionary chain are offended. We never had a crash like that before the equality lambs started bleating. When a board of people, let's face it, men, who know what they're doing run the company, the company does well. Companies doing well are the backbone of this economy. You want a decent return on your pension? Silence the nonsense. Support common-sense and let the men do their jobs.'

The interviewer, Kammy Parsons, I think it was, took a while to think of her next question. I was egging her on from my living room with Katarina sat next to me, begging for Kammy to shoot the man down.

'And before you say anything,' Peter Ward continued. 'Ward Innovation Technologies is an extremely diverse company. We have a queer on the board, and a woman. Malorie Baxter invested a great deal of her father's fortune in the company, under her husband's guidance. She is an example of a good, solid woman.'

'So, rich women only are welcome in the workplace?' Kammy Parson asked.

'Don't you put words in my mouth. That's such a woman thing to do. But in answer to that question, no. They just need to prove they can do the job as well as a man, instead of us being pressured into assuming that and screwing our books as a result. We don't want women out of the workforce entirely. There are plenty of professions designed for women. Care work, teaching, medical jobs even. But tech requires something different, and it is tech that keeps the stock market moving.'

I think I turned the TV off after that, not wanting to award him with the airtime. I see enough of his unflappable face at work.

'What's your tally for the week?' Katarina asks as I load up IMAtech. I shouldn't check it at home. I should be able to leave work and shut that part of my day away, but the red bump injected under my skin never lets me forget.

'I've made up for any lost time,' I say. 'I'm nearly two minutes up.'

'And look how tired you are.' She inspects me properly now, her made-up face full of scrutiny. 'Those dark circles are going to take a lot more than concealer to cover up. *You* need sleep. Rest. Proper rest.'

Katarina has a way of making eye contact that peels away any barrier, exposing my soul. I usually prefer to stare at my lap or computer screen.

I yawn and reach my arms behind my back and crack my shoulders. 'Once the next game is released, I'm sure they'll cut us some slack. We're ahead of schedule.'

'I'm just looking out for you. Someone has to. I was never there for you at school, and I should have been. Let me make it up to you now.'

I smile. Katarina might be crap at doing her share of the chores, but she is a friend. My only friend. 'Thanks.'

'I mean it. I'm here for you. Whatever you need.'

'You could do the dishes?'

She laughs. 'You know what I mean. It's what friends do. I just don't want you to end up like—'

'Don't say her name!' I hold my hands to my ears. 'Don't you *ever* say her name.'

Chapter Four

Layla

Katarina mentioning her name would be like a slap in the face. It hammers it home, that I'll never know her embrace again. I've tried to forget, to shove her to the back of my mind, to get over her, but it's impossible. I lost a part of me when she died. Waking every day, knowing I won't hear Isobel's voice, makes the hours stretch out for eternity. No sound is as sweet as her voice, no sight as bright as her face.

I have so few memories of her to cherish. There's a void inside that is meant to be filled with those. Instead, those memory banks are empty. The relationship that was never given the time to develop. We're still mid-way through a chess game on my phone. It's Isobel's turn. She probably would have moved her bishop.

We first spoke in the WIT staff room. Why they bother putting chairs in that room is a mystery, since no one ever has the time to sit in there. A dash in and out to get a cuppa even wastes too many seconds. On the wall are posters of smiling staff—stock images, no real WIT employee ever smiles that much—underneath written: *Be the best version of you!*

Isobel stood right next to one of those posters, making some fruity herbal tea that smelled like sweets. It was hard not to notice her. With her pink hair and flowery Doc Martens, she walked through like a breath of fresh air. We smiled at each other. She made some quip about the daily grind, and I laughed in a way that made me sound like a clown on helium. Later, she told me she thought my laugh was unique and alluring, which made me laugh even more.

I went home thinking of nothing but that staff room encounter, though I didn't so much as know her name at the time.

It was a few days later when Katarina walked into my apartment, oozing confidence and glamour. Katarina would never shy away from speaking to someone she liked. Katarina would know exactly what to say and do. It was like the universe had sent a sign, an instruction manual, for this timid and awkward person to benefit from. She moved in that evening.

The next day, Katarina, her eyes lined in smoky pencil, her hair cascading down her back in silky waves, put her mirror away and sized me up in seconds with a side-eye.

'What's wrong? Something's up.'

Less than a day we'd been living together. Was it that obvious?

'I can always spot when something's wrong,' Katarina said. 'Let me guess, you like someone? Spill.'

I bit my lip for a second, searched the floor for my voice, then told Katarina all about the woman I admired so much.

Katarina listened, nodded, and her solution was so simple. 'Just say hello,' Katarina said, as if it would be that easy without even so much as a glass of wine in my system. 'Say her tea smells nice. Complement something.'

Katarina's advice stuck, and the next day at work, I imagined being Katarina, flicking well-styled hair over my shoulder, making eye contact with those come-to-bed eyes Katarina seems to always have. All I had to do was be more like Katarina.

'Hi,' I said to her when we were both in the staffroom. I tucked my hair behind my ear and did my best to hold my chin up and meet her gaze. 'Your tea smells interesting.'

She smiled. Her lips shone with pale pink gloss. 'Yeah, it's from a little tea shop in Hackney. Supposed to reduce stress and tiredness without caffeine, although I think that's nonsense. But it tastes nice.'

I sipped at my own tea with unsteady hands as my mouth dried. 'Hackney? That's where you commute from?'

'Yeah. The journey isn't so bad.'

I could visualise Katarina next to me, egging me on. *Keep this going! Keep this going!* Her encouragement like an awkwardness filter, sifting all self-doubt away.

'There's a little bar in Hackney I've been meaning to try out,' I said. 'Some Asian street food place I heard is nice.'

'Yeah, I know it. Well, maybe we could go, if you like?'

Her eyes were locked on mine, relaxed and expectant as I fought the desire to run or faint. Twelve rounds of fight or flight were erupting in my chest. I stayed standing, and despite my face being on fire with blush, I returned her smile.

'Yeah, I mean, yeah, that. . .that would be great.'

'Cool, well, I'm Isobel. Message me, and we'll make a plan. Sorry, can't chat much now. Super busy.'

'Oh, that's fine. And yeah, I'll message. Thanks.'

I was left giddy and breathless, the conversation playing over and over again in my head just to confirm that it really happened. Just being a little more Katarina, and I had a date.

We would laugh together later about how shy I felt, how I couldn't believe it when she asked me out. I'd tell her I was still pinching myself every moment we spent together.

Katarina had impressed on me some self-belief. Just being more like Katarina had granted me a relationship. Being more like Katarina had given me so much joy.

I've often wondered if I regret that day. The joy was brief, the pain is still ongoing. If I'd never spoken to her, maybe I wouldn't miss her so much now. Maybe my heart wouldn't be shattered like broken glass.

Maybe she wouldn't be dead.

Chapter Five

Katarina

I walk to work slowly, taking in the night air. Layla's inaction has made me crave the feeling of the breeze on my face and take some time to unwind. So many evenings we've had the same conversation. I've tried to express my concern for her, my desire to help, but she shuts down and won't listen. If I push the subject, it'll result in an argument again, with Layla storming off and slamming doors. Layla is physically breaking more and more as she just puts up with the crap WIT bestows on its employees. Mentally, she broke a while ago.

We were sitting in the living room when we found out about the accident, watching some early evening news program. A car accident in Greenwich, the newsreader reported. One woman dead, he said in some deadpan voice, like he was reading out the weather. Only thirty years old. I held on to her as she bent double; the wind sucked from her, a guttural cry as her loss shattered her bones. Her soul ripped to pieces. I held on so tight, my grip left bruises.

It was weeks later we found out the accident had happened because she'd fallen asleep at the wheel. We both knew whose fault that was. We both know who should pay.

As much as I have tried to nudge Layla into avenging her death, she is weak with grief. She's so different now from how she was before the accident, as if reborn from darkness. IMAtech makes Layla too exhausted and worried about her job to resist any pressure they pile on her. If it was the other way round, Isobel would put up a fight. That's who she was. She stood up for what she believed in. Layla needs some guidance in that department.

I've been unable to convince Layla that inaction is more exhausting than action. As I stomp my way to work, hot and tense, my deep-red lips stretch thin, and I imagine the WIT building burning to the ground, the plummy voices of the board members screaming in terror, their designer cufflinks banging against the glass as they try to smash their way free. Let them cry out in pain. Let their fear make them shit themselves. How glorious that would be! All those billionaires burning while soaked in their own excrement.

A warmth ripples through me, a contentment at the thought of their suffering. That should be how justice is served for Isobel. That would teach those pricks a lesson.

When I arrive outside the bar, I note the steamed-up windows from the crowd vaping outside, and when the door opens, the shoulder-to-shoulder groups I'll have to squeeze my way past with their wandering hands. I consider calling in sick and retreating to my apartment for an evening of wine and slippers on the sofa. But then I remember I need to pay rent and buy food. I remember my salary is likely a tenth of most of the bar customers, and so a night off is a luxury I can't afford. It's only the rich who can afford such a social life since the market crash. The recovery period the country is in has only served to fatten the wallets of those few.

I take a deep breath, roll my shoulders back, then barge my way in through Little London's front doors.

Davina has the music up too loud. I lift my shoulders when I'm closer to the speakers, like somehow that will deflect the noise. I wince my way through to the stereo and turn it down a notch, just enough so I can hear myself think. Davina shoots me a look—at least I think she does. It's hard to tell with her resting bitch face and permanently downturned fat lips. I've often wondered if she's had her lips filled with lead so she can't ever smile.

I shrug off the look and leave the volume lower. The customers don't seem to notice. The wait at the bar is three people deep, and hearing their orders will still be hard enough. Weekdays are always busier than weekends, the ethos being: Why waste a weekend hungover? Weekends are for retreating to the countryside, doing obscene things like hiking or going to a spa. Layla would agree, but then Layla would also think weekdays getting rat-arsed is a bad idea.

Sometimes I wonder how I put up with her.

I serve drinks without an ounce of charm. Every glass I slam on the bar, not caring what spills over the top. I state each customer's bill curtly with none of my usual smiles and small talk. To say I'm not in the mood tonight is an understatement.

Layla's tiredness and lack of desire for revenge is eating at me. Every time I see her it's like a tap on the shoulder, a niggling itch. Every time I think of Layla being overworked and underappreciated, whenever I think about what happened to Isobel because of that company, it makes me slam the drinks down even harder. Layla needs to grow a backbone instead of letting hers turn to mush.

Three broken martini glasses later, I conclude it's time to somehow take matters into my own hands. Pent up rage is not solving anything. No way am I going to let Layla end up like Isobel. I am going to make them pay. Even billionaires need to atone.

There's no point in waiting for revenge. What is it they say, a dish best served cold? No. Better to serve it piping hot, before the desire goes stale and sour. There's a sweetness to quick action when still ripe with grief. Fuck waiting any longer. We could all be dead tomorrow. With any luck, *he* will be.

Only an hour into my shift and I've made forty jaeger-bombs and thirty espresso martinis, on top of pouring countless beers and handing out bottles of wine. The smell is disgusting. I've never been able to stand the smell of coffee or Red Bull. The two together are like a bog.

Some dick at the end has hit on me twice, like he didn't get the message the first time. Like, no means yeah maybe in a minute, or ask more nicely please, you massive jerk. God, I hate him, and I don't even know him.

I front up to him with folded arms. 'No. Hear me? No. Prick.'

He shrugs and licks his lips in such a way I want to gag.

They say the Clarity Directive was designed to allow 'men to be men' in the workplace without the worry of oversensitive female outcry. The market crash that crippled the economy was apparently only recoverable if the men in charge of big businesses were not distracted by worries of women calling them out on their misdeeds. To remove ambiguity, they said. No means no, but any other word or silence means go right ahead. All it's done is mean men treat women like their own personal playthings. It's not all men, it's *City* men. Men in banking and on boards with tailored suits and weekly haircuts, men who think the gender pay gap is something they should aspire to increase and that women are theirs to mould, and men who think they own the world and the normal people owe them a debt.

Pricks, the lot of them.

When I'm spared whiffs of the drinks, it's the eggy sulphur smell of flatulence that irritates my nose. The amount of cocaine in the bar on any one night is enough to empty the bowels of all of Zone 2. They aren't even subtle about it, as untouchable as they all think they are. I half-expect them to rack their lines up on the bar and shrug at any voice of authority. Though they probably enjoy the pantomime of it, like sneaking off to the toilets in pairs adds to the illicit excitement. I kick them out when I catch them, loudly, make them feel small—or try to—then take their stash. I often find the little folded squares frosted with leftovers discarded in the toilets, or the tiny little baggies with too little left in the bottom to be worth the effort when those rich jerks could just score a fresh load. I keep them all in a lockbox under the bar. There may come a time when that will all be required.

The bar quietens down after a couple of hours. Davina goes home, and I'm left wiping up puddles of spilled whatever and responding to the slurred orders, while also chastising some men for fronting up to each other. It's always the same. Every night.

Only tonight, some different customers arrive.

It's the first time I've ever set eyes on Adam Ward in the flesh. Little London often serves drinks to wealthy CEOs, I've overheard the dregs of board meetings and bankers banging on about the FTSE or the S&P500, (yawn) but Adam Ward is even more highbrow than I'm accustomed to serving. And it isn't just him. He's joined by his fellow board member and even richer friend, the pharmaceutical company heir, Harry Baxter. Britain's two most prolific womanisers and eligible bachelors, if *OK magazine* is to be believed. Adam Ward has the sort of designer stubble that a barber must cut for him daily. My loathing for him runs so deep I feel it in my bones. It crawls over me and makes me shiver at the sight of him. Every thread of his designer clothing is paid for by the exhaustion of his employees. The rich prick gets richer while everyone else suffers. I watch his chiselled jaw move as he speaks and imagine being that barber and using the knife to cut through his scrawny neck. How satisfying it would be, like slicing through a cake, spilling justice from his arteries.

He has that smug arrogance that only comes when your net worth requires three commas. When mummy and daddy have handed everything to you tied up with a gold bow. I smirk as I watch them find a table, Adam sitting as Harry stays standing, talking for a moment, then makes his way to the bar.

My mind goes to Layla, of how tired she is, of her heartbreak. I was never kind to her at school, never defended her from the bullies back then. Now it's time to make up for that.

I check my reflection in a mirror behind the bar, wipe some of the shine from my forehead and yank my T-shirt down a bit. The perv at the end of the bar raises his eyebrows and I give him the finger. Sometimes being alluring is an asset, and right now, I intend to use that to my full advantage.

Chapter Six

Layla

At night, I dream of Isobel, her easy laughter, the way she'd bite her bottom lip after she spoke, the raspberry scent of her lip gloss. I yearn for more memories. We weren't together long, just a few months, and so the scant few I have are wearing out like an old videotape, fading and scratching. By the time day breaks, sadness and anger rest heavy on my limbs and I'm sluggish with grief. Katarina would tell me I should avenge Isobel, that I should take action against the company that made her so exhausted she crashed her car. How am I supposed to take revenge when I'm buckled by poverty and fatigue? Revenge is a pastime for those with the means to see it through.

When ideas of action come to my mind, when I try to push myself into doing something, anything, it usually results in me choking down a screaming fit or having a daydream about taking a cricket bat to the CEO's kneecaps. I'm having bad thoughts more often lately. Violent thoughts. Evil thoughts. I never used to be plagued by such visions, of blood and pain and death. I lost four minutes on IMAtech a few days ago as I tried to imagine what Peter Ward's scream would be like. He must be in his seventies, so I imagined a gruff, throaty scream, like a long cough perhaps.

As I lie in bed now, my mind favours a higher-pitched scream, feminine and nasally. Sounding like the gender he has so little respect for. What is it he said to us when it was the IMAtech injection day, 'IMAtech especially is important for the ladies, since we train them up and then they bugger off on baby holidays. Got to get our money's worth out of you while we can.' He smiled when he said this, his sneer revealing long yellow teeth like streaks of piss.

I wonder if he's ever screamed with fear. I hope he has, coupled with bulging eyes striped with red veins from seeing true terror. That would be good, to make him scream like that.

I squeeze my eyes shut for a moment, then shake my head. These thoughts are evil. That isn't me. Isobel had the kindest soul. She wouldn't want me thinking this way. It doesn't suit me. I'm Layla Daley and I'm a conscientious worker who has never harmed anyone. I mutter this in a whisper, to remind myself who I truly am. That is what I see when I look in the mirror. The sort of person that makes my dad proud. When I was a girl, he would always tell me to get off the video games, get my head out of the sky, and knuckle-down with my work. That's exactly what I am like now. It's how I was always meant to be.

A diplomatic solution is better for any problem. I may have signed a Non Disclosure Agreement when I was first given the

IMAtech chip, but as long as I stay anonymous, I can inform the press, the council, or maybe an MP. A carefully worded letter speaking out about the dangers of IMAtech is exactly the right sort of action this requires. I can't avenge Isobel, but I can prevent further disaster. That's what Isobel would want.

My dad would still probably disapprove. Keep your head down, he always says. Don't anger the big man, is another one of his sayings. Even now, from his mobility-aided chair and only half his face still working since his stroke, he still likes to remind me to keep in line. I often wonder if he has any regrets. His work life was spent slaving away in another corporate shithole, then cut short due to the heady mix of both boredom and stress. Perhaps if my mum hadn't died, he would have sought a better balance. Perhaps, I often think, it was me who caused him the stress.

I jump out of bed with a start when I realise the time. How has so much time passed? My eyelids are so heavy it's as if I've only had five minutes' sleep. Even if I am lucky with the tube, I'll still be half an hour late. Rushing to the bathroom, my legs and feet cramp. The sleep I've had is not enough. My back and shoulders still ache from the day before, and my knuckles are swollen. A quick shower, and as I rinse, I notice scratch marks scoring my arms and I wonder if I have bed bugs and have been itching in my sleep. It's not the first time I've woken to scratched-up arms, though it's the first time it's happened in a while—not since the nightmares I had after Isobel died. In the back of my mind is a memory, hazy, the blurred outline of panic and trying to recall it makes my heart pound. A nightmare then. Not bad enough to leave a lingering fear or sadness, but enough to make me fantasise about Peter Ward's scream this morning.

I walk through to the kitchen and my whole body sags when confronted with the mess. I shouldn't be so riddled with disappointment. I should be used to this by now. Katarina moved in months ago and it's always the same carnage. I doubt Katarina even knows how to work the dishwasher or where the washing machine is. Her high heels are scattered by the door as always, causing me to almost break my ankle stepping over them. There's a half-drunk glass of water on the side, spillages all around, evidence of toast being made and eaten, half a slice left butter-side down on the counter, and crumbs littering the floor.

'Fuck's sake,' I mutter as I make a rushed effort to clean up, though I've not enough time to clean properly.

Katarina's carefreeness and outgoing demeanour had been something exotic and exciting when we were kids at school, and I longed for the sort of friendship I was too shy to obtain. When I decided to sublet the spare room, I just needed the money. I'd considered bulking up my hours testing video games for bugs, but the thought of more screen time gave me a headache. My job had killed my love of gaming.

Then Katarina waltzed in, and she had the same confidence she had when I used to admire her from afar at school, like she owns every room she ever steps foot in. She was all laughter and intensity, and I realised I needed so much more than just help with the rent. Katarina gave me a glimpse into the life of a person who was glamorous and desired and wore such traits as if she owned them instead of them being a novelty.

Six months ago, I saw Katarina's presence as a door opening, letting the light in. Now I wish she'd at least shut the damned door when it was freezing outside, and perhaps remembered to lock it once in a while.

These annoyances are small things, I know. They test my patience, but not our friendship. Little irritations that when I am more well rested, I can easily dismiss.

It's not like having Katarina around can possibly make my life any worse.

Chapter Seven

Layla

I fidget my whole way to work. The collar of my cardigan is still damp from the wash since Katarina slung her coat on top of the drying rack. Nothing I wear is ironed. I'm not even sure if my clothes match, but I don't want to look down and check. I must appear a wreck, though hopefully not as bad as the women queuing up outside the Taylor Foundation building. There's always a line there stretching around the corner. The charity offering refuge for vulnerable women was a compromise, they said, after the Clarity Directive came into force. The few victims of the changes can have fully-funded help. So that makes it all okay, the men said. *#behave.*

My IMAtech buzzes a minute down by the time I get to the tube station. I get straight on a train without having to wait, yet still my IMAtech buzzes every minute all the way to work. I can't turn it off. I can't turn my phone off because then I'll be logged as unreachable, absent, which results in many more minutes being deducted and disciplinary action. The punish-ment list is extensive, the rewards negligible. I'll likely get the sack, and with so many jobs being replaced by AI, getting the sack is something I can't risk.

My brisk walk from the tube station coupled with my dread means my heart rate is elevated by the time I sit at my desk, so IMAtech informs me, made all the worse by the orchestra of tuts directed my way. The office counter still shows the collective seconds are down, and my tardiness just cost them nearly two thousand more. My heart rate will get fed through to HR. I'll probably get an email telling me I need to look after my health, that WIT requires a healthy workforce, reminding me that AI doesn't get stressed or sick.

I practise some breathing exercises I've seen online to try to steady my heart, then dig my fingertips into my scalp and purse my lips as I wait an age for my computer to load. Thirty-six minutes down before I've even begun my day. I've no food in my bag to keep me going and no seconds to spare to run out and grab something, not even a coffee. I don't even have a moment to water the potted plant that is wilting on my desk. That was Isobel's plant. I can't even keep a damned plant alive.

To my right, Joel hasn't started work yet either. He slouches in his chair, his podge making his shirt buttons threaten to pop open while the glaring sun through the window shines off his bald spot.

I yawn and start typing.

'You okay?' Joel asks. 'Not like you to be late.'

I'm sure he doesn't want to know, and just wants a distraction as always. Why doesn't he try to talk to me when I'm waiting for my computer to load? It's like he purposefully chooses the worst time. 'I'm fine,' I say. 'Overslept.'

'You look tired.'

'Yep.' Shut up, go away, is what I want to say, but I bite my tongue and keep my head down.

'They're going on about it again. Extreme tiredness. They won't let it go. Not since—'

'Don't say her name!' I spit. Joel doesn't have the right to talk about her. He's not worthy of uttering her name. No one is. I'm not, even. I need every thought of her locked away. Compartmentalising is all that is keeping me sane.

'Sorry,' he says in a way that sounds more standoffish than apologetic.

I attempt a polite smile in return. I shouldn't snap. It's not Joel's fault. He didn't even know about our relationship until after the accident. No one did. The newness of our relationship made it easy to hide. Grief is the opposite. Its infancy makes it harder to conceal. If time heals all, then it damned well needs to hurry up.

I start typing, my hands flying over the keys, and my IMAtech begins to climb from the dip I created in the chart. I've worked so hard to catch up from running late last week and now I have this setback. I clench my jaw and wish I could work from home more, away from all the judgemental faces that close in around me like dark shadows. I used to be so much more organised. I used to be so much better at time keeping. Ever since—*no.* I give my head a little shake, clearing thoughts of her away. Isobel is gone. I need to stop thinking about her. To focus. I was always so good at focussing.

'I've got some Texi if you need it?' Joel offers.

'What?' His offer startles me. It's so brazen, and so clearly something I will say no to. 'No—no,' I stutter. 'No, thanks.'

'It's good. It helps. I've caught up on most of my time this week. Really helps you concentrate.'

Yet he is still distracting me. He's hardly a good advert for the drug. Atexamine or Texi, as it is commonly known as, is becoming more and more common in office life. A Baxter Pharmaceutical product that's now as easy to get hold of as headache pills. Convenient, I always think, since the Baxters are on the board of WIT. The pressure created by IMAtech is forcing so many to buy their medication. The great circle of life.

Antonia walks over. As much as her manner around the bosses irks me, the way she swishes her hips is an entirely different distraction and I'm like a magpie looking at something shiny. I avert my eyes and cower, ducking my head low, but it's clear Antonia's beeline is aimed right at me.

When standing by my desk, Antonia clears her throat in such a theatrical fashion, I worry she might retch up a tonsil.

'Can I help you?' I ask.

'Reason for arriving late?'

'My watch stopped.' I can't admit tiredness, not if what Joel implied is true. The IMAtech chip under my skin can tell so much, it probably knows when I'm asleep or awake, stressed or not.

Antonia makes a noise through her nose that can be likened to a squeaky floor. Disapproval not overly clear, though not in any way supportive. She logs my bullshit excuse, then walks back to her desk. I exhale my relief that she didn't give me a lecture.

She only got the office manager job because the last woman was demoted after she had a baby and her thickened waist remained. She wore Spanx so tight, she almost passed out one day. Antonia and those swishing hips were a shoo-in, that and the way she touches her neck when she giggles. I doubt she's actually fucking Peter Ward, she has way too much class for that. She just really likes to give them the impression she's up for it. Selling the dream. The sight of them standing so close makes me want to throw up.

There's no way Antonia approves of IMAtech. She's only doing what she has to because she's terrified of losing her job like everyone else. And Antonia has uterine fibroids, so at certain times of the month, she has to go to the toilet often. She's told everyone this, justifying it, many times. But as office manager, she also says why should she get special treatment when Ben and his prostate don't? Or when Carla and her caffeine addiction that causes her to piss every fifteen minutes don't? 'We're all equal under the regime.' She actually called it that.

In other words, we are all fucked.

The lines and lines of code start to blur after a while. I push my glasses up my nose every now and then, stretch my back and neck to try to get comfortable. Thirty-six minutes. I can make that up today if I just stop daydreaming and apply myself.

I tuck my chin in and keep my shoulders slightly lifted, some hunched position I'm sure makes me look like I'm working hard. I have a job. That's all that is important. Since the crash, most companies outsourced the majority of their staff to AI. I'm sure the only reason WIT hasn't is due to Baxter Pharmaceuticals being on the board and they can use us to pedal their wares.

I can improve my time management without Texi. I just need to keep my daydreaming at bay. I know this, and I can do better. It's certainly what the office posters imply. *Be better than AI! AI performs consistently all month: do YOU?*

Those posters get my back up every time I see them, the monthly performance clearly targeted at women since some smiling woman adorns the background. IMAtech tracks our cycles and ensures our performance doesn't wane when our oestrogen does. They may know we're not AI, but they certainly like to treat us as such.

'At least testosterone is consistent,' Peter Ward said to us once. 'That's half the workforce we have to worry less about.'

God, I want to gouge his eyeballs out every time I think about that. Or strap him to a chair and rip his fingernails out with tweezers like in mediaeval times. Maybe carve a cock and balls symbol into his forehead.

The bad times will be over soon, my dad always says. Don't anger the big man, be a good girl. When I imagine hearing his voice, it has the same calming quality it did when I was a child. I can work hard. I can be a good girl.

I allow the percussion of keyboards to set the rhythm as I continue to type, for the metronome of life to help my bad thoughts drift away. I'm at work, where I'm dedicated and conscientious, not some crazy woman imagining torturing people.

Across the office, someone gasps. An exhale so loud it makes everyone in the office jump. Whoever created the distraction, some blond I have never had the time to say hello to, stands and lifts her phone above her head.

'Listen to this, everyone,' she shouts.

Her phone is playing the news and I wonder how on earth she has time to follow the news. Either she has banked loads of time this week or she doesn't care.

. . .once again, our breaking news story. Peter Ward, CEO of Ward Innovation Technologies, has been found dead at his London home. . .

The shock is instant, my gasp mimicking everyone else's, my hands go to my mouth in unison with theirs.

Antonia is standing, frozen, her face reddening and wide eyes glistening.

A reflex response is quicker than a considered one. After my brain has a few seconds to mull it over, I keep my hands over my mouth, but behind those hands is a smile.

Chapter Eight

Layla

My eyes are fixated on the news all the way home. Rain splatters my phone screen, making the touchscreen frustratingly slow, and my fingers jabbing at the news site adds to the aches in my hands. Bit by bit, the press releases the details, like some page-turner book or soap opera. Every tidbit ends with a cliffhanger, leaving me hungry for more.

Peter Ward's head was too smashed in to be identified. That's what happens when you fall four storeys headfirst. The body was initially identified by his watch, still on his wrist, recording everything when he fell, yet survived unscathed. The little square that tells anyone who wishes to know how many steps he's taken, the amount of time staring at screens, his medical information, *that* survived the fall. It probably even stated his heart rate the second before he smashed into the ground. Such is the immortality of tech. I'll bet one day, IMAtech chips and smart tracking devices will be part of crematorium ashes and be scattered to the wind.

Maybe his heart paused for a moment, shooting pain through his chest like he was having a heart attack just before the end. Or maybe, instead it spiked so high it made him vomit, and the puke was mixed with his brains on the tarmac.

I shake the thought away. Another bad thought. A man is dead. I should have empathy and feel sad for his family. The bad thoughts are the sort Katarina would think, not me. But then I continue to read. The news article is like poetry, like ornate, melodic prose that makes my heart sing. I don't need the details. I can add my own embellishments. As he fell, shitting himself with terror, he experienced seconds of regret and despair at the shitshow of a company he ran, his soiled underwear a testament to his panic. Fuck empathy. Revelling in the news is far more appropriate.

Katarina is rubbing off on me. Such glee is out of character. I should feel bad for his family. Didn't he have a pet, a dog, I think? The dog will be sad.

I read on.

Four storeys. Did the fall take long enough for him to know fear? Remorse? On reflection, landing feet first would have been better. Perhaps that way, he would have known pain. His legs may have shattered before his brain shut off.

My own thoughts make me shiver. Katarina's polished nails are too deep under my skin. I need to find my inner compass that points towards empathy and morality. I need to remind myself that I am Layla Daley, a good person. Kind. Hardworking. My name doesn't suit me. It's too lyrical. It makes me sound like a porn star, one guy told me in a bar once, then seemed disappointed that my demeanour didn't match.

I read the next bit of the news article: suspected suicide.

My nose makes a similar squeak to what Antonia's had earlier. An audible ambivalence. Though I revel in the mental anguish he must have experienced over time—there isn't a man alive more worthy of despair—taking his own life means the fear at the end may have been absent. The glee I have abates slightly, and my salivating mouth runs dry as it riles me that, at the end, he may have known contentment, that he welcomed death. He died as he lived: under his own volition.

'I thought you'd be pleased?' Katarina says when I arrive home and am no more cheerful than I had been the day before.

'A man died. That's hardly good news.' I sit next to her at the table and look at her smirking face, eyebrows raised and chin tucked in, as if she is sizing up my reaction and deems it inadequate.

'The man was a dick,' Katarina continues. 'It's his company that injected you with that damned chip. He deserved to die for what his company has done. To you, to—'

'And you think now he's dead they'll forget all about it?' I interrupt before she has a chance to mention Isobel. 'They'll let us cut the things out and I'll be allowed a toilet break at work?'

I get up to fetch myself a drink, but Katarina beats me to it and pours us both a large gin and tonic instead of the glass of water I was intending. She even fills the glass with ice and a slice of lime and presents it in such a way that it implies we're celebrating.

'Without Peter Ward at the helm, things really might get better,' she says.

'Don't be so naïve.' My tone is as cutting as I intend. 'That's just how things are for you, drinking and doing God-knows-what in the evening, never even sparing a minute to put your shoes where they belong.'

'Wow. You are particularly grouchy today.' Katarina leans back in her chair and folds her arms. 'I only thought that perhaps this is a bit of justice.'

'The man killed himself. He died as he lived, getting whatever the fuck he wanted. I was going to write to the press about IMAtcch. To, I don't know, some employee rights group. Maybe there's still a union somewhere. But I can hardly do that now. It would be in poor taste.'

Katarina snorts a laugh. 'So? That picture of him in the news, that comb-over was in poor taste.'

I neck my gin, stare into the empty glass and sniff back a tear. 'It won't bring her back.'

'I know. Shit, I know that.' She stands and walks around the back of my chair and rubs my shoulders. 'But maybe if Peter Ward killed himself, the rest of the company will see that working people into an early grave isn't a good thing.'

'No chance. It's not like he had an IMAtech. All they'll do is work us harder to stop the hit on the share price. They sent us home early as a mark of respect, so now I've three hours to make up over the weekend.'

Katarina crouches as she works her fingers in deeper. My muscle knots are as hard as concrete.

'You need to relax. Stop worrying. Just leave the revenge stuff to me.'

My shoulders stiffen and shoot up. If any muscle knot had eased, it coils right back up. 'No. Christ, Kat. What are you thinking about?'

'I dunno,' she says, and runs her hands through her hair instead, looking up at the ceiling as if she were watching some old romantic movie. She often has a whimsical way about her, a distant stare like she can visualise her ideologies. 'Seducing the entire board and luring them into the woods. . .'

'What scares me is I don't think you're joking.'

'Fuck them, Layla.' Katarina is back in the room again, rigid and sharp. 'They shouldn't be allowed to get away with treating you like this.'

'This is London, Katarina. Your romanticised ideals of revenge don't apply here.'

She narrows her eyes and her lips twitch before she stomps through to her bedroom, slamming cupboard doors and drawers. 'Yeah, well. Let's see about that.'

Chapter Nine

Layla

In my chest of drawers are some of Isobel's clothes. A pale blue hoodie with a peace sign on the front, a yellow woollen cardigan, some underwear. Such colourful items for someone who carried the sunshine with them everywhere. Sometimes I open the drawer just to look at it all, to imagine Isobel standing there, still wearing it. Some pink strands of hair are still in my hairbrush. I haven't used that brush since, leaving the last of Isobel to rest on my dresser. I've been tempted a few times but haven't worn Isobel's clothes. As cosy as it would be to curl up in that hoodie and inhale the last of Isobel's perfume, I can't bring myself to do it. Isobel was her own person. I would taint that somehow, casting a shadow over her light.

There's a polaroid of the two of us on a pinboard over my dresser. Isobel took the polaroid. She loved retro things. 'Bring back the old days when life was simpler,' she'd often say. I hold the photo and look at our smiling faces. I never appreciated it before, how Isobel's smile appeared so much more genuine than mine. Isobel's outlandish colours added a splash of excitement to the scene. I miss that about Isobel. I am so dowdy. Too sensible and studious and by-the-book to ever be the sort of fun Isobel was. Life was less boring when Isobel was around. I don't look at the picture for long, I can't. It's as if Isobel would be tarnished by my gaze alone.

The first month of our relationship, we saw each other every weekend and at least one night in the week. Dinner at one of our flats on Wednesdays. A show in the Westend was Isobel's weekend choice. We visited the bar near my flat, which I pretended to have visited on many occasions, though not knowing where the toilets were gave the game away. If Isobel twigged, she didn't say. We'd share a pitcher of beer or Pimms on a Sunday afternoon and made small talk about our pasts, holiday desires, families.

We took our time with our relationship, at my request. She yearned for the physical gratification that I denied her for a while. I wanted to eek out every stage of our relationship slowly, for her to not just want me but need me.

After a couple of months, we were drinking at a pub close to Isobel's end of town and we stumbled, drunk and horny, back to Isobel's flat and had the best sex I've ever had, though with my level of experience that's not much of an accolade. We shared a sense of togetherness. I am sure now as I look back on our time together. That photo confirms it. There was a warmth and comfort there I hadn't ever had before. Two outcasts together. Isobel rejected society's ideals, dressed her own way, and walked to the beat of her own drum. I didn't choose to be an outcast like Isobel did. Everyone else enforced that upon me. My studiousness and quiet nature make me a social reject. But Isobel didn't mind that.

'You think I want some popular socialite?' she asked one evening. 'Don't be daft. You intrigue me. You're everything I want to be.'

'What? Me?' I jerked my head back.

'Sure. You get things done. I procrastinate, get distracted too easily. You put your entire self into everything you do. Everywhere you go, you make things better.'

Isobel had said this with such sincerity I blushed, then held her closer than I ever had.

We were both designing WIT's next video game, WardZone. Its development was ahead of schedule back then, though not ahead enough according to our employers. So, IMAtech was rolled out. Every member of staff was lined up and given the choice: be injected with the chip or go home. A country still in economic-crash-recovery mode is hardly a job-seeker's paradise. Everyone pulled their shirts away from their collarbone and winced through the pain of their job requirement. AI doesn't feel pain. AI doesn't grumble about a system upgrade.

'Sorry, Layla,' Isobel said as we sat in the staffroom at work. I had my usual cheese and pickle sandwiches along with a chocolate bar, another of which I had brought in for Isobel, a gesture I had taken to making a few times a week. Isobel smiled as she took it, had a bite, then glanced over to the doorway to check no one was there before kissing my cheek. It was the third weekend in a row Isobel was making such an apology. 'I'm just too tired to do much. I still have work to catch up on, and there's this anti-hunting meet I have to go to. Maybe we can have a quiet night on Saturday.'

I smiled it off and gave her a one-armed shrug. 'No worries. I'll just meet some other friends.'

'I wish I could be more like you,' she said. 'You just get everything done. I find it too hard to work non-stop for nine hours a day.'

'You're just too interesting.' I smirked.

'I hate it that I can't see you as much as I want to. This fucking company won't be happy until we're all worked to death.'

The conversation all these months later is still so vivid. I can still feel Isobel's frustration in my bones, her tiredness coursing through her. The scene plays out in front of me, like I'm watching a play. Isobel wore a tie-dye top, her floral perfume subtle, the sound of her soft boots on the tiled floor. It was unseasonably cold that day and the office air con was too high. I can still feel Isobel's goosebumps under my own skin, can still taste that chocolate bar on my tongue.

If only I had known then what was to come.

Isobel rubbed the chill from her arms. 'Once this game is finished, the workload will be less. It's just so close to the deadline.'

A deadline. That was literally what she was working towards.

Isobel nuzzled into the nape of my neck, just for a second before she pulled away and checked the time, packing up her lunch things as she did. 'You and me, we'll go to San Francisco when this game is done. How does that sound?'

My eyes lit up. 'San Francisco?'

'Yeah. I've always wanted to go. Just four months, I reckon. That's all we need.'

But she didn't survive another two.

Chapter Ten

Katarina

Tonight the bar is quiet, like the whole damned city is in mourning. Or more likely, plotting their move on how to take over the world of tech with Peter Ward out of the way. One billionaire is dead, yet a hundred more can take his place, all on their high horses believing in what Peter Ward did. What was it he said on that TV interview once? 'Too much equality caused the economic downturn. Gender assigned roles happen throughout nature. We should stop trying to change women.'

Oh, excuse me while my heart bleeds for the man.

I doodle on a napkin, rearrange the spirits, and wipe every surface a second time as my eyes search the ceiling, inspecting my thoughts and memories. I wash my hands a hundred times, file down broken fingernails, and rearrange my hair. Though a distracted body does not translate to a distracted mind.

The door opens and in walks one man. Alone, face drawn like he hasn't slept a wink since I saw him the day before.

'Usual?' I ask.

Harry Baxter gives a small nod and sits at the bar, holding his head in his hands. I pour out a double whiskey and put it in front of him, which he doesn't acknowledge for some time.

'I saw the news,' I say. 'Condolences.'

'Thanks.' He necks the entire whiskey. 'He was like a father to me. I just can't believe he's dead.'

I don't yank down my T-shirt this time. Being alluring for a grieving man is an entirely different technique. My heart races with excitement at the sight of him, but not for the reasons he's probably used to.

'I'm sure he loved you like a son,' I say, filling my voice with every ounce of compassion I can formulate.

This makes his tears flow freely, and I rub his biceps. Hard as a rock.

'There, there,' I say, then pour him another whiskey. 'This one's on me.'

He sniffs and wipes his eyes on his cuff. 'You're so kind.'

I shrug and polish the surface I just used. 'Just my natural demeanour, I guess.'

I allow the conversation to stall, giving Harry a few seconds to take in a moment's silence. I lean back against the bar, turning a glass over in my hand, drying it with a dishcloth. It squeaks occasionally, a subtle noise, just to remind Harry I am still here.

In the press, Harry Baxter is always pictured with some svelte darling hanging off each arm, a couple more of society's finest walking just behind. Low-cut designer dresses, smooth skin stretched over their bones glistening with reflections from their diamond jewellery. Such socialites frequent Little London often. They order drinks, looking down their surgically reduced noses and giggle their haughty laughs at whatever the men are saying.

Gold-diggers.

Almost as nauseating as the gold itself.

I couldn't give a shit about Harry's money. I need his trust. Drawing him out is like sucking on a snake bite.

'I don't know why I'm here,' he says after a while, red-rimmed doughy eyes looking my way for a moment, then back at the bar as he slouches lower. 'I think I just don't want to be around my usual crowd, you know?'

'It must be so hard for you.'

'None of them knew him like I did. God, I can't believe I'm saying that in past tense.'

'Such a shock.'

He sniffs and wipes his eye again. 'All of them saying it was suicide, which is nonsense, by the way. Peter would never have killed himself. He just wasn't the sort.'

I knit my brows and nod, leaving him in silence a moment more. I shift my weight on my hip to accentuate my arse slightly. A subtle change, but one that causes him to flit his eyes up for a split second. I don't meet his gaze but maintain a solemn face, still holding the glass with one hand, tucking my hair behind my ear with the other.

'We had a connection, you and me, last night, I think,' Harry says. A neediness about him. 'You're not like my usual friends.'

I give him a pained smile. He spins his now empty glass around, and I take a fresh one to pour him another whiskey. He drinks it in one gulp.

'You're not drinking tonight?' he asks.

I shake my head. 'Not tonight.'

'Last night,' he says, 'when we had that drink, I said we should see each other again. I meant it.'

Last night, Adam had left early, sober as he always was these days, apparently. Three stints in rehab being quite enough for a thirty-one-year-old, I learned. The rest of the bar was empty, even the perv who had been hitting on me all night had gone home. But Harry Baxter, eyes unfocussed with drink, speaking with a slur, cocaine dusting his nostrils and not even bothering to wipe it away, leaned in close and whispered in my ear, 'Come home with me.'

I said no, of course. I am Katarina McKenzie, not one of the floozies he picks up in the Diamond Lounge or wherever it is he hangs out. Surprise lifted his face and he said—probably accurately—that any other woman would give their left tit to get such an offer.

I eyed him up and down. He is handsome if you like that poster boy clean-cut look. He could do with a tattoo or blemish. With his level of precise grooming, he looks like a Ken doll.

'Maybe some other time,' I said with a smile.

I don't want a fuck from Harry Baxter. However hot he is, a quick drunken shag in his deluxe abode will solve nothing but scratch an itch. I need more from him than what's in his trousers.

I step a little closer to him now. 'I felt the same,' I lie. If I felt I have a connection with every drunk guy at the bar I'd rejected, I'd be overrun with dates.

He picks up the whiskey and necks it again, sniffs back another tear, and I refill his glass.

'Sorry for your loss. It does sound like he was a great man.'

He downs the other whiskey and again, I pour.

'You understand. I knew you'd get it. I don't believe he killed himself. I just can't.' His voice has the elongated vowel sound of early inebriation, a higher pitch.

Another whiskey. I lean against the back of the bar, listening. Always listening.

'No way was it suicide.' He fails to stifle a hiccup. 'I don't care what the note said. It didn't say anything really. . .' He swallows another whiskey. 'He hated heights. If he was going to kill himself, that's not how he'd have done it.' He gestures a lot with one hand, swaying as he does. 'He wasn't even poor. Share prices are excellent. He had no reason to kill himself.'

I rest my elbows on the bar and my head in my hands, giving him a decent view down my top. 'Sounds like there needs to be a proper investigation.'

He scoffs. 'Yeah, right. Once they decide suicide, that's it. They just want to draw a line under it. Save the bloody taxpayers money. The company doesn't want the focus on it. They'd rather reassure the shareholders that everything is fine.' He hiccups and wipes his nose on his hand. 'You know . . . you know what I might do? I'm going to get a man. A professional, a private investigator.' I'm sure that's what he says, but it comes out as investeeglator.

I rub his forearm now. 'What would Peter want?'

He drinks another whiskey. His eyes are no longer aligned, one pointing more towards his nose than the other. He hiccups, then huffs a breath. 'Revenge. That's what Peter would want. I'm going to get revenge for Peter.'

I smile, then bite my bottom lip. Revenge is something I have been thinking a lot about lately. This sounds fun. 'Who do you think did it?'

His grip tightens around his empty glass, veins protruding along his forearm. 'There's only one person who could have. Adam. His son. My so-called best mate. Adam fucking Ward.'

Chapter Eleven

Layla

I sit at my desk, gnawing at the skin around my fingernails and stifling what would otherwise be a constant stream of yawns. It's not just me. A quick glance around the office shows me everyone is tired. Antonia is walking around, fidgeting as she does, skittish and jumping at every noise. Red-eyed and pale-faced. Perhaps she's grieving. Perhaps she really liked that dickhead.

I'm four hours down on my IMAtech total, and despite working my arse off to make up the lost time, I'm struggling to catch up. I'm distracted, the light beaming in from outside is more enticing to stare at than my computer screen. The chair digs into my sit bones and I can't wriggle enough to get comfortable. My blinks are slow, tiredness robbing me of any motivation. Worrying about Katarina is making me even more tired. I rub my temples. A constant headache is bearing down on me like I have a hat on too tight. My eyes water from the glare of the screen. One more thing to make my IMAtech tally worse.

An email came first thing, about my lateness, commenting on my elevated heart rate, how I am one week past my menstrual cycle and they are noticing a pattern in women's behaviours. If I was one week before my cycle, I may have taken that level of snooping on my personal life a whole lot worse. I should watch my iron, it said, to keep my energy up and fight fatigue. As if I have time to eat a balanced diet. As if I can afford red meat. The email came with a link to Baxter Pharmaceuticals' iron tablets, and with a heavy breath, I clicked and ordered some.

AI doesn't have these problems, the email reminded me. Men don't either. I need to do my bit to aid the economic recovery. I need to continue to prove myself, was the last sentence. Or at least the last bit I read before I deleted the email and pain shot through my jaw from gritted teeth.

'They're monitoring all hormones now,' Joel says.

'What?'

'Cortisol, adrenaline, endorphins. You not read the email?'

My inbox is blinking at me, and I click the one Joel is referring to.

As part of a new initiative by Baxter Pharmaceuticals, IMAtech is monitoring all hormone levels in the staff to check for signs of stress and to offer tailor-made therapies if needed. This will ensure we have a happy and functioning—

I don't read any more. I don't need to learn about Big Pharma's innovations in the world of tech and what this means for corporate efficiency. I've read such spiel before. What's the tiredness hormone? There'll be plenty of that in my system.

I strain to remember where I am up to in my work. My forehead tenses as I search my brain, but it seems like so long ago. The words blur on the screen, the colours swimming. If it wasn't for the software reminding me, there is no way I'd know. My body aches as if I've run a marathon since yesterday, my brain lost in a thick fog, like a week has passed in between. The monotony of it is haunting me. The daily repetition of typing code makes every hour seem like a week.

Video games were fun when I was a kid. It was pure escapism back then. When I played, I could be anyone, take on the roles of the heroes and warriors. I could be the best person there is, the bravest, the most beautiful, the fiercest. When I first got the job at WIT, I imagined rekindling my love for gaming. I thought perhaps one day, I'd be designing the games and using my own imagination. But it hasn't worked out like that. When I'm programming, I'm fulfilling someone else's specification. It requires no creativity and I'm only ever one person. I'm no hero or warrior. It's as dull as nagging Katarina about the dishes.

Joel, for once, keeps typing as he talks. His groans still filter over, but he taps his foot with impatience rather than slouching with lack of motivation.

'The Texi really helps,' he says. 'I was sceptical too, but it works. You really should try it. Pretty much everyone is taking it now. And it's totally allowed. Says so on that email.'

I make a quick mental note of all the other medications I've taken in my life. I'm off it all now, though I briefly considered starting again after the accident. But there is something about my mind being my own, free to explore its depths on my own terms. My raw emotions are real instead of being cooked and watered down and squashed under layers of drugs. My sadness and stress have an authenticity about them, some sense of ownership. Texi would be like I was taking a step back.

'I'm fine, thanks,' I say.

'Really?' He looks at me with a furrowed brow, noticing my state. My clothes are so crinkled I must look like a tramp. Luckily, a childhood of being teased about my appearance has left me resilient to such looks, and in any case, hardly anyone would notice. Once I'm sitting at my desk, it's not as if I have the time to walk around the office ever. A far cry from the days when I first met Isobel. My clothes were tidier then, crisply ironed and stain-free. I was so much better at managing my time then. Nowadays, it's a constant struggle to be the Layla everyone knows and expects.

'I don't think we've got anything to worry about anyway,' Joel says, still typing away. 'I figure they won't sack us if we're a little down. They might be able to replace us like that,' he spares a typing second to click his fingers, 'but it would take time to catch someone up.'

'Yeah, just as soon as the game is finished, we'll be out.'

'Well, that gives us some breathing space. Hey, how about we go for a drink after work?'

My flinch is impulsive and costs me a precious few seconds on my IMAtech tally. As my gaze darts up for a second, I catch Joel looking at me, offering a smile. My hesitation is stretching out in all directions, time slowing as it does. Caught off-guard, I still don't reply. I keep typing. Perhaps he'll think I'm too busy working, though I can feel his eyes still looking my way. We made eye contact. He knows I heard. Time is now so slow, the rippling tingle of awkwardness is like individual jabs with a needle, like the touch of each molecule is perceptible. I search my brain for words but find nothing except blankness. After another second or two passes and the ground hasn't been kind enough to swallow me up, I say, 'Sure. Okay.'

Even as the words leave me, I regret them. There isn't a more powerful persuasion tool known to humankind than an awkward silence. Katarina wouldn't have buckled. She wouldn't have allowed such a silence to happen. She would have laughed and said, hell no, or something confident and amusing. Katarina wouldn't even have had the social time free for an unwanted date. She probably has a million others lined up.

My insides cave in, weak and spent. Agreeing seems less confrontational than saying no. It's the coward's way out. But now I have to go, which means if he asks again, it would be even more awkward to say no. *Stupid! Stupid!* I chastise myself as I type, while Joel's presence next to me is an ominous reminder of my lack of backbone.

I spend the rest of the afternoon typing with one hand, using the other to rest my head in, leaning on my elbow. This keeps Joel out of my eyeline. My IMAtech marks the seconds, not climbing as it should as one-handed typing is so much less productive, and minutes slip by. The extra work to catch up on isn't the worst thing in the world right now, since it will delay any evening plans.

Joel stands to leave bang on six o'clock. 'I'll find us a table. Meet me there when you're finished.'

'Yeah, great. Thanks.' *Stupid!*

He steals a peek at my app, then exhales loudly. 'Four hours twenty down! This drink will do you some good.'

My eyes glaze and focus on the mid-distance. How is it that I now have more time to make up for than Joel? That bloody drug makes me feel cheated. Staying late and making up the time will do me more good than sitting in a bar, and it's a good excuse to cancel.

'I'll probably be quite late,' I say, attempting a wispy tone of regret. 'I should really make a dent in that time.'

'I've got an idea,' he says as he leaves.

Twenty minutes later, when I'm starting to think I'm rid of him, he arrives back with some pre-mixed cocktail cans and a selection of pastries. I stop typing to look at it all. There's some fruit as well, bowls of pre-mixed salad and take-out cutlery, and some bottles of juice. My mouth hangs open and my eyes sting and blur. It's the nicest thing anyone has done for me in ages.

A rush of emotions well up from my chest, and I cry.

'Oh, come here,' he says and offers his arms for a hug. I fall into them. 'It's stressful, I know. Just got to soldier on.'

I lean away, my back clicking as I do, and I pull a tissue from my pocket to wipe my eye. 'I'm so sorry. I just feel so broken lately. Since the accident.'

'You guys were close, right?'

I nod. 'And with IMAtech being so demanding, it's tough. My housemate is such a handful. She's great in so many ways. It's just. . .' I scrunch my sleeve in my hand and shift my weight. 'Do you ever feel like the world is showing you how you should be, instead of letting you be how you are?'

'I think everyone feels like that sometimes.'

He opens a can of pre-mixed mojito and passes it to me. I sip, the sharp fizz better than I thought it would be.

'Now, don't mind me,' he says. 'You do whatever work you need to do. I'll make sure you're well fed and hydrated.'

I swallow some more cocktail and wipe my eyes. 'Thanks, Joel. You're a good friend.' I place a slight emphasis on the friend. A brief glance up confirms that he registered it.

After a bite of a pastry, I face my screen again and resume the tedium of typing code. Two hands this time. My app ticks the seconds away and after my second can of mojito, I start making a few typos that take time to correct, but I'm making a dent in my time debt.

Joel sits quietly, scrolling through his phone and keeping my side plate stocked with snacks. If I had such a service every day at work, maybe I wouldn't get so behind. When they have board meetings up in that glass box, they're often catered with staff handing out food and drinks to the investors and bosses. They are catered for and they don't have IMAtech. The best of all worlds for them, the worst of all for the office staff.

As much as I am concentrating on work, I can't help my wandering mind, the anger bubbling through me as I clock the time, and my seconds on IMAtech, mentally calculating my journey home time, how little time I'll have to sleep later, how many more nights I'll have to work this late.

It's almost nine when I think I should call it a day. Joel has sat quietly for hours, and guilt claws at me since he has also wasted his evening, and as kind as he is, I am definitely still not interested.

We walk to the tube station together. 'Thanks, Joel. That was so nice of you. I needed a friend tonight.' I put emphasis on the F word again, just to remind him.

'Anytime. We're all in this hellhole together.'

I nod and we both scroll through our phones as we wait for the traffic lights.

'Whoa! You seen the news?' he says.

'No. More board members jumping off buildings?' I can't hide the optimism in my tone.

'Ha! No.' He laughs. 'Some sicko breaking into morgues and cutting bits off bodies.'

I grimace. 'Nice.'

'Also loads of old obituaries still for our ex-boss. They're still saying suicide.'

I sigh. 'I just find it hard to believe that he hated himself more than anyone else hated him.'

'Yeah, especially after Antonia. . .' I wait for him to continue, but his mid-sentence pause turns into another awkward silence.

'What about Antonia?' I eventually ask.

'Forget I mentioned it. He killed himself and that's that. Makes you wonder what drove him to it? I guess if he had IMAtech, they'd have known what his hormones were doing. That smartwatch likely did heart rate, right? I'll bet they'll say—'

Joel rambles on, but my attention is elsewhere. His subject hopping and filling any hint of a pause with unnecessary words is only moving the conversation further away from whatever he almost said. And that's all I'm thinking about. What he almost said. Something about Antonia.

Chapter Twelve

Layla

Katarina is nowhere to be seen when I get home. I could have sworn it's her night off. She's probably out socialising, dating, doing all the things single women should be doing. Having a life, instead of working to exhaustion and pining over a previous relationship. Katarina is too gorgeous to grieve for long. No doubt she has people drooling over her at the bar.

I've never been attracted to Katarina. She's so confident, and I cower from her rather than fancy her. Katarina would suit someone who can handle her reckless and loud ways. She's too attractive for the likes of me. Too desirable. Chemistry can't exist between a slug and a peacock. I often stare at her in awe, admiring the way she holds herself, grooms herself, then look away afraid and intimidated when her confidence shoots out of her like lightning bolts. All of these reactions are frequent, but attraction, never. It's not right to fancy someone I want to be like, that would be too narcissistic. And I am in no way a narcissist. That's Katarina's domain.

The blissful peace of the empty apartment is comforting, and I'm grateful for the time to myself. I spend half an hour washing up and tidying, then begin to wonder what Katarina would do if she had an hour or so in a quiet house to herself. She has all day, every day to herself when I'm at work, but given her late nights at work, I assume she mostly just sleeps.

I rummage through some of her makeup. Katarina always says I should help myself whenever I want, telling me I could do with a little spruce up. One look in the mirror at my sallow complexion and it's clear she's not wrong. Making up my face, though, is a step too far. Isobel liked me as I am. Natural and pasty. I find some red nail polish instead and I paint my toenails, just like Katarina's.

I shower before bed and roll my damp hair up into socks to curl it, a way Katarina had shown me ages ago, but I've never gotten around to trying. Being a little more like Katarina, a bit bolder, is going to take more than styled hair and pretty toenails, but maybe it's about time for me to start looking after myself. Being asked out on a date, albeit with a man I'm not interested in, has lit a little fire inside.

Perhaps people see me in a way I don't see myself. Isobel had been attracted to me, so I can't be a total pig. Not that I'm interested in dating, it's still too soon, but maybe it's time for a little reinvention. To make some friends. To have someone besides Katarina to offload on. The irony is, in order to make some friends, I'm going to have to be more like Katarina.

Despite the socks in my hair making my pillow uncomfortable, I sleep well, better than I have in ages. Maybe it's the dent I made in my IMAtech debt, or it's the emotional release of crying. I wake on time, feeling the freshest I have in ages, and take the socks out of my hair. The waves bounce up, defying gravity as Katarina's do. It looks so much better, I'm self-conscious and I blush at my own reflection. Someone might comment on my extra effort. Katarina wouldn't mind standing out. She'd lap up the attention. I splash my face with some cold water and decide that is how I'm going to react too.

I walk to work with my eyes forward rather than staring at the ground. Isobel always picked up litter on the street and put it in the bin. It's a habit of hers I adopted, but today, I don't see the discarded rubbish on the ground. Instead, I focus on the people, the buildings, the sky ahead. On the tube, I keep my head up, not scrolling mindlessly through my phone to keep my gaze away from people. I keep my back straight, reminding myself the whole journey that I can be confident, that I have no reason to curl up and hide away.

When I get to work, no one pays me any attention as usual. I sit at my desk and begin to type, quickly, my hands gliding over the keys with a lot less weight bearing down on me.

Antonia is patrolling, peering over shoulders and uttering encouragement when needed. She's still jumpy, wringing her hands and stumbling over her words. My mind is still reeling from what Joel didn't say last night. Maybe she hated Peter Ward as much as me.

For every minute or two I spend typing, I spend a second looking her way. She's wearing a tight fitted skirt that shows off the kind of curves I wish I had. She walks to my desk and hovers behind me a moment, and my heart pounds like a jackhammer. I want to ask her, to look her in the eye and bitch about Peter and loudly delight in his death. Instead, my face heats up, and my throat turns dry as I try to swallow.

The sound of her breath makes my extremities tingle, her subtle perfume intoxicating, and I want to lean back in my chair, to bury into her. Has there always been this tension between us? This is more than just someone catching me watching her as she walks. There's a bond between us, some nexus. Our mutual hate magnetising. It's a stifling and inebriating presence. I reach for my water bottle and sip, choking a little as I do.

I stand to go to the bathroom, and as I walk away, my arm brushes hers. It's the slightest contact, but it's enough to turn my knees to jelly. By the time I reach the bathroom, sweat is collecting across my hairline, so I shut the cubicle door and lean against it, taking some deep breaths while fanning my top.

Has Antonia always made me feel this way? My whole body is excited, riled, on-edge. I sit on the toilet and take a moment just to cool down, to calm my racing heart.

When I'm in somewhat more control, I make my way back to my desk, and with Antonia now on the other side of the office, I cool down more and curse the lost seconds.

Adam Ward arrives shortly after. As always, I hunch forward, letting my hair shield me, hoping he doesn't look at me. Why I bother, I don't know. No one ever notices me. He's been in the office far more than usual since his father's death. He normally graces us with his presence maybe an hour or two a week, just long enough to shout out something condescending, then goes about his day. But the last couple of days, he's been parading around the place as if he's also linked up to IMAtech. No doubt he'll be taking over as CEO. He'll march around the aisles and look down on the staff even more then.

He loiters next to my desk, peering down his nose at me, then over at some colleagues opposite. I hunker down and let my hair conceal me, deploying the childish tactic of if I can't see him, he can't see me.

He clears his throat. 'A little more pride is needed in the workplace, I think, don't you, ladies?'

The response is only keyboards tapping away. I glance up for a second and clock eyes with a woman sitting across from me—her face wears all the hatred and dread I feel inside.

'A dress code, then. I'll get a memo drawn up. You work for a great company, it's about time you looked like it.'

He walks away, and I lose two seconds balling my fists. He's every bit as bad as his dad was. What had Peter Ward said when he was interviewed on TV, the reporter saying going to strip clubs for board meetings was inappropriate and should be stopped. 'Over my dead body,' he said. Ha! Seems ironic now.

I don't temper my thoughts this time. I don't fear the gore I wish I could see. It's okay to imagine bad things happening to bad people, I tell myself. It's cathartic. And in any case, it's only thoughts.

So, as he walks, I imagine him choking on his morning muffin, collapsing to his knees as no one rushes to help. I picture the scene in perfect clarity: his face turning deep purple, his hands grabbing and clawing at his throat, his mouth forming the word help, and the hopelessness he feels as no one does. I can picture his body then, sagging and lying on the ground next to his half-eaten muffin, and all I can think is what a waste of a muffin that would be.

I lick my lips and smile. Perhaps I would go to him, make him think I was about to help, only to pick up the muffin and take a bite while I stand over him, and as my mouth pulls back into a snarl the crumbs scatter down like ash over his choking body.

It's only thoughts, I remind myself as I smile. Thoughts are secret, they're mine alone. Nothing bad can ever come from just thoughts.

Chapter Thirteen

Layla

Condolence gifts have been piling up in the office, all addressed to the board members. They arrive every morning and evening and by the next day, the pile is significant. When the delivery person arrives, someone has to sign for them, and with no one wanting to lose the seconds that would take, the delivery guy starts tapping shoulders.

Flowers are displayed all around the office like the whole place is a mausoleum. Adam's PA is constantly arranging them, making sure they're in prominent positions with enough sun, though not too much. If only the staff were afforded such considerations.

It's eventually my turn to sign for a parcel and I lose thirty-six seconds in doing so, and another forty walking it over to the pile.

Some of the other board members arrive mid-morning. Parin Shah and Jan Novac, still dressed in black, shake hands with Adam as they arrive, and they all note the pile of gifts before walking towards the stairs at the back.

It's easy to hate Adam Ward the most, but the rest of them are just as deplorable. Parin Shah is probably next on my want-to-die list. He's known in the tech world for game development and is the one who set the deadlines. *Better, faster,* are two words he says more than any other. Apparently, his family run sweatshops throughout Asia and he's brought the same attitude to WIT employees. He looks like a runt next to Jan Novac. The size of Jan makes me wonder if he punched and threatened his way onto the board. Since he has previous business in media, such bullying tactics are probably spot-on.

The three of them stop for a moment, right in front of my desk, and the other two follow Adam Ward's gaze as he looks around the office floor.

'You're right, Parin,' Adam Ward says. 'I never noticed it before, but you're right. The Baxters warned me about this.' He clicks his fingers towards Antonia and she runs over, the tapping of her heels snagging my attention, and it's an effort to keep my eyes away.

'Like meerkats or sheep,' Jan Novac says as he eyeballs the room.

Antonia joins them, adjusts her fitted skirt and awaits instruction.

'What's the gender ratio in the office?' Adam asks her.

'Near-on fifty-fifty,' she says. 'We are a wonderfully representative office—'

Adam holds his hand up to shush her, so dramatically it's clear even from the edge of my vision. 'We need the office more spread out then. Split the women up.'

'Erm. . .' Antonia stutters a moment. 'E . . . excuse me?'

'Synchronicity, you women do it. Like sheep. It's a problem. Put you all in a small space and you share hormones or something. They spread. Hugo Baxter was saying something about this a while ago. Baxter Pharmaceuticals have done a lot of research into hormones, as you know. We can't have fifty per cent of the office staff all hormonal at once.'

There's a grunt from Jan, and Parin puffs his scrawny chest out like some proud soldier.

'The women need to spread out,' Adam continues. 'Use the men as buffers. Maybe there's something we can put in the air con units to neutralise the contagion or whatever it is that causes it. But in the meantime, alternate male and female throughout the office.'

I hadn't realised I'd stopped typing until my IMAtech buzzes to tell me I'm another minute down. Still, my hands won't tap at the keys like they were just now. My fingers are too tense, my biceps too taut to reach for the keyboard. Antonia's heels clip-clop down the office, though I don't see her now. I can't see anything. Black spots cloud the periphery of my vision until I'm left with only a pinhole view in front. And in that small patch of vision, I see Adam Ward, his smug face faltering into despair. In my rigid fingers, I feel his flesh beneath my nails as I rip his skin from his bone.

Sweat trickles down my brow and burns my eyes. I blink, and my daydream is shattered by the functionality of having to wipe my forehead. I attempt to temper my rage with some breaths, sip some water, and crack my knuckles.

The three board members have circled the office and are back by the pile of gifts. All their lips are curled in the same smug way, like they think they've just saved the world. I swallow back bile and allow my imagination to override my anger. Perhaps they'll slip on the floor and break their necks. Perhaps they'll overdose on testosterone and their dicks will fall off. Perhaps they'll all have heart attacks from an overload of narcissism. I wish that was a thing. I wish whatever makes them so fucking egotistical is also terminal.

The three of them begin opening the gifts and cards, reading the condolence messages out loud, name-dropping and quoting the highbrow senders' words.

They pass the cards to their fussing PAs whose faces wear such permanently pained expressions, I often wonder if they are capable now of ever smiling. What did my dad used to say? If the wind changes, your face will stay like that. Those staff must have been head-on in a gale.

The first gift is a magnum of champagne, another is a case of whiskey. I smile to myself as I consider these gifts to be more representative of congratulations than commiserations. Maybe Peter Ward was also hated by other big company owners, and his awareness of the loathing was the reason he killed himself.

Thank God he's dead, I hope they're all thinking. Perhaps they saw him as the tyrant I did.

Adam Ward opens the next gift. A wooden box sealed with a brass clasp. He lifts the lid and puts his hand in, then recoils, jerking his arm back like whatever is inside just bit him. His hand comes out wet and trembling. He gasps and drops the box, and its contents spill across the floor.

I sit more upright and lean to the side to get a better view, then my breath catches. I blink a few times, trying to see what's really there and not what I'm imagining. Because it can't be real. Surely. In the stillness that envelopes the office, I think Adam Ward's gasp is his last, his death rattle, and that what appears to be on the floor belongs to him.

More bad thoughts. Vivid bad thoughts.

I shake my head, but the image doesn't change. The sight is real. Out of the box and among the puddle of red-tinged ice is a severed human hand.

Chapter Fourteen

Layla

I jolt back in my chair. The gasps from those who have seen it are enough to snatch the attention of those who have not. The hand lies stationary on the floor, the fingers curled upwards, the skin grey with its fleshy end flapping with sinewy innards, the bone protruding farther than the meat. It isn't bleeding, it's too old for that. The state of decay leaves only a few red splodges among the rotting tissue. It smells like roadkill.

Some staff member screams, the blond who played the news a few days ago, her shrill cry commencing the panic. The sound of retching follows, an echo of heaving stomachs and gagging throats, then the staccato of feet skidding across the floor in a frantic run for the toilet. Joel is still at his desk, his mouth buried into the crook of his arm. Across the office, Antonia is standing, her back pressed against the wall.

My stomach holds, my core muscles taut and rigid. I glance down at my IMAtech app. Still ninety minutes down and counting. I can't spare the time for this distraction.

'I'll call the police,' I say, in a tone so authoritative it surprises me. No one looks my way, all eyes are still fixed on the hand or looking anywhere but the hand. Funny, I think as I dial, human reactions. To stare or to look away. Fight or flight. I note my own lack of either, instead I'm connected with my own calmness. As I speak to the operator, I concern my thoughts with how much time on IMAtech I will lose. I'm certainly not going to waste seconds cleaning up the puke that a colleague ejected just a couple of metres away.

Gore doesn't phase me at all like it should—I'd seen death at a young age. My mother's brains on the floor is an image burned into my mind. The smell of the vomit is more intrusive than that of the hand, but nothing a sip of water and my mental abilities to compartmentalise can't handle. Or perhaps IMAtech conditioning has aligned my focus in such a way that I prioritise work too much and it allows me to shut out all else.

Perhaps it's Katarina's influence. Katarina would laugh at this sight, would revel in the dismay of her bosses. Her delight in their horror would trump any squeamishness.

Less than two minutes after the hand rolled onto the floor, I resume my typing as the office continues to turn to shit around me.

The police arrive, flashing blue lights bursting through the front windows, announcing their presence and still I don't look up. One officer taps my shoulder, so I have no choice but to pause working and give my statement. The office empties then as everyone is sent home after giving their statements and permission to make up the time at home is given. I check my app. I'll have to work till late to make up the time.

The police need to do a search of the building, they say. In case any other body parts are lurking. I wonder who will clean up. The poor, overworked and embittered PAs, or maybe the police have staff to deal with it? No doubt someone on shit money will be doing the worst job.

All the way home, my usual hunched shoulders droop lower as disappointment bears down on me. I can't rid myself of the wish that the hand belonged to Adam Ward himself. Perhaps it was one of the Baxter's hands, or Diego Smith's, as unlikely as that seems. The hand was obviously from a body that had been dead for a while and there's nothing on the news about any of them croaking it. Shame.

I play the moment over and over again in my mind, and grin when I do. The way Adam Ward's complexion turned green, the little yelp Parin Shah made like he'd had an electric shock. Jan Novac even jumped. There was a hint of fear about them, their egos a little dented.

After replaying the scene a dozen times, I walk taller, my hair still looking good and my spine a little stronger. No fan of WIT would send a severed hand as a gift. This is a sign that someone hates them. That someone is taking action.

***

Katarina arrives home a couple of hours after me, a little drunk by the smell of her. I hold a gin and tonic and she helps herself to a mouthful.

'Check out the news, Kat. You seen it? A severed hand. An actual severed hand!' I have been glued to the TV since I got back. My laptop is open. I've clocked a few minutes but not enough. Being sent home early is going to count against me, but right now I fail to care. The news is far too exciting.

'I saw. It's spot-on, right? Hey, your hair looks great.'

'Thanks,' I say, and flick it over my shoulder. 'I was right there next to it when the hand fell onto the floor.'

Adam Ward's face, a bizarre mix of pinched and puffy, is on the screen now, giving a statement, and I turn up the volume.

…after what I have personally been through, and the company. This is a pointless act of homicidal vandalism. Disruptive for the workforce, and spare a thought to the girls who will have to clean up the mess…

Eurgh, *girls*. As if the two syllables of the word women are too much effort for him. I mute the TV.

Katarina pours herself a drink, then sits next to me, also tutting at the news. 'Did you see the words? FREE written across the knuckles?'

'No, it was facing the other way. But yeah, the news says it said that. It must be an employee. We're all trapped by that bloody company. You see the note that came with it? Stop IMAtech, it said.'

Katarina sips her drink and nods. 'It makes a statement. Maybe it'll work.'

I turn my attention to my laptop and start making up some seconds. 'Peter Ward's memorial is coming up. The publicity that will get will outshine this. But maybe there's some momentum . . . I was going to send my email to the press, but now if I do, they might think that hand was me.'

Katarina snorts a laugh. 'No offence, but your letter wouldn't do anything anyway.'

I fold my arms and furrow my brow.

'You can sulk all you like, but it won't,' Katarina continues. 'Stuff like this is far more impactful. Stuff they're not expecting. A bit of chaos is what it needs. It catches those pricks off-guard. IMAtech is too regimented. People don't work that way. It's like a scale, see?' She stands, then holds her arms out either side of her. 'Order and chaos. Too much order and the chaos is suppressed and squashed down.' She bends her knees, as if I don't know what squashed down looks like. 'But it's a pressure cooker.' She jumps up. 'The chaos bursts free.'

I laugh at her theatrics. 'Maybe, but at least it's not just me who hates that company. At least it seems someone is on our side.'

Chapter Fifteen

Katarina

Sex with Harry Baxter is as aggravating as it is satisfying. It's not that it's bad, quite the opposite. It's more that it irritates me how good it is. I want the notorious womaniser Harry Baxter to be a flop, so I can roll my eyes and smirk at the news reports of whoever his next squeeze will be, so I can feel sorry for the next idiot who lifts her skirt for him and his bank balance. But he's generous in bed in ways his tax return is not.

The worst thing is—he knows how good he is. 'I've a reputation to maintain,' he says. 'Couldn't very well have the media saying I'm crap.'

I could hate him properly if he was some minimally endowed, inattentive, hastily ejaculating squib. I'd love the chance to laugh about how fucking Britain's most eligible bachelor is like a prod with a broken massage chair.

But no. He is amazing. The git. I grit my teeth through my final orgasm, my groan as much out of annoyance as satisfaction.

When we are both more than spent, I lie down, slick with sweat, panting in the bed next to him as I purse my lips and stretch out my shoulders, frustrated with my contentment.

I bend my legs and let my feet glide back down the sheets, so soft and smooth against my cracked heels. I've never stayed in such a fancy hotel before. We didn't even drink more than a sip of the champagne Harry had sent to the room. It tastes divine, but there's some decadence in the wastage. The chocolate-covered strawberries are untouched, so I reach over and grab one, biting down, letting the sharp sweetness linger on my tongue.

Harry's partly closed eyes are on me, a half-smile on his lips. 'We're like kindred spirits. I feel that,' he says. 'You're just so different from other girls.'

I look up at him through my eyelashes. 'Well, I suppose you're quite charming yourself.' I push myself up, then start to dress.

'Stay,' he says, and reaches for my arm.

'I can't. I need to get back.'

'You got kids or something?'

I laugh. 'No. God, no. It's just . . . a rule. I don't stay over.'

'Why?'

'It's complicated.' I lean in and kiss him on the mouth.

When I pull away, I tilt my head so I can take in his profile. So damned good-looking, like an artist crafted him from stone. But he's just a shell with a hollow inside. And I'm not feeble. I can break that pretty-boy nose if I want to.

Then he starts crying.

For fuck's sake. This level of emotion is not what I signed up for.

I suppress my sigh and roll back onto the bed, stroke that rock-hard bicep, and make the sort of soothing noises I would normally use to tempt a cat to give me a cuddle. 'There, there. It's okay.'

'Sorry. I don't mean to cry.'

'It's okay. Let it all out.' I wonder how much his therapist costs. He's getting a bargain right now.

'I could never cry like this in front of my usual friends, women, I mean girls, you know?'

That's maybe the fifth time he's said something like that since we met up a few hours earlier. The veiled flattery is wearing thin. Harry stumbled into the bar right after Peter Ward's memorial. Videos of the event were playing on the news. A grandiose affair that looked more akin to a corporate sales pitch than a funeral. The who's who of the tech world were there, mostly inebriated men being supported by bored-looking women. All lining up to piss on his grave.

It was Davina's night to finish late, so when Harry arrived at the bar alone, puffy red-eyes and looking like a depressed puppy, I thought, well, why not?

I realise now the snot bubbles are why not.

'I'm just so sorry,' he says between sobs. 'I feel so sad one minute and so angry the next.' He says the last few words through his teeth, a sound I can imagine him making when he lifts weights.

I upturn my mouth and caress his hair. I should win a fucking Oscar for this show. 'You angry about Adam?'

'He did it. I'm sure of it.' The redness on his cheeks morphs to a deeper purple with rage. It seems there is nothing like a decent shag to invoke some inner fire. I could use that fire. I could harness it, join it with my own anger to make an inferno. 'He left the bar early that night, remember? He benefits so much from Peter's death. They never got on. Adam said to the press that they did, and during his funeral speech he said they had a bond, but they didn't, not really. Peter always wanted him to be better instead of the lowlife he is.'

'Sounds like you were the real son to him.' An Emmy award is deserved, at least. I've been through Harry's socials, and he supports the Clarity Directive and spread *#behave* as much as every other rich dickhead in London. Being nice to him is killing me.

My sympathy makes Harry's crying worse, and I make a mental note to stick to soothing noises next time instead.

'He needs to confess,' Harry says when his crying has lessened. 'It's the only way. He has to admit he killed him. It's the only way I can get revenge.'

I wet my lips and snuggle in closer. That R word arouses me in all the right ways. 'I hate seeing you like this. How can I help?'

Harry's face is so blotchy from crying, even his chiselled features soften, which seems a pity. 'Why?' he says. 'Why would you want to help?'

'A deep inner sense of justice. I hate it that he's made you so sad.' I run my fingers over his neck. 'Plus, I have nothing to lose.'

Harry nods at my last point and knits his brows, no doubt calculating how much he has to lose: his reputation, his fortune, his position on the board. Clearly one of the things he finds most attractive about me is that I'm a nobody.

As expendable as the bottle of champagne.

'I have an idea,' he says, 'how to make him confess.'

I put one leg back over him and rest my chest on his. 'Yeah? Tell me more,' I say and lick his lips. 'Let's hear how vengeful you can be.'

Chapter Sixteen

Layla

A work memo arrives on Saturday morning, alerting me with an obnoxious ping as I eat my breakfast. For a brief moment, I consider not opening it. It's Saturday after all. Surely they don't expect me to check work emails on a Saturday. I almost laugh at the absurdity of that assumption. That level of reasoning implies it's still in the days before the market crash, or even before broadband and smartphones. Sheer lunacy. The age of communication tech means no one is afforded such weekends. Every employee is only ever a click away.

With heavy arms, I open the email, and instantly my gut twists with regret. I roll my creaking shoulders forward and hold my head in my hands. It confirms that, due to the office staff not making their time target, we won't receive our bonus this week. My neck tenses, pain shooting around my head. I flip over the blister pack of headache pills next to me, but it's empty.

The rest of the email drones on about the need to support the company and the market recovery. It bangs on about hormones and efficiency, how soon they expect the tailor-made pills to be ready, what an invaluable service we are doing for the worlds of tech and pharma by allowing our levels to be monitored.

As if we have a choice.

I massage my temples. We were sent home early after Peter Ward's death and then again when the police came about the severed hand. How the hell are we meant to make up that much time? Joel's offer of Texi is sounding more tempting, but I can't. Living day to day under the guise of medication rather than my own free mind is still not worth thinking about. It's only one week's bonus, I tell myself, sniffing back my frustration and rubbing some positivity into my forehead. Only one week. I can afford one week's loss.

Then there's the last bit of the email. A sneaky addition, as if it makes it a small cheeky request. The new dress code for women, to be more presentable, it says. Well-fitted tops and skirts, heels at least two inches and at least four items of makeup applied. The last sentence says that it is currently voluntary, but no doubt such attention to detail will prove to make WIT employees even more productive.

Yipee.

I don't think I own four items of makeup. Katarina does, but I'm not about to dress myself up like her. It just wouldn't be me. I mentally flick through my wardrobe and without raiding Katarina's closet, I've nothing suitable. It's a while till payday so I'll have to wing it until then. I'll tuck my top in, perhaps. No one will ever notice me anyway.

I log onto my bank app and groan as my balance is lower than I thought. A lot lower. I never spend money on anything other than food and rent. How can I be so broke? I'll never be able to buy new clothes. A thought flashes, a bad thought I shake away instantly. It comes back though, like a mosquito buzzing around. Maybe Katarina has taken money from me. I shake my head again. No. Katarina isn't a thief. She's a friend. She has a good, loyal heart.

She does manage to buy quite a lot of clothes and makeup for someone on a bar staff salary though.

Suspicion gnaws at me, creeping up my spine and making me shiver, though I fight it off with solid reasoning. I shouldn't worry. I should trust her. Katarina is everything I wish I was. Confident, self-assured, in control. She isn't the sort to steal. She was there for me after the accident. She helped me move on, to find myself again. She's such a support, teaching me how to be strong, how to bounce back. Katarina makes out that a heart is made of putty and can be remoulded instead of breaking. She rises above pain, where I wallow. She's an inspiration.

I reconcile the glaring and obvious fact that I'm simply bad at budgeting. London life is expensive. I shouldn't rely on my bonus. It's never guaranteed.

This inner monologue is something a therapist explained to me years ago, a method of talking myself off the edge, reasoning with life's barriers instead of head-butting them. There is always a solution. Find some patience and perspective.

It's all fine, Layla. You're fine.

I exhale a slow and steady breath. No big deal. All is well.

I need to spend the weekend catching up the minutes I missed, or I'll risk losing next week's bonus too. Katarina, though, has other priorities. As I resume my usual position of staring at my computer, she sits next to me at the table, fresh out of bed at midday, wearing a loosely tied silk nightie, and provides a distraction I desperately don't need.

She stirs her coffee loudly. The tinny ring of the teaspoon against the china as she does is so hard she could be trying to break the cup. She huffs in boredom when I try to ignore her, then puts her feet up on the table to paint her nails, right next to my screen. I have only one hundred and thirty minutes more to make up, and that will take hours if I'm not left alone. By 1 p.m. I've run out of different ways to tut.

'Kat,' I snap. 'Seriously. There's a perfectly good sofa over there.'

'I like company. You look like you need it.'

'No. I need to finish this.'

Katarina stands, then walks around behind me. She bends over, her chin inches away from my shoulder. After a moment inspecting my work—or lack of—she stands in my eyeline and folds her arms instead.

'You know what we are, Layla?' Katarina's tone is one that I know too well. It's one that indicates some life lesson is coming. 'We're big lumps of biodegradable slurry. That's it. We're here one minute, worm food the next. The worms will be more grateful for us than employers will ever be.'

Yep. A life lesson. 'Worms don't pay the bills.'

'But they will remember you far longer than the dickheads who employ you.'

'I'm not sure about the memory ability of a worm.'

She flicks her hair, then folds her arms. 'I am certain of the memory ability of a billionaire towards his minions.'

I smile at that. 'Touché.'

'Can you even comprehend what a billionaire is? Why they are so…repulsive. Think about it. A million seconds takes about 11 days. A *billion* seconds…over thirty-one *years*. That sort of wealth is off the scale. They definitely don't give a shit about anyone whose net worth in seconds would pass in the blink of an eye.'

I knit my brows, numbers swimming in my mind. 'Anyway, I still have work to do.'

'So stop this incessant good-girl act,' Katarina pleads. 'Live a little.'

Live a little. That's never been the aim. Growing up it was always, 'What do you want to be when you grow up?' 'Study hard, no time for fun.' 'Don't anger the big man.'

Always on and on, like after trudging through childhood, I would be greeted by the big climax that is adulthood. Like there's going to be some mighty pinnacle in life and I'm scaling that peak.

The reality is, my life flatlined from birth. For the first thirty years, the most excitement I had was finding a ninth hash brown in a bag of eight.

Isobel was easily distracted. Isobel would probably have allowed Katarina to lead her astray, to get mixed up in things she shouldn't, to procrastinate. But that isn't me. I am diligent. A good worker. Isobel admired that about me, she said so many times. She said I make everything better. She said she wished she could be more like me.

'Let's go take some drinks to the park,' Katarina says. 'We'll take umbrellas. Sod the rain.'

'I've got work to do.'

'Let's get a train—anywhere you want. We can visit another city.'

I angle my laptop so I'm facing away from her mischievous eyes. 'I still have an hour to make up. That takes so much longer when I'm distracted.'

'You're even more of a swat now than you were at school. Isn't it about time you had some fun?'

'I have work to do.' I would have loved to have fun at school, but Katarina wasn't my friend then. No one was.

'You're always trying, Layla. You always try so hard to be what everyone else wants you to be. You should do something for you. Just you. A makeover, maybe? Let me do your hair. Your nails.'

'No.' I never do my nails. My toenails are still painted red, but no one sees those. Nail polish on fingernails is garish, too showy. Not me. Not Layla.

Katarina sulks, sticking her plump bottom lip out before stomping around the flat for a bit, then she sits next to me once again. She passes me food, sugar, refined carbs, cheese, alcohol, all the things I probably shouldn't eat so much of, but Katarina devours without a thought. Every two minutes there's a plate or glass of something wafting under my nose, like when Joel was there, but Joel wanted to help. Katarina wants the opposite. My waistband is cutting into my midriff these days. I can't indulge like Katarina and get away with it. Katarina is the essence of excess.

As much as I need to get my work done, as much as I am annoyed by her, I have to acknowledge life is less dull with Katarina around. When Katarina hands me a second plate of brie she sliced for me, a second bar of chocolate, another too-large gin, I accept with less of a fight. Katarina knows how to wear me down, the exact formula to lead me astray. However much of an annoyance she is, she adds some flavour to my otherwise bland life.

Several hours later, when my work is done, I sit and giggle with Katarina on the sofa, bitching and laughing. I tell her about Adam Ward's fear of women's synchronicity, and she replies with all the expletives I should have said. I tell her about my not-date with Joel, and she tells me how she would have replied. Feisty, assertive, with a sanguine smile, and a bucket-load of glamour.

Despite our rapport, my shoulders tense as much as they do after a day in the office. I can't get comfortable. I jump at every noise and shiver when it isn't cold. Whatever I eat or drink, it can't fill the hollowness inside me.

Katarina, though, glows with relaxing radiance. She gestures animatedly at our conversation as if her limbs are lighter than feathers. No weight of worries pushing down on her. No furrows across her skin from stress.

After another gin, we play a game of chess. It was my idea. I always have to beg Katarina to play. She is good though, as good as me. The game ends in a stalemate, as it always does.

We drink some more, and I concede to Katarina's nagging and allow her to tong my hair and paint my nails. A deep red, the kind of colour that draws attention, just how Katarina likes it. Katarina compliments my hair. Vacant compliments, I'm sure, though I accept and repay. When she's done, I look at my hands, the blood-red polish lurid in the evening light. My hair bounces from the waves Katarina has styled in. I flick it over my shoulder and it flies through the air as if weightless, just like Katarina's.

Too much sugar and it rots your teeth. Katarina is like cholesterol, destined to live hidden inside me however much I try to oust her.

Bit by bit, I have let Katarina in, and there's no brushing her away.

Chapter Seventeen

Layla

Walking to the shops Sunday, the pavement is congested and stuffy. The stale scent of others irritates me as much as their shoulders slamming into mine. I'm not very tall and the lack of view makes me feel even smaller, with only the tops of the highest buildings visible over the array of bodies.

There's the odd brush of a hand that isn't by accident. It's the same most days since the Clarity Directive was passed. It's impossible to deny consent in a crowd. Katarina jokes we should have T-shirts printed with *No* written front and back. As if something like that would be acceptable attire at work. At her work, maybe. *#behave* is no longer trending, but the mentality lingers on like some bad fashion trend that refuses to die out.

I use my hands and elbows to push away the occasional leach. There's not many. Most people aren't on board with the Clarity Directive, since it serves to protect the few men at the top of the corporate tree who want to protect their reputations. Despite the dickhead behaviour of those few, most people are still respectful.

Katarina is out in the evening at work or on a date with her new guy she's shared meagre details about, having the sort of social life I have never been blessed with. I never had friends at school. None, not really. At lunch, Katarina and the other kids would sit and talk about TV shows I'd never seen, fawn over celebrities I'd never heard of, clothes I didn't have the means to buy. There's no manual for adolescents telling them the right things to say and the things they should watch on TV. They all seemed to absorb it like osmosis. Like now, Katarina always looked perfect and knew all the latest information about the latest things. For me, I existed in a ditch, shielded and stained with *loser* written all over me.

In the evenings, they'd all have plans to get up to mischief I couldn't even comprehend. When exam grades were released, there was no expectation or disappointment. Katarina and the rest of them were who they were meant to be, and everything that happened to them was meant to happen. They were born for this, whatever it was.

There was never any place in the hierarchy for someone like me. Not smart enough to be one of the geeks, not pretty enough to be popular. No clique had a slot that fit me. Welcoming me into a group would require a hammer and a shoehorn.

'You'll find your tribe,' my dad said once.

The question I still ask is, when?

Is Katarina it now? She's the best and only friend I've ever had. Perhaps she and her roguish ways are as good as it gets for me. The bad times will be over soon, my dad always said. Perhaps this is the most I can expect.

Instead of having fun over the weekend, after my grocery shopping I get to work drafting and re-drafting a letter to the press, telling them how terrible IMAtech is, how the entire workforce are on their knees with stress, how it invades our privacy by monitoring our blood mineral count, hormone levels, as well as what they consider to be productive work seconds. As cathartic as it is to rant on the page, it's pointless, as Katarina says. Such a mild reaction will never generate change.

'You have to move the earth in order to change it,' Katarina said once. 'Seasons happen because the earth is off axis a few degrees. Play straight and nothing changes.'

I can't pick holes in her logic, but my desire to rattle the cage is just that. A tap on the bars, a jingle of the lock. A coward's way.

I briefly consider speaking with the other staff. A joint letter from all of us might have more impact. Surely, they can't sack us all? But then, how do I know if I can trust any of them? If one decides they want to snitch, I'd lose my job for sure.

I click through some emails. There's nothing of note, but Antonia's name comes up. Antonia and her fitted skirt. Antonia who makes my heart race. Antonia who. . .something happened. Something Joel somehow knows and I don't. Like there's some gossip in the office that I've been excluded from. That shouldn't be too surprising. I'm more than a little standoffish at work. I should just let it go. Why do I care if something happened?

But I do. I can't shake that feeling. I haven't felt such desire since Isobel.

I shake my head. I need to push Antonia out of my mind and concentrate on Isobel, on achieving some justice for her.

IMAtech may have been partly responsible for Isobel's death, but it wasn't like the board aimed to kill their employee, however much Katarina thinks they're completely to blame. I mustn't think like Katarina. The bad thoughts need to be kept at bay and diplomacy is my tactic.

When Katarina says that something like a severed hand is a good idea, a pulsing sensation begins on the side of my head and my palms go clammy. She says such things with an air of nonchalance, so much so, I can picture her dagger in hand, scoring welts down the chest of the board members. I'm sure she's not really evil. She has a loose tongue and a deep sense of purpose. She is trying to be a good friend.

What would Isobel say? It seems so long ago I last heard her voice. I remember how her face became animated when she spoke about her passions, only now, it's like viewing her looking up through water, wavy lines blurring out the details, features merging, her voice losing its clarity hidden behind the sound of a lapping shore. Like she's swimming farther away from me, trying to get away. I can't reach her hand anymore, her grip lost to the cool slipperiness of departure.

I stare at my laptop screen, my fingers still as I try to imagine what Isobel would write. Isobel was dedicated to her causes and would be willing to do a damn lot more than just write a letter. But she believed in the power of words. Diplomacy, she said once, is one step on the road to retribution. Fox hunting was what she was protesting about last. She wrote to MPs and councils before she took to blockading hunts, getting up early on weekends to drive out to the countryside to try to stop the slaughter. If she'd had more time, more energy, if IMAtech hadn't exhausted her to the point that she crashed her car, perhaps she would have made a difference.

There's more to remembering someone than just the outline of their expressions and the pitch of their voice. It's also a feeling, the tingle that resonates inside when I think of her. A longing that will never abate.

What would Isobel's letter say? She would tell the facts with a dash of hyperbole—just the right mix of methodical and harebrained. She would write with passion, whereas I'm more of a bullet pointer. I wrote part of the training manual for WIT once and HR told me it was too bland and lacked enthusiasm. Maybe I need to be just a little different, a little less Layla and a little more Isobel, or Katarina. If you mix the three of us together, perhaps we'd make the perfect woman, or at least, what everyone else thinks is the perfect woman.

Thinking about Isobel inspires me. It gets the blood flowing through to my fingers and I slam away at the keys. As pathetic as my letter probably sounds, it comes from the heart and the statistics. Though I don't send it. Not yet. Isobel would. She would print it and send it by recorded post as well as email to all the major newspapers and business bloggers. But I am not Isobel.

I'm more cautious. Layla Daley doesn't make rash decisions. Methodical is the game. To use facts and tread a well-planned path. Like my dad says, I'm a good girl, a hard worker.

Isobel's clothes are still idle in the drawer, unworn, belonging to no one. It won't pay to be like Isobel now, nor like Katarina. Katarina is impulsive and hasty. If she ever thinks things through properly, it doesn't show. She considers consequences as rarely as she considers doing the washing up. I am not ready to be so reckless just yet.

Chapter Eighteen

Katarina

I may be reckless in some walks of life, but I am not without the ability to plan. When I first applied for my job at Little London, I researched not just the hours and pay, but also the bar and the clientele. No way did I want to end up in some dive bar where I was expected to get my nipples out for tips.

Now I need to research once again.

Harry is an open book, easy to tease information from. You'd think someone in the public eye would be a bit more guarded with his information. The rumours of his lack of intelligence are absolutely correct from what I can tell. The man has all the wit of someone who survives on good looks and family fortunes alone. Funny that.

He tells me he can be so open with me because I'm an outsider, not his usual crew who will judge and ridicule. I'm supportive and interested in him, not just his family name.

Oh, sweet naïve man.

I pour the last of a bottle of wine into the cleanest glass I can find, then open the laptop. Layla is sleeping and I tap softly, searching for the names of the rest of the board members.

His parents aren't seen much, preferring a more silent role in WIT. Any internet search on the name brings up ninety-nine per cent Harry articles with just the odd picture of those two. Their time is taken up with Baxter Pharmaceuticals, and Harry is their constant source of disappointment. How much they would have preferred a goody-two-shoes swot for a kid, an ugly thing with more promise in the books than in the bedroom. Shame for them.

I load up one interview with them and almost spit out a sip of wine when I read about them singing his praises, trying to paint the image of the son they would have preferred, using words to describe him such as bright, intelligent, an asset. Oh, God. It seems naïvety in that family runs deep. They allow him to speak on their behalf at most WIT meetings and delegate their responsibilities to their dim-witted golden boy, proving their trust in him.

How does so much wealth end up so stupid?

Somehow, Harry has escaped rehab. It seems he understands a whiff of moderation, in contrast to the many episodes of his best mate Adam Ward hitting rock bottom with a tourniquet around his arm.

Adam Ward. I click through images and every time I see his picture I can't help but sneer. I clench my fists and salivate at the thought of his neck within my grasp. How I'd love to look him in the eye as he edges closer to death. How I'd love for my smiling face to be the last thing he ever sees.

He's the sole child of Peter Ward and probably also the late billionaire's only disappointment in his lavish life. Glossy magazine articles, videos, news columns, so many inches dedicated to Peter Ward giving free rein to Adam disgracing himself. I click through link after link and each time I read about Peter Ward's opinion about his son, I wish his death was slower than the four-storey fall allowed.

Not that Adam Ward isn't a prick, but somehow his dad pointing it out at every opportunity makes Peter Ward even worse. He never spared a word to excuse his son's actions, only to remark that the boy (he always referred to him as 'the boy') would learn his lesson one day, by hook or by crook. I can only imagine the reprimands he saved for in private.

'That's why he killed Peter,' Harry said the other night. 'Peter was writing him out of the company, he wasn't going to let him be CEO. He knew Adam would fuck it all up.'

'It's a compelling motive,' I agreed.

I watch video after video of Adam Ward on YouTube. The man is as wet as they come. His voice resembles that of a disgruntled cat, mewing his way through interviews. He's like soggy moss clinging helplessly to the mighty tree.

I sip my wine and tap my fingernails on the sofa as I try to psychoanalyse Adam, then scratch my head. Why would anyone with that much wealth give a toss about being in charge of a company like WIT?

Power. That's the obvious and simple explanation. His perception of power, at least. But all Adam Ward's power gives him is the ability to boss people around, to give those cringe-worthy speeches at the office that Layla winces through, and he feels like he's inspirational. The twat.

But that's not power. That's being bossy, like some older sibling or territorial dog. Real power is more elusive. A snake has more power than a dog because you don't see its bite coming. I bare my teeth at pictures of him. I want to push him off a height, to rip his flesh from his bones, to hunt him down like a wolf. Instead, I have to wait in ambush.

My wine glass empty, I put it on the coffee table, then scroll through the last of the board members. The other three are less newsworthy but evil in their own right. They may duck the spotlight a little more than their younger colleagues, but their lives and wealth still hinge on public opinion. That realisation makes me smile. These rich idiots think their fame and notoriety are power, but they're wrong. It makes them weak. They are at the mercy of their own influence.

I look at the pictures of the board members, all fat little piggies living in straw houses.

And the wolf is huffing.

Chapter Nineteen

Layla

WIT's share price took a hit when Peter Ward's untimely death was announced, a mass sell-off which is yet to recover. As soon as I sit at my desk, everyone's inbox gives a cheery ping, which forces a resounding groan from all of us. Parin Shah has been rummaging through his crappy ideas box again.

To support the company during this turbulent time, WardZone will be released ahead of schedule. The new specification details are listed below.

I read and re-read the specs. The second read-through counts against my seconds tally, but I have to be sure. My eyes sting from too much computer time. Perhaps they watered and I'd misread the first time. But no. The second read-through confirms what I thought. New levels, extra features including a two-player mode, and some new characters to boot.

How typical of them to make this announcement via email, rather than the usual morale-boosting speech. Fucking cowards.

'If everyone is on Texi, maybe it's possible,' some woman says. She's sitting on the other side of Joel where a man used to be. 'Or maybe there's a new, improved Texi.'

I sit up and count the number of heads in the office working on game development. Their nine hours a day IMAtech time isn't going to be enough by that release date. For a fleeting moment, I think maybe they're planning on bringing in some extra staff. How ridiculous to have such optimism. I know there are only two possible outcomes. Either the current workforce is to work longer hours, or they're transitioning more towards AI.

Whenever I complain about IMAtech, I have to remind myself that I should be grateful to have a job, since so many companies are over fifty per cent artificial workforce now. It seems there's no plan for the future. If no one but the company directors get a wage, what about everyone else? Even AI is designing AI. The developers shot themselves in the foot there. Calling them idiots is probably unfair. Short-sighted or just old enough that selling off their designs was enough to see them through. No one gives a shit about everyone else.

A glance around the office shows the women have indeed been split up. What's next? Hormone suppressors, mood stabilisers, caffeine injections? The tailor-made pills are to come in any day. Forcing us all onto our knees at Baxter Pharmaceuticals doesn't seem that far-fetched. Next, they'll probably be cutting our arms off and replacing them with robotic limbs. We may not be an AI workforce, but making the office artificial to aid productivity would be as surprising as one of the board members having a facelift.

What had Katarina said everyone was? Big lumps of biodegradable slurry. Now the big lumps of biodegradable slurry at the top of the food chain are asserting their ability to chomp through the masses.

The worms will remember you longer than your dickhead employer.

I smirk as I remember Katarina's words, emboldened by their brashness. Katarina wouldn't put up with this. Katarina would tell them to stick that email where the sun doesn't shine.

I pinch the bridge of my nose and shut my eyes for a moment. I take a few breaths and remind myself that I am a lot more responsible than Katarina. Isobel would have encouraged my letter writing first, whereas Katarina would say to get a baseball bat.

I rub my eyes and take some more deep, grounding breaths, ebbing away from the worries and anger that are rippling through me. Perhaps this means I'll be given some more interesting work. Most of my programming is for the menu screens and credits. The most boring bits that no one ever pays attention to.

I repeat my usual mantra in my head, over and over, searching the gloom for some calm. I am Layla Daley. I am a hard worker. I can do this.

What choice do I have?

Katarina's voice echoes in my head, like a fly that won't buzz off. Sunday afternoon, she leaned into me, and whispered in my ear so delicately—it was as if she was wind blowing through grass, the hibiscus of her perfume, the flowers in the meadow.

'I can help you, Layla.'

'Help me what?'

'Let the anger in. Let it rise up.'

'But—'

She held her finger up to shush me. 'All that effort in keeping it shut away. It's no good for you. Open the door. To your bones. To your gut. Feel it.'

As I bite my nails now, flaking away at the red polish that Katarina convinced me to apply, her words repeat like an ear worm. That wind blows hotter, burning my ears and chest. Katarina's voice is so clear in my mind it's as if she's still sitting next to me speaking, the sound of her tongue moving in her mouth like it's my own. Her perfume still carries on the breeze.

Let the anger in.

My unblinking eyes are streaming, dry and smarting. Stifled tears of anger trail down my cheeks, no makeup for them to smudge.

Let the anger in.

'No,' I say out loud, as quietly as I hear Katarina's voice. A whisper of defiance directed at Katarina, not at the company.

Katarina implies that somehow powerless employees can go for blood. I am more realistic and know that such revenge is impossible. Nothing will bring Isobel back, and stopping IMAtech will take a miracle that someone in my position is unlikely to be able to conjure up.

Rage will solve nothing. It's an emotion for the impulsive and the wealthy. Those with time on their hands and a therapist on their payroll. And a lawyer. I have no such luxuries.

Keep your head down, don't ruffle any feathers. Don't anger the big man. Be a good girl.

My dad's voice comes through with less passion than Katarina's, less persuasive with its lack of intonation and slurred syllables. I cling to it, repeating it. The tried and tested lessons of the wise are harder to grip onto than the latest fad ideas. I grasp his words, absorbing them.

My heart rate slows, and the air thins.

I read the rest of the memo, and a sliver of optimism wriggles its way in. The IMAtech global launch is also to be brought forward to encourage consumer and investor confidence.

Maybe if I send my letter, the timing won't be so bad. Maybe that level of action is all that is required. Bad mouth the new tech enough and other companies won't want it. A tarnish on its reputation and maybe they'll take the IMAtech chips out.

I saved the letter on my phone. I load it up, attach it to an email, and after a second of hesitation, I click send.

The last few lines of the email from Parin Shah are even less positive, with WIT insisting that every staff member must have a hundred per cent of minutes logged. No more five minutes a day leeway, no working from home without prior permission.

I curse into my coffee cup, which costs me another couple of seconds, then I resume typing.

'Can you believe this?' Joel says.

'Yes,' I say. 'I definitely can.'

'Fuck this shit. I'm quitting.'

'Good for you. There are no other jobs anywhere. AI does everything now.'

Joel makes his usual sound of annoyance, groaning louder than his chair as he rocks back on its rear legs.

'If we can't match AI output and more, we're done,' I say. 'That's just the way it is.'

He stops rocking and commences typing again, still cursing but quieter. 'Someone should teach these dicks a lesson.'

I would roll my eyes if I was able to look away from my screen for that long. 'Have you forgotten about the dismembered hand that landed right next to me?'

'Well, it's not enough,' Joel hisses. 'More needs to be done to put a stop to this. Someone really needs to stand up to them.'

I bite the inside of my cheek, tensing my muscles, and remember the wording of my letter. Scathing and truthful. It has just the right amount of emotion mingled with facts. It's a stepping stone on the road to retribution. Surely, that will result in some action. I smile. 'Maybe they already are.'

Chapter Twenty

Layla

The board are in the office again, and as they stand up there in their glass office, I imagine smashing the glass in, the shards raining down on them, cutting them to pieces. I dwell on that thought for so long I can almost smell the blood and hear the screams. I have a rope, of course, or some sort of restraint to stop them escaping the glass shower. Maybe I squirt something slippery on the floor like in old slapstick movies, make their legs splay in all directions, maybe they tear a ligament before they fall and land so hard their bones snap. The splinters of glass puncture their hands as they put them down. Maybe some fully impale their hands, others embed deep into their backsides. Some fall face down, the glass spilling their guts.

What would Adam Ward's groans of pain sound like? Pathetic, I imagine. Like some kid who's just had a nightmare. I would laugh so hard my eyes would water like rivers down my cheeks, but even in the blur, I'd be able to see the panic in his eyes, wide with terror, cheeks flushed with fear.

My IMAtech buzzes. Four minutes that little daydream cost me.

Such bad thoughts. When did my mind start spiralling to such thoughts? They're people, I try to remind myself. I've never hurt a person. I shouldn't be thinking that way. Though when they walk back through the office floor, it's hard to see them as anything more than cattle. Meat waiting for slaughter. Is that how they view their employees too?

I am a good person. I should think good things. As I try, Antonia across the office catches my eye, and the tension in my back eases until I resemble a puddle of mush. She looks my way, and we clock eye contact for a moment. Long enough for her to smile, long enough for my face to become as hot as the sun. When I next take a breath, I swallow and look away.

After losing so much time on my daydreams, I'm too preoccupied to notice one of the board members has returned. I've had no time for a toilet break so far today, no seconds to spare, but right now I realise I have no choice but to take the hit on IMAtech or risk pissing myself. I leap from my seat and bolt for the toilets, just as Diego Smith is next to my desk, hot coffee in hand. I barge into him, sending coffee flying through the air, most of it landing on Diego Smith's cream shirt.

'Oh, my God. I'm so sorry,' I say. Every set of eyes is on me. Out of the corner of my vision, the minutes totals are visible and the seconds on the collective tally stagnate, then decline.

'Jesus Christ,' Diego says in his thick Spanish accent. He's a tiny, squat man with grey ringlets that go out in all directions, and is rumoured to be a force to be reckoned with in board meetings. The eldest now that Peter is dead. He looks at me with eyes that could cut through glass in a way like I'd just been imagining. As I fluster and apologise, the part of my mind that had been having the bad thoughts imagines taking the little man's neck in my hands and squeezing until his eyeballs bug out.

'It's fine,' Diego eventually says when I apologise for the umpteenth time. 'What's your name?'

I blink some clarity into my vision and find my voice hiding, meek in the back of my throat. I lean in and whisper my name, hopping on the spot, my need to pee even more urgent.

'I never forget a name or a face. I expect you won't be so careless next time.'

My app buzzes. Three minutes this has cost me so far. 'I need to go. IMAtech. . .anyway, sorry again.' I dart off.

For the rest of the day, I can't tame my roving mind. Diego's scent lingers in the area next to my desk, mixed with the aroma of coffee still strong from the mark on the floor. Diego's nose is tiny, like a child's with an underdeveloped bridge. Would that make it easier to break? The insubstantial thing would be concave, just a bloody hole in his face where his nose used to be. He's probably had surgery on that along with the face lift that has left his forehead so stretched it looks like the skin would easily rip. I've rarely heard Diego Smith talk before, but now, his voice plays over and over again in my mind. How breathy it would be if I had strangled him. How would that wiry, curly hair feel when caught within my grasp around his neck? If I were to pull it, a whole fistful, how hard could I yank before it rips from Diego's skull?

Being so close to him is like an opportunity wasted. I could have shouted at him, grabbed another hot drink and chucked it on him, poked him in the eye. I've never punched anyone before, and as I crack my knuckles with my free hand then tighten my fist, I salivate at the thought.

I rub my palms over my arms, just wanting to feel some flesh in my grip. I squeeze my wrist, imagining how different that would be if it were a neck.

At six o'clock, my IMAtech buzzes. Two hours down today.

Chapter Twenty-One

Layla

I stay late again to make up time. Somehow it's easier to concentrate on work rather than daydreams when the office is devoid of staff. No Joel huffing and groaning next to me, no board with their beady eyes scrutinising our every move. I can go to the toilet without a percussion of tuts on my way there. It still baffles me how it has come to this. How one company has normalised anger at colleagues having to change a tampon.

Everyone wears comfy clothes to work, except Antonia, who still spends time each day walking around the office. Despite Adam Ward's request for more fitted clothes for the women, no one has complied. There's a sense of togetherness in that. A mutual defiance. There's little point making an effort when cowering behind a desk all day and little energy to put in the extra effort. We all look the same: complexions devoid of sun exposure, eyes red from strain, wet hair tied back, clothes with elasticated waistbands so as not to put pressure on our time-costly bladders. All the same. Like mass-produced humans churned out of some factory line.

Like androids.

My walk home is laborious on legs made of jelly as my brain struggles to wade through any logical thought. The direction of the tube station eludes me for a moment, which card I need to tap at the turnstile, how many stops until mine. All of it should be muscle memory after doing this commute for so long, but autopilot is taking a day off after such mind-numbing work.

The *Big Issue* magazine headline on the cover catches my attention: *Peter Ward—his Legacy?*

The question mark at the end makes me think that perhaps, this article won't be pages of praise and accolades. I rummage in my bag and find enough change to buy a copy from the vendor.

'Thanks again, miss.'

'No worries,' I say. Quite unsure what he means by 'again'. I've probably bought a copy before, since he's the vendor closest to my house. The vendor's memory is better than mine, which is turning more and more to mush by the day.

With the magazine tucked under my arm, I join the line of people ambling down the street. Finishing work so much later means I have a bit of elbow room and breathing space, yet the crowd is dense enough to allow me to blend in. Not that anyone will ever recognise me or know me, such is my lack of friends.

I wonder how things will change if everyone in London has IMAtech. The morning rush will be more frantic, the evening commute pushed back later, my current journey home will be more like it was at six o'clock with the heaving masses of people standing shoulder-to-shoulder, the air thick with body odour and exhaust fumes. There's not much politeness around London anyway, and if everyone has IMAtech, the barging and shoving will be more of a ruckus. As if Londoner stress levels aren't high enough.

At the moment, it's like I'm the most stressed one in the crowd. A few tuts when people are impatient is as bad as it usually gets. I can allow my stress to diffuse slightly, to radiate away from me. My journey home is often the most enjoyable bit of my day. Will WIT take that small piece of serenity from me too?

The city pollution is thick, a yellow mist descending. At least it's dry, though the particle matter coating my skin leaves me sticky and grimy. I fancy a bath, but my apartment only has a shower. Maybe I could go to a spa at the weekend, to stew in some hot water and try to dissolve my anger. When did I get so damned angry? Was it after the accident? Is it Katarina's encouragement? Maybe it's just tiredness, lack of appreciation, or stress?

There's something my dad said to me years ago, after a stint in hospital. 'You need to let some things go, Layla,' or something like that. It's hard to remember. Seems like a lifetime ago. It was a lot of medication ago.

The street is not as dense as it is at rush hour. There are gaps in the crowd, open spaces for limbs to spread. The stranger's hand reaches through to grab for my breast. His grasping hand curled over like talons at the end of an outstretched arm and before I register, he squeezes hard,. My discomfort is his pleasure.

'Ow!' I yank myself free, elbowing him as I do.

He's salivating, chest rising and falling with rapid breaths, and he goes for another grope.

I step away. 'Fuck off, pervert.' This slows my pace and the other pedestrians step around me. No one pays my drama any regard. Why would they? It's such a common sight, no law has been broken.

'You didn't say no. I have consent.'

'Fuck you. No.'

'Oh, come on. Might as well let me feel the other one.'

Katarina's voice comes to me, loud and clear and making more sense than ever. *Let the anger in.* I can't see the city any-more. The people and buildings are all lost as my peripheral vision closes in. Her voice repeats, over and over, as my pulse throbs in my ears. I clench my fists. I don't picture punching him, not his greasy grey curtain of hair, the dandruff spilling down his shoulders, or his lazy stubble. I picture what's behind him, as if I can punch right through his skull. He's reaching for me again, the spittle collecting in the corners of his mouth bubbling, and he licks it. His narrowed eyes stare only at my chest. I reach my hand back and with every muscle in my body tense, I land a punch on his nose.

The cracking sound is magnificent. Although some of that was certainly from my fingers.

He yelps in pain, stumbles backwards into another com-muter, who curses and shoves him forward. Blood is pouring from his nose, too much for his hands to collect. 'Fucking bitch. You fucking cow. You broke my nose!'

I'm weightless, giddy, any pain gone with the warmth of joy. I don't notice the lack of view from my stunted height, don't feel the shoulder barges of people trying to get past. I am taller than I have ever been, soaring high.

'I'm going to get you, you fucking bitch. You need to learn to behave.'

Snapped back to reality, my feet find the ground again, and I run. Unable to stop grinning, I laugh as I run, ducking and diving around people until my lungs are burning and I find a newsagent to dart into. I lean against the wall, catching my breath, sweat pouring down my face.

It's like Katarina is with me, laughing with me, telling me well done.

As my heart rate stabilises, my joy dissipates and dread chills my warmth. My joy sizzles away like water poured on hot coals. I hurt that man. Will there be cameras? Will he find me again?

He deserved it. Katarina's voice comes through clearly again, and she's right, of course she's right.

The pain in my hand is pulsating now, across all of my fingers and knuckles. I shake it out. My hands were already sore from work and now this. It was stupid. I shouldn't have done that. It's just not something Layla Daley would do.

It's something Katarina would do, something she'll be proud of me doing.

When I restart my journey home, I decide I won't tell her. She doesn't need to know she's influential, that she's getting under my skin. Not that I'll do such a thing again anyway. It was a one-off.

I can keep the anger away. I can keep Katarina's influence at bay.

Chapter Twenty-Two

Layla

When I get home and take off my coat, I realise how mucky it is—London pollution and now a grubby handprint. Most of that brushes off at least, and as his fingerprints fade, I decide to erase it from memory. I won't think about it again. It's in the past. I can compartmentalise. I'll take my coat to the dry cleaners when I get a second.

Katarina's shoes are haphazardly scattered by the front door as always, as if she takes them off mid-stride. I walk through to the kitchen and sit for a few moments to stretch out my back and contemplate dinner. There are some cold cuts of meat in the fridge, some pickle, mustard, and crackers. No-cook food that I can prepare in a moment and eat while sitting on the sofa, but then I open the fridge, and my stomach growls louder.

Katarina emerges not looking ready for work, wearing joggers and a plain T-shirt. I fight back my desire to shout at her, but my stomach is loud enough without my voice adding to it.

'Do you think you can do a bit of food shopping?' I say in my most diplomatic voice. 'I bought loads and there is literally nothing left. Looks like you ate tons when you got back at whatever hour last night.'

'I'll go out and get some in a bit. It's my night off. I was just so exhausted, worked up quite an appetite last night.' She bounces her eyebrows.

Katarina's joviality is catching, and I laugh. 'This guy you're fucking sounds quite the catch. Who is he?'

'No one you'd like.'

'Well, maybe get him to take you out for dinner and save some food for me.'

Katarina leans across the table on her elbows and peers closer at my face, like she's looking for spots. 'What's wrong? Something's different about you? What happened today?'

I stiffen and twiddle my hair through my fingers. 'I just. . .' I spent way too long fantasising about strangling a board member at work and then punched a guy in the face for groping me, is what I should say if I am being honest, though somehow, admitting that doesn't sound right. It doesn't sound like me. 'Just tired as always. Work. The board came in. I had a run-in with Diego Smith and spilled my coffee on him.'

'Ha!' Katarina's face lights up. 'Was it hot? Did it burn him?'

'What? No. I mean, yes, but no. I don't think he was burned.'

'Shame.' Katarina clears her throat, then stands. 'Diego Smith may not be as evil as his soon-to-be ex-husband, who's going after every penny he has thanks to his infidelity with his soon-to-be wife, Francesca Moreti. As penniless as his ex, it seems Diego preys on those with less than him, preferring to feel superior rather than indebted.'

My eyebrows shoot up. Her speech is clearly rehearsed or read from some blog. 'Why the hell do you know so much about Diego Smith?'

'Just doing my homework.'

I narrow my eyes. 'Anyway, that was an opportunity missed. I should have said I bumped into him because I was in a rush because IMAtech is exhausting and doesn't even allow us time to piss.'

'But you said nothing?'

'I just apologised.' I look down at my hands. Shame heats my face, although the source of the shame I can't pinpoint. Shame I didn't punch Diego Smith or shame that I wanted to? Somehow, the lines that divide my brain into good and bad are blurring. Looking at my hands, they're clean. My bad thoughts leave no stain. Yet my fists are clenched so tightly they throb. The usual pain from typing so much, but the pain grounds me. I can imagine it's Diego Smith's pain. I wonder how much a broken jaw hurts.

'I need to rest,' I say. 'My mind is becoming wrong, all twisted. I feel like I'm going mad. I keep having these thoughts. . .it's like they're going to burst out of me, like I can't control them. Bad thoughts. Ever since the accident—'

'Hey.' Katarina sits again and puts her arm around me. 'I know. I know you so well. You don't have to worry. Those bad thoughts, that's what I'm here for. Tell them to me. Offload.'

I shrug free from her arm and lean away. 'It doesn't matter. I'll find something for dinner. I just need some food.'

'You need to let it out, Layla. Be angry, it's okay.'

'I don't know—'

'It's like. . .' Katarina stands, then gesticulates as if she's explaining her thoughts in mime. 'Like you've had a heavy weekend, and it's Tuesday and someone is moaning at you, and you feel so damned sober because you were so stupidly pissed at the weekend, and all you want to do is have a drink. You get it?'

'Not really.'

'It's the peaks and the troughs. You want to be happy. Everyone just wants to be so fucking happy. But you'll only find true happiness when you have experienced true hatred. You'll only know peace when you have embraced all the anger you keep inside.'

Katarina's eyes are wide, almost pleading, trying to hammer her point home. That elation I felt after punching that guy. . .she's right. But I can't go around punching people all the time.

As much as I try not to be influenced by her, it's impossible. Katarina can claw her way past any barrier I put up. I stand, then look in the fridge again, like there's something I missed before, some dish of delicious leftovers that's hiding behind the soggy lettuce and off milk.

'I just need to keep my head down, work hard,' I say. 'I need some rhythm, some routine, that's all. I used to be good at this, timekeeping, keeping up, I used to have no problem with it. It's just lately, it's harder. But I'll figure it out. Or else I'll look for another job. I mean, I looked a bit already, but there's nothing right now.'

I trawled job sites over the weekend, and there really is nothing. I open up my phone and check again.

'I don't know why you bother,' Katarina says.

'You never know.'

Katarina looks over my shoulder. 'Cleaner, bar staff—hey! You should do that!'

I roll my eyes and elbow her away. 'All the companies are going to roll out IMAtech after the launch anyway. Out of the chip pan and into the fire.'

'Yeah, well. I have a plan.'

That grabs my attention. 'Oh, God. No, Katarina. What have you done?'

'Trust me. You just need to let me take the lead on this.'

'You always take the lead.'

'You know what I mean.'

I slam my phone down so firmly, I fear I've smashed the screen. 'No, I don't. I literally have no idea. Are you going to come to my work and cause mayhem?'

'Ew. No.' She winces. 'I just think the world needs to see WIT and IMAtech for what they really are.'

My persistent headache returns as my body temperature spikes. 'You can't keep me in the dark like this! I need to know.'

Katarina puts her hands on my shoulders. 'Calm down. Let off some steam. Trust me.'

I meet her gaze, her eyes twinkling with excitement, whereas mine water with fear. I wipe my eyes on my sleeve, then search Katarina's face for answers but find only a smile.

'Come with me,' Katarina says. She takes my hand and drags me towards the front door.

'Where are we going?'

'Out.'

'Where?' I try to pull my hand back, but her grip tightens. 'Can't we just stay in and play chess? I'm tired.'

'You'll say no if I tell you, so just trust me and come.'

Trust me. That's such a big ask from someone like Katarina. But still, I have nothing else to do. Perhaps I can grab some food while we're out.

I scrabble for my shoes, Katarina choosing some flats for a change, then we dash out the door.

Chapter Twenty-Three

Layla

We arrive near Hyde Park. A quiet street made up of three-storey townhouses, each one large enough to be a hotel. The sort of residences that house London's richest, complete with Bentleys attended by chauffeurs waiting outside.

At the roadside opposite, Katarina and I sit at a bus stop flanked by well-tended to bushes. I picked up several pieces of litter and put them in the bin on the way, but here, there's no litter at all. We peer through the streetlight glare at the tidy houses on their manicured street.

Katarina is pressed against my side and points across the road. 'Look at the size of these places, Layla. I mean, how many millions does each house cost?'

I fold my arms. The night is cold, and I should have grabbed another layer. Katarina has a thin cardigan over her more revealing clothes. She doesn't even shiver. Not a single goosebump. 'God knows,' I say.

'That's how the world works. That's why it's all so wrong. There's no Taylor Foundation for vulnerable women around here. These people all want to be the richest, but they can only be the richest if everyone else is the poorest. You see what I mean?'

'Not really.'

She leans so her face is closer to mine. 'These people can't live in pokey apartments and worry over every wattage of electricity. Like IMAtech, they assign that job to everyone else.'

A car purrs its way along the street and stops in front of one of the largest houses. An excessively grandiose thing with high ceilings and a few steps leading up to its oversized front door. Out of the back of the car exits Diego Smith. My hands go to my mouth. 'How did you—?'

'I've been doing my homework, like I told you. If only we had some more hot coffee now!' She laughs.

I shush her and elbow her in the ribs.

'You need to see. It wasn't an opportunity missed, today with the coffee. It's easy to hunt these people down. They're so public, so brazen with flaunting themselves, they think they're invincible. But they're one match away from being wiped off the earth.'

I jerk away. 'Kat! You can't even think like that.'

'It's just thoughts, like the ones I'm sure you have. So don't feel bad about your thoughts towards him and his cronies. Don't hide who you are. Who you truly are. *They* don't. Because he does a lot worse to you and everyone. However revenge presents itself, it's never going to be enough.'

There's venom in Katarina's voice, a hiss on every S. Her hatred comes through every syllable, sending out shockwaves. My hatred sends shockwaves only internally, ruffling my own feathers, fizzing my own bones. My skin is a barrier to all my emotions. For Katarina, it's a catalyst.

'Men, they're like herpes,' she says, recoiling her lips. 'Men in power anyway. They're invasive. They infect and linger and come back to bite you whenever you're down. They're a blight on your immune system. They're only good for one thing, and most of them aren't even any good at that. Women birth the entire world, yet men take ownership of the lot. If WIT was run by women, IMAtech wouldn't be happening. If women ruled the world, the Clarity Directive would never have passed. Those dicks in charge think it was quotas for women in top jobs that caused the market crash. But they can't see the problems began because there was a *need* for quotas. And who are the only ones reaping the rewards of the recovery now? Wealthy men. They won't stop until they've rinsed the rest of the world of every penny and felt up every woman. So, we have to stop them.'

I look over at her, at the sparkle in her eyes as she watches Diego Smith outside, in the open. It's as if her eyes are a sniper rifle. Katarina licks her lips, like the thoughts she has makes her thirsty. And it seems like they are the same sort of thoughts I've been having. Bad thoughts. Wanting to harm people thoughts. Only, Katarina reaches for them, embraces them, parades them. She feels no shame in them.

I clench my jaw, narrow my eyes, shutting out my peripheral vision. Shutting out the predator.

A rustle behind, and the high-viz of a police officer walks towards us. Katarina jumps behind a bush, but I'm not quick enough. I stay sitting at the bus stop, my face blank as my eyes search the ground for an excuse.

'What are you up to?' he asks. He's well over six feet tall, and I feel like a misbehaving child next to him.

'Sorry officer,' I say with a tremulous voice. 'I'm just waiting for the bus.'

'I heard voices.'

'I was on the phone.' I get my phone out of my pocket to show him.

He nods, then stares at me a moment before replying. 'Well, off you go. No buses use this bus stop this time of night. You'll need to head to Lancaster Gate.'

I get up, thank him, and slowly walk away, exhaling a long breath. After a moment, Katarina catches up, giggling.

'Where the hell did you hide?' I ask.

'The bush. I think I've got leaves in my pants.'

I laugh and link arms with her.

'Imagine on our street if someone was hanging around hiding under bushes,' Katarina says. 'Would anyone say anything?'

I think for a moment. 'No. No, they wouldn't.'

'We're fair game in this dog-eat-dog world. It's time someone sorted that out. Don't you think?'

My anger warms up again. Katarina is right, we were only sitting there. In any other neighbourhood, no police would give a shit. But here, where the richest live, we are shooed away like rabid foxes. I swallow and stare straight ahead into the night. Katarina's words sinking in, getting under my skin, and lighting a fire inside me. 'I guess so.'

Chapter Twenty-Four

Katarina

Harry's apartment screams wealthy bachelor. Dark leather upholstery, suggestive art hanging from the walls, some woodsy air freshener that probably makes him feel like a salt-of-the-earth, blue-collar man. The black crystals of the chandelier jingle as the oversized bed bangs against the wall in time to our rhythm. The bed is so comfortable, I'm sure I could fall asleep instantly, even from my position on all fours. It's more comfortable than the hotel he took me to last time. I scrunch the silk sheets in my hands as I have the need to, and when we collapse side-by-side afterwards, I stretch my arms out over the softness of the mattress and imagine how it must be to wake in such luxury every day.

I prop up on one elbow, resisting the urge to give in to relaxation. The condom packet is on the floor, ready for the cleaner to tidy up, another half-wasted bottle of champagne is still in its ice bucket.

One wall of the bedroom is entirely made up of a bay window. We didn't bother to close the blinds. There's little point from so high. The view of the city from so many storeys up makes London look like a toy town. There's no sound from below. A silent display of little lights twinkling in lower down windows is the only sign of life. I check the time. I'm due at work soon. My shoulders droop as I know the comfort can't last.

I smooth back my hair, sure our escapades have flattened my waves and stuck my roots to my scalp with sweat. Harry is composing himself, a satisfied half-grin plastered across his mouth. I wonder how many women he's fucked in this bed. Hundreds probably, if the media are to be believed. Where some might view fucking Harry Baxter as an accolade, I view it as an inevitability of odds. At the rate he ploughs through women, my turn was bound to come up.

Still, I am in this for the bigger picture, not just the short-term satisfaction.

There are no family photos that I can see around the apartment. Strange, I thought at first, since his entire lifestyle is made up from the wealth his parents' company bestows upon him. The bedroom door is open and through the hallway there's a large-framed photograph of Peter Ward, hanging next to some vintage arcade games.

When Harry has ejaculated all of his masculinity, has taken his moment of contentment, then cooled off, he glances towards that photo and becomes an oversharing babbling mess of a man again. A box of tissues is on the bedside table and I pass him one.

'Everyone still just believes it was suicide because of the note. But all it said was, *Adam, I'm sorry.* That's it. He could have meant to write more. I know he did. That note was going to say that he was writing Adam out of the company.'

I sit up and reach for my underwear, a matching black lace set that cost more than I'd usually spend and is likely still a fraction of what Harry's women's underwear usually retails at. Still, it all looks the same in a crumpled heap on the floor. 'So,' I say when I am more modestly presented. 'It's like you said. Adam needs to confess.'

Harry blows his nose, then tosses the used tissue towards the condom packet. 'I'll make sure he does. After the IMAtech launch.'

My acting performance has found its limit. There is no way I can pretend to be okay with IMAtech. I fold my arms and look away. 'That stupid launch for that product that is so bad.'

'Hey! It's a great invention. Everyone bangs on about waste these days. Plastic waste, food waste. What about wasted time? That's important too. IMAtech makes workers much more time efficient.'

'They're knackered.'

'It's fine,' he says in such a carefree tone I want to smack some sense into him. 'We've thought of everything. Employees can take Texi if they're knackered. The new hormone balancing medication is going to get everyone geared up for work all day and totally able to chill at home.' He reaches into the bedside table and takes out a packet of yellow pills. 'Want one? I got my best score on Pac Man after taking Texi. When the new Ward-Zone game comes out, it's going to be in even higher demand. Everyone who plays video games will take it.'

'Kids taking drugs to play a computer game. Sounds sensible.' My tone drips with sarcasm that I make no effort to hide.

'It's the 21st century. It's just how the world is.'

It's his family's pharmaceutical company who are pedalling Texi. Board members at WIT cashing in from IMAtech, and the drug that keeps the minions trolling on. No wonder he loved Peter so much.

I've seen the pills before, heard people talking about them in the bar. The drug has found its place in the mainstream. More socially acceptable than cocaine and amphetamines, this is totally legal and pharmacy-approved. Someone from Baxter Pharmaceuticals must have screwed the brains out of the boss at the Drug Administration Department to get those little yellow pills on the shelf in every supermarket.

Baxter Pharmaceuticals' stamp and patent make it as naughty in the workplace as a double espresso, and a whole lot more effective. It's a game-changer, they say. It puts all your distracting thoughts away, allows total focus, and is given out like sweeties by the pharmaceutical giant who profits from employees taking toilet breaks.

I don't need the extra focus at work, since pouring cocktails is hardly mentally taxing. My arms and feet ache, but Texi won't help with that. Perhaps though, it will help channel my other thoughts. The plan-making thoughts. The revenge-plotting thoughts. I wet my bottom lip, then take one.

Harry gives me a peck on the cheek. 'See. It's all good.'

It's hard to say no to him with cheek dimples and a jawline like that.

Layla has resisted Texi so far, on my advice. It might stifle creativity, or ramp it up too much, prevent sleep, all sorts. She could overdose. She's been on pills for other ailments before and they didn't help at all. I hope she stays off them for good, for both of our sakes.

'Launch is next week,' Harry continues. 'That will shoot up the share price and will be a perfect time for Adam to step down, after his confession, of course.'

'And you think he really will confess?'

'He will. I know how to make him talk. How many stints in rehab has he had? I've lost count. But the guy is weak. One slip up and he'll blab like a baby. You just need to play your part at the CEO party. Think you can do that?'

I smile. 'Be sexy and alluring? Sure. I'm Katarina McKenzie. That is precisely what I can do.'

Chapter Twenty-Five

Layla

The nights I spend indoors alone give my mind too much room for regret and grief as I attempt to summon up the feeling I had when I held Isobel close. When I try to learn some lessons from her, when I can still smell her on my pillow.

When it's not loss that rids me of sleep, it's nightmares. Tonight, I wake suddenly, clammy and alert. It wasn't all a nightmare, some of it was a pleasant dream too. A faceless person giving me pleasure I haven't known in a while. It's as if Isobel is still with me, reaching down, caressing, her body's warmth permeating, her touch soft yet assertive, knowing exactly the right places to tease. But then, my fantasies of hurting people come through: squeezing warm flesh till it goes cold, a sharp knife cutting through skin and tissue, the slight resistance from the tangle of an artery, the hard stop when I hit bone. Diego Smith's bones may be brittle with his age, but one saw of that knife and I'll turn them to dust.

With an unsteady hand, I reach for the bedside lamp switch and turn it on, rubbing my eyes while they adjust to the light.

I wipe the sweat off my face. I must have had a drink last night, since my hands are sticky and my skin is tacky all over. I need a shower. The little clock on my bedside table flashes the time. I've ten minutes before my alarm will beep. At least I'm not late this time.

The *Big Issue* magazine is on the floor, open on the page I was reading late last night. It wasn't as damning as I'd hoped. They'd gone for a balanced approach on the arsewipe that was Peter Ward. They stated his net worth and how little philanthropy he did, a little about some tax avoidance over the years, a few paragraphs about what a waste of space his son is.

There's a quote from when the Clarity Directive first came in: *Since the market crash, gold diggers are everywhere. Poor women trying to find ways to milk us for all we're worth. The Clarity Directive offers the most important people the protection they deserve.*

I can hear his voice saying those words, its scratchy timbre making every word sound like he needed a cough.

The article doesn't comment on that quote. They printed it under a picture of him with his arms folded, looking exactly like the arrogant prick he was. I can't imagine any woman trying it on with him, however rich he was. Even that picture makes my stomach heave. I can still smell his aftershave.

There's nothing about IMAtech. It's not public knowledge yet. The tech world knows WIT have something big up their sleeves, but until the launch it's mere rumours, and the whisperers are excited.

On my way to work, I remember the date. My dad's birthday. I should go visit him. I should jump on a train and get the hell out of London, sit next to him on the sofa, and watch those crappy game shows he likes so much, while I eat all his biscuits that never seem to run out. I haven't even had time to send him a present. He'll understand. He always does.

I dial his number, just a voice call. My hair is still wet from my shower, my unmade-up face looks an impossible combination of gaunt and chubby. If he sees what a mess I look like, he'll only worry.

My eyes brim with tears when he answers. His speech is bad since his stroke, but I can understand him. Just the intonations in his tone are enough. I can hear his smile.

'You okay, dear?' he asks. 'You sound different.'

'I'm fine, Dad. It's just nice to hear your voice.'

'Your brother popped 'round yesterday. He seems well.'

Dylan always seems well. No changes there. I'm just glad I missed him. The last time I spoke to him was when the Clarity Directive was being voted through and he was all for it. Said it was necessary after the market crash, that men were saving the country and they needed protection. He blurted out the mantra of the wealthy pricks at the top, such is the impressionability of such a shallow mind. Perhaps he thinks if he talks like them, he'll be one of them. As if they are something to aspire to.

You really get to know someone when some big policy change like that comes in. We never got on anyway, and after that, I wanted to rub broken glass in his eyes. The brother who I could never compete with. The brother who was the perfect child in our mother's eyes. Mum never put pressure on him to do anything. He was free to do what he enjoyed, play football, rugby, date, whatever. 'Boys will be boys,' she said. 'Women need to apply themselves more or else you'll end up at the sticky end of some pervert for the rest of your life.'

'Glad to hear it,' I say to dad. Why does he have to mention Dylan at all?

There's a pause. 'Maybe you could come visit at the weekend? I'll pay for your train if you're worried about money.'

I could go at the weekend. I could work on the train and at his if I have minutes to make up. Dad will probably be less distracting than Katarina. But I know I can't go. I'd want to stay all week and home working is banned since I have no way to justify it, and then it would be too upsetting to leave. My excuses for not going come to the forefront of my mind too readily. My reasons for going are sparse and insubstantial. As if an indescribable pull is keeping me in London. There's something about this city, like it's surrounded by iron gates. Once in, it's nearly impossible to escape.

'No, Dad. Sorry. I'm just too busy at work. When this new game is out, it should ease up a bit.'

'If you need to speak to someone,' he says, 'or you need to have a break somewhere, like before, I can pay. I can get that nice doctor, Doctor Cottrell, to write you a prescription. You remember him? He's a friend of mine. I'm sure he'll help. You just need to say. If you're in some sort of trouble—'

'No, Dad,' I say before he can tempt me anymore. I need a clear head. I need to get my work done. I need to be near where Isobel once was. 'I'm fine. Really. Just work is nuts.'

He pauses another moment, and I can almost hear his thoughts ticking over. 'Okay. You're such a hard worker these days. I'm so proud of you. You're such a good girl. Not all work and no fun, I hope? You getting out much?'

Sadness heats my face, and I swallow back my emotions. 'I have a friend. She helps me.'

'That's good, sweetheart. I'm glad you have someone. You're such a hard worker these days. It's like it's given you some perspective.'

I wipe my watery eyes with my sleeve. It's all I've wanted for so long, to make my dad proud, to keep my head down, to be responsible. Make the big man happy, so he always said. Since the accident, when Isobel died, I really have knuckled down and worked hard, despite my timekeeping going off the rails. Hearing him acknowledge this makes at least some of the laborious hours worthwhile.

Chapter Twenty-Six

Katarina

My new dress is perfect. It fits like a glove over my curves. It's black satin with a slit almost as high as my crotch, with just the right amount of boob on display. Quite what to wear to a CEO bash I'm not really sure, but I figure skin on show always goes down well. I want to stand out, and to have all eyes on me. As I pose in front of the mirror, I'm sure they will be.

'Wow,' Harry says when he sees me, his lustful eyes bulging. 'You look great. That dress is going to work perfectly.'

I smirk. 'Functional was my aim.'

'You know what I mean.' He winks and wraps his arms around my waist. 'Every girlfriend I've ever had, Adam has hit on. He can't stand to let me have anything. So you just have to let him believe he's in with a shot.'

'I think I can do that.'

'Just remember, Adam killed Peter. He's a murderer. Just in case you were tempted.'

'Gotcha.'

I check the time, wishing we have a few moments spare for me to take the dress off and his suit too. No such luck. I haven't even finished getting ready yet. My eyes are dry but I put my contacts in anyway, a few eye drops and a ton of makeup. I look at my reflection once again in the mirror, front, side, and rear views. If Adam Ward makes a habit of hitting on Harry's women, I'm definitely dressed well enough for him to find me irresistible. I still look tired though, dark circles under my eyes, a pallor to my complexion that lurks under my foundation. I'm dehydrated, probably.

I drink a pint of water, then regret it as peeing in such a fitted dress will be a chore. I manage a final toilet stop before we leave and as I do so, I take a moment to think of Layla. My heart goes out to her, and all her colleagues. They'll be spending their day behind a desk typing away without a drink, as they can't afford the seconds lost for such pit stops. Since when did taking a piss become a luxury of the wealthy? That is what IMAtech is doing. It's making human rights a thing of opulence.

It's not only avenging Isobel I have on my mind, it's saving Layla. Saving all of them.

I wash my hands and stare at myself in the mirror once more. I am Katarina McKenzie. And I am going to fix this broken world. Whatever it takes.

Chapter Twenty-Seven

Katarina

There are plenty of press at the party, all snap-happy with their cameras and shouting questions to Harry as he enters. I walk in behind him unnoticed by the media. Harry gives the cameras a sage smile, though undoes any wise image by posing for photographs while making a heart shape with his hands. I suppress my desire to cringe. One thing he's obviously learned from the likely hours and hours he's had of media training—keep quiet in front of the journalists, though it seems that training didn't extend to cheesy hand gestures. He probably saw that in some TikTok video and thought it was cool. The idiot. At least he does keep his mouth shut. It's unlikely the press want to know about his vintage arcade games or thoughts on Peter Ward's alleged suicide. He says nothing after he finishes his childish pose as he walks past the cameras, leaving his PA to spew out a pre-rehearsed statement.

Other investors and tech giants file in behind, their staff commenting on how it's an exciting time for WIT despite the circumstances, and how the entire tech world is on tenterhooks awaiting what WIT has in store for them next.

I don't roll my eyes and scowl at them all, as much as I have the urge to. I'm here to be alluring, but what I really want is to punch every one of those dickheads in the face. My arms shake a little with pent up rage as I try to diffuse my thoughts, to stay focused. Funny how all those bigwigs in their expensive suits arriving by individual chauffeur-driven cars, smiling showing off their six-figure teeth, comment on how exciting this is for the big companies. None of them take a second to thank the staff working themselves to death for fuck-all reward. An extra zero on their own bank balance is all they care about.

As we walk farther into the hall, away from the press, I block out the rest of the people, concentrating all of my thoughts on Harry and WIT. It would be too easy to get distracted, to get side-tracked and start trying to take every blood-thirsty company down. I wonder how many other companies have employees who are worked, quite literally, to death. I wonder how many other companies want their staff to behave like soulless robots, to turn them into machines that print money? How many of the CEOs support the Clarity Directive? Every company CEO must be as much of a weasel as Adam fucking Ward. All those men look just like the fat little piggies I've imagined them to be. Shove an apple in their mouths and douse them with butter and I could roast the lot of them.

No. I need to concentrate. One herd of dickheads at a time, although herd doesn't sound quite right. What is the collective

noun for a group of wealthy city CEOs? A plague of pricks. . .
A bell tower of dickheads. . .

Focus Katarina! It's only WITs invention that caused the
accident. I can't take down the entire damned bell tower. Although I can't help imagining though. . .a world where sky-
scrapers don't come at the cost of the sanity of so many, where
reward is fairly distributed instead of inherited, where women
are treated as equals. It's a clean thought, a non-violent one.
The sort of diplomatic thought Layla probably has from time
to time. Such thoughts are dull and uninspiring. I purse my lips
and my arms tense as I replace such mundane thoughts with
pictures of their bloodied faces and broken bones instead, their
naked bodies rotating over fire on a spit roast.

I keep a few paces away from Harry, no holding hands or
linking arms at his request. 'Going public is a big step,' he said
on the journey here. I smiled it off and feigned a mild offence.
As if I care. It's hard, though, to pretend to be someone who
gives a crap. That BAFTA award had better be in the post.

I settle in a spot at the edge of the room. Not hiding away,
but also not wishing to engage. I practise my posture in front of
the window, leaning my weight on one hip, displaying the slit
in my dress. I don't pout like the InstaBimbos Harry normally
hangs out with. Instead, I appear impressed and interested in
the entire shitshow. I'm the best dressed here by a mile, by best
dressed, I don't mean pricey labels and frigid coverings. I look
like the one men would most like to talk to.

Nibbles are served on silver platters by fussing staff. Crystal champagne flutes are handed out, though they are filled with sparkling grape juice in support of Adam Ward's current sobriety. Adam's stints in rehab garnish many pages of glossy magazines. As an addict: alcohol, drugs, gambling, he flits between dopamine causes as fecklessly as he does women. Or men, if some less credible sources are to be believed—not an interest his father approved of.

That was the only indiscretion his father vehemently denied. 'The boy is not bent,' is one such remark I've come across in some magazine archives, alongside his unwavering opinion that the economy stagnated when equal rights became law. 'Women insisting on promotions is what tanked the economy of this great country,' he said to some *Financial Times* journalist once.

It's a wonder that any cards of condolences came after Peter died. The man was a dickhead of the highest degree.

So, thanks to Adam Ward's current bandwagon, proper booze is served by special request only. I consider it for a moment, then decide a clearer head is sensible. And there is a chance that booze-breath will fend off Adam Ward rather than attract him.

The suite up the glassy towering spire of London's Shard building rivals Harry's apartment for views. Sipping on my grape juice, I swallow back my awe, keep my posture upright instead of giving in to the temptation to press my body against the glass, and stare down at the city below. Up here, I can understand why these people feel powerful, with the city so far beneath them. London appears so small, it's as if I could reach down and place the cars and buildings exactly where I want them. I close one eye and reach my hand forward, holding a tiny stick-figure of a man on the street below between my thumb and forefinger, then I press them together. It's as easy as that to squish someone from up here.

People in glass houses shouldn't throw stones. And this tower is ninety-nine per cent glass.

Harry's parents greet him, and he doesn't introduce me. I stay a few steps behind, like some subservient wench. They likely think I'm another PA. It's obvious they're his parents, even if I hadn't researched them beforehand. Harry is the spit of his dad, only taller with less of a scrutinising look about him. It's his mother, though, who has the hardest face of them all. No amount of collagen injections can plump out those scowling lines.

I maintain my downward gaze, inspecting the tiled floor, though I lift my eyes for brief moments to observe. They both fuss around Harry, asking questions parents would normally reserve for adolescents: are you eating enough, not drinking too much, has the cleaner been, have you been going to work?

The rumours of Harry Baxter being mollycoddled by his parents are often rife in the media, and he's always keen to present himself as some independent man, self-made. *Yeah right.* His chosen lines of philanthropy are charities set up for millionaires gone bankrupt and arcade game salvaging. Shame he doesn't think to invest some time and his not-so-hard-earned money in addiction charities, since his family's business peddle so much misery in that department. Adam Ward's misadventures notwithstanding. I might have respected him a bit more if that were the case. But watching him here, in the presence of his parents who are, in effect, his financiers, it's clear he is their puppet, and such a move would slap them in the face. He answers their questions in a pleading way, as a naughty child would. I've never fancied him less.

After a few minutes, Harry's parents leave him alone and he passes me another flute of fizzy something and stands next to me. Adam Ward is across the room, talking to someone in an equally sharp suit and nodding with a furrowed brow. He looks as serious as he always does. I wonder if he's ever laughed properly. If he even knows what jokes are.

Harry leans over to whisper in my ear, though I don't catch what he says, too distracted making eyes at Adam Ward. I giggle, holding my hand to my chest as I do so, taking a sip from my flute. Despite Adam's attention on the person he's talking with, I can feel his eyes on me, a warm tingle on every part of my skin that's under his gaze. I side-glance at him, a split second at a time to note his unblinking eyes are directed my way in an unwavering stare. I lick my bottom lip and turn my gaze back to Harry.

Behind Harry is Diego Smith, coffee-stain-free, and easily the loudest in the room. He stands with the other board members, Parin Shah and Jan Novac. I've studied their pictures online, have read about their roles in the company, and others, and know their collective net worth has too many zeros to say in one breath. I bristle at the sight of them, all immaculately dressed in suits that likely cost more than a month's rent, tended to by an array of staff and they've not a polite word for any of them. The way they address their PAs and staff is a manner in which someone might speak to a misbehaving dog.

Across London, the office staff at WIT will be sitting at their desks, slaving away, that damned IMAtech buzzing every time they stretch their backs out or go for a toilet break. These board members won't have any such tech nagging or berating them. Their workday consists of lunches, drinks, guffaw laughing and counting their billions. I push that to the back of my mind. Instead, I revel in how human they look. Burned flesh all smells the same, however rich the person is. Store budget butter or fancy branded stuff—the same knife cuts through it all.

Harry doesn't approach his colleagues. I notice it then, the reluctance in him, a social anxiety he hasn't displayed to me before. He's not part of their clique. The sight of him biting the inside of his cheek, his hands squeezing his glass a little tighter, rolling on the balls of his feet as if summoning the courage to walk over, almost makes me feel sorry for him. Almost. I remind myself of what I said in the mirror. I am here to fix the broken system, and Harry Baxter is part of what has broken it.

Diego Smith walks over to us, Harry visibly stiffening as he edges closer. He leans heavily into each step, his short and stocky frame rocking like some pendulum. Cuban heels are a ridiculous choice for a man of his age. The slightest nudge and he'll roll an ankle or fall flat on his face. What a shame that would be. I sip my drink to hide my smile.

'Afternoon, Harry,' Diego says. 'I see your parents are here to wet nurse you.'

'Fuck you, Diego.'

'Wouldn't let Mummy and Daddy hear you talk like that. You'll be grounded.'

'Seriously. Give it a rest.'

My mouth hangs open. Diego is a sixty-something business tycoon, yet he sounds more like some playground bully. One more reason to hate him. One more reason to burn his eyeballs out.

'And I see you've bought an escort.' Diego looks at me with cattier eyes than I could ever manage. I almost admire how much of a bitch he is. He sets the bar high.

I take a mouthful of drink, and it takes all my strength not to spit it in Diego's face.

'She's not an escort, actually,' Harry says, and sounds pathetic as he does.

Diego looks me up and down. There's no subtlety in his scrutiny. 'If you say so.' He scrunches his nose like he's about to hiss.

I lock eyes with him, maintaining a blank expression, and say nothing, the tightening grip on my glass is my only tell. Diego probably expected some pleasantry, a complement from some awe-struck uber fan. I give him nothing but a blank stare, as if Diego were no one. A shadow. A ghost. I hope he soon will be.

Diego struts away, and I glance up at Harry. He sips his drink, his has the tang of real champagne, and as he swallows, I note the tension in his jaw, his cheeks rippling over grinding teeth. Perhaps all the teeth-grinding is what's given him such a defined jawline. When Diego arrives back at the group with Parin Shah and Jan Novac, they all laugh.

'Why do you let him talk to you like that?' I ask him.

'What? It's just how things are.'

'Only because you let it.'

'You don't know what you're talking about.'

Harry's tone is curt, and I don't continue the conversation any further. Harry Baxter is a sap, that is what I have learned. Some spineless mummy's boy who won't stand up for himself. That isn't all bad news. It makes it easier to hate him.

Adam Ward eventually makes his way over and shakes hands with Harry.

'Big day, mate. Congrats,' Harry says. 'Shame about the circumstances of course. How're you holding up?'

Adam nods. 'Okay, I guess. Well, it is what it is.' Adam lifts his shoulders when he speaks, shrugging off any emotion. He's shorter than he looks on TV, less good looking than Harry, his features softer. His complexion is mottled from teenage acne. All of this explains why he tries to steal any woman Harry has an interest in. Less good looking, a few hundred million poorer. Small man syndrome comes to mind. I look at him with narrowed eyes and imagine what his skull looks like if all his flesh has rotted off.

'Meet Katarina.' Harry steps to the side to present me like I'm some gift.

'Pleasure.' I offer my hand, which he accepts.

'So, Harry, this is what has been occupying your time.' He gives Harry a gentle nudge, keeping his eyes on me.

My smile tightens, as if I'm made of something inanimate like Adam clearly thinks I am.

'I like to stay busy, as you know,' Harry says, grinning.

'Well,' Adam steps a little closer to me, his eye contact boring through me. My face heats, and I hope he doesn't notice the blush. 'It's criminal that Harry has been hiding you away.'

I smile my most alluring smile. 'Oh, he hasn't been hiding anything.' I detest how much of a flirt I'm being. Letting these men think they're powerful, that they somehow have influence over me, that he'll think my reddening cheeks are from any emotion except anger. Adam Ward radiates such arrogance, it's as if he believes he's some god. He needs no more self-gratification than the desert needs sand. I could do with a handful of sand—to rub it in his eyes.

Adam and Harry's conversation blurs into background noise, something about their mutual friends, designer clothes, and a new car some socialite crashed. Every muscle tenses as anger rises within me. These people are the most shallow and conceited shits I have ever known. It's like some old boys' club from a century ago. Men bred to feel powerful, parading their testosterone around like it makes them stand taller. How is it that the world is geared that way? Nothing has changed in years.

With my rage comes determination, and the vivid certainty, all that makes them powerful, in fact, makes them weak. I bite the inside of my cheek to stop from smiling too broadly. With the gene pool so limited and unchanged, they are exposed. This bunch of brats aren't capable of evolution. They'll never see me coming.

Parin Shah comes to join them, almost pouncing on Adam like some jealous dog.

'Decent enough turn out, don't you think, Adam?'

Adam nods. 'Yeah, I think so.'

'Anyone would be an idiot not to come and congratulate you. This is huge for the tech world.'

I stifle my retch. What a brown-noser. Parin Shah came up the ranks following in his father's footsteps, starting out with smaller gaming companies across Asia before setting his sights on the UK. IMAtech is the brainchild of the sweatshops he oversees in Mumbai, if the rumours are to be believed.

The jovial background chatter coming from Diego and Jan's group comes to a sudden silence. Their faces morph from re-laxed to red-faced and taut. They all look at their phones with such anger in their eyes I can almost see steam coming from their ears.

Diego, Jan, and their entourage walk over to Adam, footsteps thudding in unison against the floor.

'Adam, you seen this?' Jan asks.

Jan Novac angry is an intimidating sight. He's the only one of the bunch who actually scares me. The size of him is enough to make anyone think twice about crossing him. I am relying on his sheer stupidity to aid my scheme. His dialogue mostly consists of grunts and snorts like some mud bathing boar.

'It's ridiculous,' Diego says. 'This shit is going viral.' None of them address Harry, I note.

Adam takes Diego's phone as Harry gets his from his pocket, turning it on with a shrug. 'What?' Harry asks.

Adam looks in silence as Harry scrolls through his social media a while before he finds it.

Adam's lips purse, his sinewy biceps tightening under his shirt. I stand, slouching on my hip and sip my drink, mostly keeping my focus mid-distance.

'So damned disrespectful,' Adam says. 'The man died five minutes ago.'

The video, I can make out from the corner of my eye, is some AI deep fake of a naked Peter Ward, arse fucking a line of peasants. Seven of them, each wearing a T-shirt that spells out IMAtech.

'The comments—' Adam says, a quiver in his voice.

'Don't look. Fucking paupers think they have the right to say such things.' Parin's nose is in the air. 'After all we've done for the markets, this is how they repay us.'

'We'll get PR on this,' Jan says. 'Get it all taken down.'

'It's everywhere,' Adam says, breathy, as if defeated. 'It's literally everywhere.'

Chapter Twenty-Eight

Layla

I startle as Katarina comes bounding through the front door. No wonder the handle and hinges are getting loose if she makes entrances like that. She can call the lettings agent again, since they never listen to me anyway, and she seems to have endless free time. I'm on the sofa going over what I need to do at work tomorrow, while Katarina has clearly been out having fun, being exciting, living her best life.

'Did you see that video?' Katarina asks with a giggle.

I put my phone down and rub the sleep from my eyes. 'Yeah,' I say, the sound effect from the video is ringing out—a panting old man and little piggy squeals. 'Funny video.'

'Oh, come on!' Katarina says with a groan, bending her knees like she's going to beg a reaction from me. 'It's hilarious, and it's gone viral. Shows how sick to the teeth people are of WIT and their damned IMAtech. It's not even launched yet, so this will ruin its reputation before anyone even knows what it is. With that and the severed hand thing too, maybe it'll turn the tide with the press a bit.' Katarina bends to take off her shoes before slumping on the sofa and rubbing her feet. 'I hadn't even noticed how much my feet were aching. Too busy revelling in the look on those board twats' faces from that video.'

My head flinches back. 'How'd you see their faces?'

Katarina takes a second before answering. 'I can just imagine it, can't you?'

'I guess so. They'll probably dismiss it and announce some new WardZone game spec to get people excited about that instead. This will blow over like every bit of scathing press does to them.' I pull my head back some more, taking in the full sight of Katarina. 'You look really fancy, by the way. Been somewhere nice?'

'Yeah. New guy.'

'All right for some.' I yawn. 'I'm so shattered. So bloody tired I can't even remember what I did at work today. I was trying to think—'

'Why were you trying to think about work?'

'Mentally preparing for tomorrow, I guess.' I don't mention that I actually had some good news at work today. They gave me some more interesting work to do. Adding the finishing touches to the main characters. I know the job will still suck and Katarina would also point that out. This new work is not much more interesting than a colouring book, but at least it's a rung up the ladder.

Katarina helps herself to my glass of water, then rubs my arm. 'You need a good night's sleep, maybe a massage. Shall we go to that place down Prior Street? It's still open.'

I glance out of the window, the blackening sky threatening rain, then remember I still haven't even done the dishes and there's zero chance that Katarina is going to do them. Plus, however much her feet ache, I reckon mine hurt more. 'No, no. I really can't be arsed, nor do I have the money. I do need to concentrate at work tomorrow though. Thinking of getting some Texi.'

'Don't!' Katarina snaps.

I jolt back and blink a few times. 'Why not?'

Katarina folds her arms, and her eyebrows arch. 'The Baxter family's pharmaceuticals? Come on, that's double standards.'

I yawn again and stretch out my neck. 'Yeah, I suppose you're right.'

'Just like I'm right about this video. The tide is changing for WIT. Just you wait and see.'

I peer at her with narrowed eyes, tilting my head to the side. 'Why do I get the feeling you're up to something?'

Katarina's plump lips stretch into a smile. 'So, what if I am? You wrote your bloody letter. I have my own methods.'

I groan and rub my eyes some more. Whenever Katarina mentions WIT and revenge, my stomach sinks. What is she up to? She has a mischievous look about her, though with her people skills and making others do what she wants, she probably only has to make a phone call to Adam Ward and ask him nicely to stop IMAtech and he'd agree. My letter may not have generated any sort of response yet, but Katarina has powers of persuasion that I can only dream about.

'Just tell me you're not doing anything that's going to get me the sack?' I ask.

'I am only using my many charms,' she says with a wink.

I laugh and shake my head. 'I guess, at least whoever's doing this is on our side. We're less alone somehow. We're not just some weak protest. The more of us there are speaking out, the stronger we are, right?' Inwardly, a little fizz of excitement stirs inside me. Whatever sweet talking Katarina is doing may help, but there's also someone out there who's being even more drastic.

'Sure,' she says. 'But remember, even you, Layla, are strong. You alone are a force to be reckoned with. They might be born into money, but that doesn't mean you were born weak. You have a voice. Those who are ordinarily incredible are fakers, always trying to be something they're not. It's the everyday people, the incredibly ordinary, who can create real change.'

I lean a little closer and smell her for alcohol. She's talking like she's pissed, but I can't detect a whiff of booze. Her face is flushed though, crimson with enthusiasm. I lie back on the sofa and rearrange the cushion behind me. Whatever has gotten Katarina riled up isn't catching.

'I mean it, Layla,' she continues. 'It's what we do and how we learn that define us. We're adaptable. Women are, we have to be. We can present the best version of ourselves whereas that bell tower of dickheads in charge, they never learn. They're all the same and have been for generations. They don't evolve, and that's what makes them weak. Impact sports make bones strong, right? Those men, they've been wrapped in cotton wool their whole lives. They've never had even a single knock, so now their bones break too easily.'

I sit up a little straighter, the ache gone from my back for a moment. Katarina's words are like a hoist, lifting me up. 'Yeah,' I say. 'Though my dad always said, whatever doesn't kill you makes you stronger.'

'Exactly,' she says, her sly grin widening. 'Kill them before they evolve.'

I swallow and stare at Katarina. A shiver fingers its way across my arms. Katarina sounds earnest. Surely, she understands it's a metaphor.

Surely.

Chapter Twenty-Nine

Layla

The video makes no difference on the share price, not that I'm surprised. No publicity is bad publicity, so they say. Or, at least, some meme isn't bad enough. Fill the press with other news stories and they have other stuff to talk about. Share prices rising, the rich getting richer, there's always some other trouble caused by poor people somewhere.

The press the next day use a handful of words to mention the displeasure towards WIT, the rest of the column inches heap praise upon Adam Ward for stepping into the big shoes that were his father's, how WIT is a solid company steering the stock market the right way, how the country is grateful for their service, blah blah blah.

I grimace at my phone, reading the accolades handed out to Adam Ward and WIT. No doubt the press are to be first in line for IMAtech when it's launched. Their reporters, interns, cleaners, everyone will have every second of their workday recorded or deducted, Texi handed out like sweeties to make them keep up. The press are cashing in like every other big company. WIT's most advanced technology yet, it's hailed as. They'll be queuing up to get their hands on it. It's going to change the world.

What had Katarina said? A few degrees off-kilter. I think it's going to need to be more than a few degrees to stop the roll out of IMAtech, especially since WIT have all the might and are planning to make the same shift in their favour.

My arms tense, elbows pressing into my sides when I imagine the world of the working classes all as efficient as AI. Texi during the day, combined with blood mineral count monitoring and rectifying by Baxter Pharmaceuticals. Mental cyborgs at desks all day, no conversation, bodies fixed into desk posture, eyes unable to look any other way, the company hailed as heroic for continuing to employ flesh and blood yet paint our skin silver, and we'll all resemble every robot movie ever made. A two second glance around the WIT office and it's clear we're part way there already.

As quickly as PR try to take the video down, it's re-circulated. Jan Novac shouts his booming voice down his phone so loudly, it's audible from the office floor. It's a welcome distraction from the percussion of typing, and the anger in his voice makes me smile.

Adam Ward comes in, his little fairy feet scurrying across the office until he stands at the back and shouts, 'Everyone, can I have your attention a moment.'

Me, along with everyone, do what we are told, though all eyes are on the IMAtech tally rather than Adam Ward's rodent-like face. How many seconds is his speech going to cost us? Adam Ward's short frame is barely visible across the room behind so many chairs and desks, though his voice is screechy enough to be heard. More's the pity.

'Some of you may have seen a video circulating online. Our digital forensics show the video was created right here, on the office floor. If the person who made the video would like to step forward and admit it, perhaps we will consider not suing. Rest assured, we will find out who made the video, and that person's employment will be terminated.

'We are monitoring all your social media accounts and if any WIT employee is found to be sharing the video, they will also be sacked. Such a childish and insolent video will not sway WIT from its course. This is a great company and now, with me at the helm, I will steer us to an even more prosperous future.' He pauses, as if he's expecting some round of applause, but only silence replies.

He clears his throat. 'The results are in from us closely monitoring your levels with IMAtech, and the tailor-made supplements will be available this afternoon. IMAtech will instruct you when a dose is required. A dispensary is being set up in the back corner. This is a great innovation we are trialling and will allow you to work at your best while being closely monitored to ensure maximum output. Now get back to work. You have seconds to make up.'

Forty more seconds each are needed thanks to that little moan. There's the slightest murmur of groans as everyone starts typing again. I spot a few red-faced employees as they hastily fumble through their social media to delete the evidence trail. I had not been so daft.

Supplements. That's actually what they're calling it. I glance to the corner and the dispensary is being constructed. There's a desk with a screen on top, someone in a white coat standing behind with boxes upon boxes piled up next to them.

Joel leans over to my side of the desk. 'Wonder what they'll give us? These supplements.'

I shrug and face my screen again. 'Couldn't give a toss.'

'Maybe it'll be happy pills. To be honest, that doesn't seem like the worst idea.'

A quick glance his way and I note his drawn face, pale and unshaven. He looks as miserable as I feel. I probably look worse.

'You okay?' I ask.

'Same old, same old,' he says with a sigh.

I bite my lip a moment, the question that has been plaguing me for days on the tip of my tongue, and decide to just ask. 'What is it you were saying the other day, about Antonia?'

'Huh?' He looks blank.

'The other night. We were saying how. . .' I lean in closer and dip my voice, '. . .how loads of people hated Peter Ward, and you said especially since Antonia. But then you didn't say anything else.'

Joel tucks his chin in, his mouth hanging open. 'You don't know?'

I shake my head.

He puffs his cheeks out and makes a long exhale. 'Okay. . .I thought everyone knew. I'll spare you the details, but just to say she *really* hated him. With good reason. There was an incident. Let's just say it was a Clarity Directive grey area involving her and our late-boss.'

My hand goes to my mouth, and I sit upright. I should have guessed. Peter Ward assuming consent and taking liberties is exactly the sort of thing he would do. My nostrils flare. As if I didn't hate that man enough already. Poor Antonia. I hope she fought back. Maybe she threatened legal action afterwards, and that's what drove him to jump. I hope so. I hope she cut his crusty old dick off. I hope she kicked him so hard in the bollocks the pain never went away.

I arch around the partition wall again and lean in to Joel to whisper. 'So, you think she killed him?'

'What? No. I mean, couldn't blame her if she did. But if he was like that with her, imagine how many people he has angered over the years. Not even counting this IMAtech shit. He had a lot of enemies.'

I sit up straighter again and nod.

Across the office, I make a second of eye contact with Antonia. My stomach erupts with butterflies and I smile this time. I should speak to her, to tell her I'm here for her, that she's not alone in her wrath. That's what Katarina would say I should do, and I am sure it's what Isobel would do.

I load up files, but it takes a moment to figure out where I was up to yesterday, then I resume the finishing touches for the main characters of WardZone. The digital exoskeleton and the bulk of the work has been done by someone higher up the food chain. I just have to add some texture. The characters are all so dull. Ripped army guys and a woman with ridiculous tits. There's no magic in games anymore. No imagination. I look at the faces of the fake people and I hate them. I want to give them all wonky noses and black eyes, to make them have the injuries I wish upon Adam Ward and his cronies. Somehow, I am nearly four hours down on the week. How is that possible? I've been working non-stop.

I open up a file I don't recognise. Perhaps there's some work saved in there by mistake. No way could I be this far behind. There must be some work moved into some random file or—

My hands freeze, my body turning to ice for a second before breaking out into a sweat. Just moving my eyes, I glance around. No one is looking, thank God. I can't let them see this.

In that file is the video. The viral, peasant-fucking video. Pre-production, in its building blocks.

I didn't put it there. Someone put that on my computer.

My IMAtech flashes from orange to red. I'm losing seconds as my body is too shocked to move. I blink, rub my eyes, then get to work deleting. Could there be more?

I search file after file, all the while this work isn't registering as productive and my IMAtech falls. I curse under my breath, then wipe sweat from my forehead.

'You okay?' Joel asks.

'Yes, fine.'

'You're all red.'

Why the fuck doesn't he just look at his screen instead? I don't answer. My tightening face should let him know I am not in the mood to chat.

When I'm sure no trace of that video remains on my computer, I take a moment to calm my nerves and look around the office again. Besides nosey Joel next to me, no one has noticed my panic.

Will they trace that to my desk? Someone must have used my computer out of hours, someone trying to stitch me up. I must have forgotten to shut it down properly one night. That's the only explanation. If the bosses trace it to my desk, denying it won't do any good. I'll lose my job for sure.

Bile burns the back of my throat, and I wash it down with my last sip of water. My IMAtech is buzzing again and Joel frowns as he looks my way.

I keep my gaze on my screen, my eyes stinging and dry. What was I doing again? The characters, that was it. With shaky hands, I get back to work, my heart still so quick it's more like vibrations than a beat. I try to calm, to reassure myself over and over: *no one saw. It's okay. It wasn't me.*

It wasn't me.

Chapter Thirty

Katarina

I didn't expect to see Harry tonight. I haven't seen him since the CEO party and have heard little from him. I haven't chased, haven't nagged. I'm sure other women would beg and cry when his affections waned, but I care more about my eyelashes than about Harry Baxter. A relationship with him is useful to my plan, but not essential. He can drop dead now and save me the bother.

Out of the blue, he turns up at the bar, his face in a half-smile, his shirt unbuttoned.

'Hey,' he says when I clock him.

'Hey you,' I say. By the needy look on his face, I realise ignoring him might have the opposite effect to how it was intended.

He looks at the floor for a while, his hands in his pockets, then his gaze locks on mine. 'I just wanted to explain. I assume you saw that article in the press?'

I nod. Of course I've seen the article. Some rumour about Harry and some gorgeous socialite hooking up. I read it without an ounce of surprise and didn't give a toss. He can fuck every person in London if he wants, and I wouldn't give it a second thought.

But then, he's still a useful man to have around—in many ways.

'It's not true,' he says. 'She's an ex. Nothing happened. She's having a tough time. We were just talking. That's all.'

'It's fine,' I say, trying to convey a little hurt when I really don't give a shit. I can make out his muscle definition through his shirt. Even downcast and sorrowful, his face looks gorgeous. His sad doughy eyes alight my excitement though, and not for the usual reasons.

I can't go home with him after work. I have plans this evening. The kind of time-sensitive plans that I can't fit around Harry and his bedroom. No time like the present then, so they say.

At the far end of the bar is Davina, busy on her laptop doing a stock order. I know from experience she'll take ages.

'Just going to change a barrel,' I shout over, then walk down the stairs to the cellar. I hold Harry's gaze for a moment, raise my eyebrows, and give him a little nod so he follows.

The cellar is damp and cold, like a dungeon. My rucksack I need for this evening is stored there, full and bulging. Harry pays it no attention. There's plenty of other paraphernalia around. Boxes of snacks in the corner past their sell-by date—crisps, peanuts as old as time, and a few fruit flies gliding around. The heavy door to the far end of the cellar is held open by a barrel that locks from the outside if shut, and the only window in that door is barred. The bar has some history in mediaeval London I'd be able to recite if I'd read the stories framed among the artwork around the place. I always check the barrel is safely in place when I go down there, only this time I adjust it, allowing the door to half close, offering us a touch more sound insulation.

I undo his trousers, then hop up on the chest freezer.

Harry gasps as we fuck, making me think, to wish, no—to yearn for them to be for another reason, and the idea of that arouses me all the more. They should be his last gasps, asphyxiated as he's buried alive. His groans of pleasure should be of pain.

I dig my nails in. The scratch marks give me satisfaction beyond what his dick is capable of. I bore into his flesh, and he groans some more. 'Bad girl,' he says.

Just before he comes, I pull away, leaving him exposed and gagging. 'What?' he says, panting, desperate, so weak it makes me smile.

And men think they're powerful.

I let him inside to finish, then bring my mouth up to his ear and bite down on his lobe as he comes, wishing I could rip the thing off then and there, wondering what his blood tastes like. 'Bad, bad girl,' he says again.

You have no idea.

Chapter Thirty-One

Layla

I've stayed late at work every day to catch up and to stop anyone else using my computer. I glare at every colleague with suspicion. Someone did that on my computer. Someone wanted me to take the blame. No further action has been taken against any staff, but every day I arrive at work, I brace myself for a reprimand. It doesn't matter how many times I practise my 'it wasn't me' speech in my head, I sound pathetically guilty.

The whole office staff are due in the auditorium at Tower 42 for the launch today. The email memo we all received beforehand instructed us to cheer and clap, to show how great we think WIT and IMAtech are, the undertone of our jobs depending on it ringing loudly and clearly. Be grateful this wonderful company has given the likes of you a job, is what I read between the lines. The launch will count towards our minutes on IMAtech if we partake in such a way.

'It's bullshit,' Joel says on the walk over, kicking a few cans as he scuffs his feet on the tarmac. 'I feel like such a fucking fraud.'

I take some deep lungfuls of the foggy London air, just grateful to be away from my desk for a moment. I tut at him kicking the litter, and pick it up, then bin it instead. 'Bullshit it is, but just appreciate the break.'

'There's not even a dispensary here. I've had to take my pills with me.'

The dispensary has been in full swing for a few days. On top of the IMAtechs buzzing through the office, there's a new ping, every couple of hours from those who are recommended a dose of. . .something. I don't get the chance to find out as I don't partake myself. But there's a shuffle of staff throughout the day who make their way to the dispensary, deadpan faces, walking like zombies after their next hit. I wonder how much Baxter Pharmaceuticals are set to bank over this.

My brows knit and I look his way. 'What shit is it they're giving you?'

'Me? Just Texi during the day, I think. It's different for everyone. The end of day ones are good. I sleep like a baby.'

He does look more well-rested. He walks with more spring than I do. I've still not indulged in Texi or the dispensary at all, but by staying late and not looking up from my screen the entire long working day, I'm back on track for my minutes. Though my vision fogs and my myopia worsens without me being able to take a single break, and I'd love an appointment with a chiropractor but can't imagine finding the time to see one.

'Maybe we should grab some lunch after this?' he asks. 'There's a great sandwich place just near here.'

I look at the time on my phone and my IMAtech tally. 'They're giving us twenty minutes for the walk here and twenty minutes for the walk back. Any more than that and we'll lose time off our total.'

'So?'

'So? I'm at break-even.'

'Just take some Texi. You'll make back the minutes in no time.'

I frown and look him up and down again. His shirt is correctly buttoned for once, and stain-free, like he really has more time at home to sort himself out.

'Trust me,' he continues. 'It really helps with the Powerhouse of Productivity.'

My eyes widen, and I lean away from him. 'Jesus Christ, Joel. That's literally the shitty phrase they say.'

'Yeah, but we've taken ownership of it. Our terms now, not theirs.'

I tut. 'Whatever. You're drugging yourself to meet their targets.' I mock him with a double thumbs up. 'You rebel.'

'Yeah, well. Beats going along with it and working yourself into the ground just like—'

'Shut it, Joel,' I snap.

We walk the next few minutes in silence. The drone of never ending footsteps and traffic from the rest of London breaks up the awkwardness. Why does he always have to bring up the accident? He knows how much it hurts me. I never mention it. He should take the hint. Everyone else needs to compartmentalise like I do. It's not fair.

'Hey, sorry. I didn't mean it,' Joel says, once the background noise fails to create the needed distraction.

I don't say anything. The guy is a jerk at the best of times, not counting our post work office picnic. I only ever speak to him because his desk is next to mine. If I sat anywhere else in the office, I'd have the same relationship with any member of staff. And by relationship, I mean terse exchanges and general ambivalence. Friendships aren't for the likes of IMAtech employees. Friendships cost precious seconds.

Across the crowds headed to Tower 42, I look out for Antonia. She walks ahead with some others. I want to catch up and speak to her, but what would I say? 'Sorry for what that dickhead Peter Ward did to you.' That sounds callous somehow. Small talk isn't really my area of expertise. Asking her out for a drink after work is what I want, I think. I'm not really sure what I want, except to work out this tension that tingles over me whenever she's near. Whether that feeling is reciprocated, I've no idea. It's likely she's never even noticed me. Probably avoiding her is for the best.

Arriving at the auditorium, we're directed to our seats by the WIT events management staff. They appear more stressed than any of the office staff on a normal workday. I glance over at their collarbones for the reddish bumps of IMAtech but see none. Such a job probably doesn't work for IMAtech. They must be motivated by other factors—angry bosses, poor pay, and withheld bonuses, or just too exhausted to do anything but obey.

Me and my colleagues take our seats, which are a hell of a lot more comfortable than our usual work chairs. These are padded with soft armrests instead of the bone-poking plastic we have at WIT. The room is dimly lit and stuffy, and I know if I so much as blink, I'll fall asleep. I sit upright, not allowing a single muscle to relax. IMAtech would pick up if I fall asleep, and I can't afford to get behind just for a catnap. A few colleagues have thermoses filled with coffee and I curse at my own lack of planning.

On the stage, a large projector screen covers the back, a podium with a microphone stand is just in front. As I sit, my phone pings with an alert from the events management to remind us again to clap and cheer. I clock eye contact with some of my colleagues, who all sigh heavily and pocket their phones.

It's a cheap bribe but no doubt an effective one. I wonder if we're all replaced with AI, will they have robots in attendance to clap and cheer or use recorded applause to bolster the ego of the presenter? Besides the office staff, the hall is filled with the salivating faces of corporate brass. All buttoned-up shirts and ruddy faces, scowling at their phones, but all fake smiles when they converse, the brightness of the screens lighting up their receding hairlines. Attentive assistants take notes, hanging off their every word. All of it is theatre. Everyone looks stressed and miserable. There isn't a grain of happiness in the entire auditorium.

There's a part of me that's almost fooled by their anticipation, like the atmosphere created by those profiteering from the tech is enough to convince me it's a good thing. Happiness isn't required when the forecast of fatter wallets is dangled like a carrot on a string. If the richest are enthused, surely it must be a worthwhile bit of tech? Perhaps that's why the product is tipped to be so successful. Everyone is just swept up in the hype.

I rub the red bump on my collarbone and grit my teeth, though there's no point in my anger. My emotions might as well belong to an ant. It's the billionaire's reactions that matter, since they're the ones that have the kind of cash that can swing charts and grab the attention of the press.

The huge stage lights up, motivational music blaring through the packed hall, and the audience stands and claps as Adam Ward takes centre stage. Me and my colleagues join in, as instructed, pasting on smiles and slapping our hands together like performing sea lions.

Adam Ward laps it up. Quite how anyone can be so comfortable in front of such a big audience will always baffle me. My own tolerance for being the centre of attention peaks at having to order at Starbucks with a queue behind me. It probably has something to do with the confidence his net worth bestows upon him. He values human presence by the sum of their bank balance, his own included.

He grins widely and holds his hands up, air-punching as if he's just scored a winning goal. If arrogance can be harnessed, he's giving off enough electricity to power of all of London.

His image fills the two giant screens on either side of the stage, several times larger than the real Adam Ward. I grimace. I don't want to see one Adam Ward, let alone three.

When he comes to a halt next to the microphone stand, he takes up the most space his meagre height and build can possibly manage, spreading his legs and holding out his arms like he's some alpha messiah as the roar of the welcoming calms. Looking down at his audience, I wonder if he sees people or bank notes. I wonder if he hears cheering or money clinking. The company's stock price is expected to rocket up as the curtains close. WIT share price is touted to continue to climb over the coming days as companies everywhere will no doubt flock to buy the latest gadget that's going to make their business more efficient and more profitable.

Adam Ward's face has the sort of smile that only someone in their element can wear. Eventually, like conducting an orchestra, he lowers his arms, and the noise falls silent. He picks up the microphone and the projector behind fills with the video game logo for WardZone.

'WIT video games are the biggest games on the market,' Adam says, as he takes excessively long strides across the stage. 'And they are released at a rapid rate. How? Because of our staff.'

Cue the moment everyone who works for WIT is to be commended. The applause is stunted and lacks the passion that Adam Ward received.

'But what motivates our staff?' he continues. 'What makes our staff so efficient? For months, rumours as to how we've made such great improvements in the efficiency of our workforce have circulated. Well, I am here today to explain and give you all the opportunity to make your staff a Powerhouse of Productivity.' Another round of applause, this one with more gusto than the staff mention received. 'For the past year, the staff at WIT have all been trialling WIT's latest invention. IMAtech. You only have to look at our figures to see how effective it is. And now the time has come to share our secret.'

The stage lights dim and the projector screen backdrop lights up, a pale sky blue with rows of desks of smiling employees, glowing with joy and satisfaction with their work. When I remember the time I was first shown that presentation, I'm still amazed I didn't throw up.

'Imagine a world of perfect corporate efficiency.' The voiceover for the video has the sort of tone that might be used in guided meditation. 'Where every employee spends a hundred per cent of their work hours, a hundred per cent dedicated to their duties. Zero hours wasted. Zero minutes wasted. Let that sink in. No more idling at the water cooler. No more time wasted on bathroom breaks. Every single employee fulfils their contractual duties in full. Every day. This is not a dream. This is reality. This is IMAtech.'

The projector screen dims, and Adam takes the centre stage again. If the corporate bigwigs in the audience lean any farther forward on their seats, they'll fall off. Adam leaves a pause and simply nods for a few seconds. The silence is so thick with anticipation, a cough echoes as intrusive.

'And in this utopia,' he says, 'every employee can start at 9 a.m. and go home at 6 p.m. No overtime is necessary. Nine solid hours of work a day.'

Can, I repeat to myself. If every second is deemed productive. If we don't look away from our screens, don't stretch, don't need the bathroom, don't slow down, don't dare say hello to another member of staff. I glance around at my colleagues, their pinched faces showing what they all think of that word. *Can.*

'And not only that, but IMAtech can be tuned into employees' internal health. It can make sure that hormones are balanced for maximum functionality, that mineral levels are adequate, and that vitamin count is effective. As soon as licensing allows, we'll be able to tailor-make suggestions to keep employees at the top of their game, behaving exactly as they should throughout the month.'

The stress he puts on the word behave sends heat coursing through me and I clutch at my sleeves, my curled fingers creasing the fabric. WIT aren't waiting for licensing. IMAtech is already monitoring our blood. The WIT staff are the guinea pigs. I might as well shout and scream at them and let them know exactly what I think. There seems little point in hiding my anger since my insides are as visible to them as my outsides. *#behave* was just a trending hashtag once, WIT's plan is to make behaving obligatory.

Adam Ward drones on, images of the implant and the app play on the screen as he touts stats and figures, how they have the health of their employees at the heart of their decisions. My head screams like a wasp is stuck in my brain. The edges of my vision fog, and all I can see is Adam Ward's body at the end of some tunnel I have to crawl through to reach him. My hands clench into fists. My legs, arms, every muscle is poised to punch, and my chest shudders as I fight to control my breath. I want to hit Adam Ward, to cut his face up, to kick him in the crotch so badly, he goes down and doesn't get back up again.

A clanging noise snaps me out of my hypnotised rage. Another clang, from the rafters above the stage. Adam Ward steps to the side, just out of sight from the stage as another clang resonates, followed by a thud. And that is preceded by another. A shriek from the front row. I squint to see, then blink, as I don't believe my own eyes. The aroma is like soured fruit at first before the stench of death encases me like some rancid fog.

Raining down onto the stage are many severed hands.

Chapter Thirty-Two

Layla

Each hand lands with a dull thud as the pudgy limbs splatter to the ground. Some of them split open, gashes ripping through the decaying flesh and chunks littering the stage, the sound of decomposing fingers breaking on impact. I swallow back vomit. Even from my position towards the back, I can smell the rotten cabbage scent of corpses.

The big screens on either side of the stage zoom into the hands. My own go to my mouth when I see, and my stomach lurches. Saw marks streak down the wrists, the effort of each cut visible in striations across flesh and bone. Retching noises come from the front rows, the old cheese scent of vomit adding to the aroma. It is overwhelmingly hot, too hot, sweat beading across my brow and top lip.

This is so different from the hand in the office. I could shut away one, I had a computer to look at, work to do. Now I am swimming in the stench, surrounded by rotten body parts. I need to get out. I need to breathe some fresh air.

Everyone runs for the exits, a clot of people blocking the corridors. There are a few panicked screams, though mostly swearing and retching. Shoulders slam into other shoulders with similar sounds to when the hands landed. Everything reminds me of that sound. The squelch of shoes, the huffs of impatience, the tapping on the walls like breaking bones.

I really need to get out.

The auditorium exits onto Old Broad Street, where clouds create hazy light and too much humidity. The cool breeze I need takes an age to come as outside, I still have to wade through the throng of people, all pale with shock or green with nausea. I step in a puddle of thick sludge, the lumpy vomit coating my shoe.

I make it to clear ground before my own chunks surface and after I bend double, spewing out all my disgust, I reach for a bottle of water in my bag, but the few sips left are not sufficient to cool me down. I remove my jacket, fan myself, then give in again and throw up once more against a bin.

With my empty stomach comes a weakness shaking its way over. I walk a few steps away and sit on the cold tarmac, leaning back on my hands and lifting my face to the sky. I try to imagine a frosty breeze of winter, a meadow, the scent of wildflowers, and the sound of bees. I squeeze my eyes shut to try to feel it, to barricade the horribleness away. It's no use. I am still in London. The stench of sick, the cigarette butts, and the dog turd next to me will not allow my mind to be fooled. The angry sound of horns beeping, swearing cyclists, buses' dump valves, and exhaust pipes spitting out fumes will not let me escape reality.

My phone buzzes. IMAtech has kicked in and now the seconds are counting against me.

I want IMAtech over as much as anyone. But someone must have sawed those hands off corpses—off actual dead people. I can hear it, the sound of a saw cutting through bone. I can feel the vibrations of the fleshy grind through the arm.

My stomach roils again and only its emptiness saves me from vomiting once more.

'You okay?' Joel appears before me, looking almost as bad as I feel, though it seems like he's at least managed to keep his breakfast down.

'Not really. My God. Can you believe that?'

He sits on the tarmac beside me, his body odour adding to the onslaught. 'I'm just sorry they all fell so late,' he says. 'Would have been better if at least one slapped Adam Ward right on the head. Better still, if it was his hand.'

'Joel!'

'What? Come on, the board are pricks. Everyone thinks so. If only they all fell off that building with Peter Ward, the world would be a better place.'

My mouth hangs open, but I can't argue with that. There's something so lurid to hearing my own thoughts out loud, to know someone else has the same thoughts. My own flaws are displayed. I take some deep, putrid breaths as I mull it over, imagining the sight of one of those hands splattering against Adam Ward's head, the death goo dribbling down his designer suit, his own arm gushing blood from the wrist.

Chapter Thirty-Three

Layla

When I get home, I need a drink. A stiff one. The washing up hasn't been done for days, though I fail to care and the smell of unwashed dishes isn't enough to upset me given the day I've had. I buff lipstick marks off what appears to be the cleanest glass, then pour some gin, leaving less than half the glass free for tonic. I open cupboard doors, then slam them shut when I'm greeted with empty shelves and an even emptier fridge. The cupboard doors are all wonky, and slamming them only makes it worse. The hinges still need tightening and aligning. I called the lettings agency again a few days ago to send a handyman, but they made excuses as usual.

I find some tepid tonic in a cupboard, half gone and flat, but it will do. Nothing that a little ice can't improve. I open the freezer, the whiteness of each tray reminding me that even here, there's no food, but I've a small glimmer of hope I'll find some ice among the frost. I open one tray, but it's empty so shut it again, then open the other, then jump back, spilling half the gin

I had poured as my arms jolt in front of my face, like somehow that will ward off the evil that lurks within that tray.

My head angles away from the open freezer. Seconds pass before I can move. I'm as frozen as the frost. But then I swallow and slowly turn my head, just a degree at a time, to see I wasn't mistaken or hallucinating.

In the freezer are more severed hands.

I stand, staring, unable to move, unable to even vomit again as I haven't replaced what I spewed up earlier. The cold of the freezer isn't enough to keep the sweat from collecting across my brow. My glasses slip down my nose and I can't even move to push them up.

From Katarina's bedroom comes a rustle, a clang of hangers.

My mouth moves but no words come out, and my throat rasps. I try to swallow, but it's as if I have gravel instead of saliva. I swig the neat gin, the sharpness almost making me heave and I call again, finding my voice this time. 'Katarina!' I yell, then drink some more neat gin, wincing with the burn. 'What the fuck?'

Katarina emerges, picture perfect and walking as if gliding. 'What?'

My wide eyes stare at her, then the freezer, then at her again. 'You! You did that. It's sick!'

Katarina's lipsticked mouth tightens into a smile, and her eyes sparkle. 'Yeah, but it makes a point.'

It still hasn't hit home. It can't. My brain can't accept something so awful. I finish the gin, then look again at Katarina and the hands. *The hands.* I blink. They're still there. I'm not imagining it. 'There are corpses' hands in my freezer!'

'Oh, relax.' Katarina waves her own hand in front of her face like my disgust is a fly buzzing around. Even the sight of her hand turns my stomach. 'They're frozen. They won't bite.'

My knees wobble and I grab a chair, sitting so hard the legs creak. 'Oh, my God. Oh, my fucking God.' The room spins and I hold on to the table.

Katarina wraps some hair around her finger, twiddling it like this conversation is the most normal thing in the world. 'You wanted revenge. I'm delivering.'

I hold my head in my hands, then recoil from my own touch. My lungs struggle for breath. I need more gin but am shaking too much to pour a drink. 'How. . . how does this avenge any-thing? How?'

'The big IMAtech launch was sabotaged, that's how. It shows how much people hate IMAtech. It takes the spotlight off Adam fucking Ward and his shitshow company and puts the attention back where it should be.'

'On the grieving families who have had their deceased loved ones dismembered?'

Katarina tuts. 'Why would they care? They're still dead. No. It puts the spotlight on what IMAtech really means. Death. As we well know.'

I wish she'd close the freezer door. The tray is still open, the grey fingers poking up like they're fumbling their way out of their icy grave. I glance up at Katarina, her perfect face, her styled hair, her manicured nails. She has somehow done this. She has somehow sliced through dead bodies. That red nail polish has never looked redder.

'It's not going to stop them,' I say, breathless in my despair. 'It's sick. And pointless. It won't bring Isobel back.'

Katarina sits next to me and reaches for me, but I yank my arm away. 'I miss her too, you know. Like mad some days. I'm entitled to my revenge, not just your pansy stupid letter writing.'

My eyes sting, but no tears will come. I am all cried out. 'It's what Isobel would do. Isobel would never want this. She'd be appalled.'

'I miss her, not her methods. My way is more effective. Just wait and see. This will teach them. I'm going to make them pay.'

I squeeze my fists against my temples. Katarina can't be saying this. I can't be living with someone who mutilates bodies. 'No. No. Nothing more. You can't carry on like this.'

'Just relax. Stop worrying. Leave the avenging to me. You have enough on your plate.'

I slam my fists down on the table so hard, my glass wobbles. 'Listen to me, Kat. Stop. This is sick and wrong. Stop it!'

'No. I'm fixing things. You'll see. Remember Goldilocks and the three bears?'

I flinch and stutter with confusion. 'W. . . what?'

'Goldilocks. We should have learned our lesson from that story as kids. She keeps tasting the porridge, being all gentle, until she gets eaten by bears. Women who take their time, who rely on trial and error, get swallowed up. That's the moral of the story. She should have kept hold of that hot porridge and thrown it in the bears' faces.'

I stare at her, blinking a few times. I'm used to Katarina's life lessons, but now she's really gone off the rails. Yet she truly believes it. Her face is full of resolve and the confidence she always oozes. Her self-assuredness isn't faltering at all. She actually thinks this is the best course of action. Her charm appears glib, like a psychopath justifying their kill, a cat playing with a bird. My heart sinks, and I have to search to find my words, the right words to make Katarina see sense. 'You can't fix things. You have to stop. Or I'll. . . I'll go to the police.'

Katarina stands and laughs. She looks so tall, so self-assured, like she's never been more certain in her life. 'Oh, shut it,' she says, all matter-of-factly. 'No, you won't, Layla. Don't be daft. You'll be as culpable as me.'

Chapter Thirty-Four

Katarina

Harry messaged to cancel our date this evening. He's busy doing damage control with the rest of the board. That's all he says, he doesn't divulge further. *Damage control.* The words make me grin so widely when I read his message. I want more than damage though. I want terminal wounds. To be the iceberg to the Titanic. I hope the ship is sinking.

Things have gone to plan so far, but I could have planned it even better. The hands should have rained down sooner, before that God-awful presentation. I should have added some bricks in with them to pelt Adam fucking Ward in the head, to dent his squirmy ratface and cut gouges out of his craterous complexion.

The hands, though, are just the start of my plan. The four left in the freezer will have to stay there for now. I'll box them up and post them off to the board members when I get a moment. Layla certainly isn't going to move them. She's far too squeamish. I've been hoping to impart some hardiness in her, to give her a sense of strength, but the look on her face when she saw the hands in the freezer tells me I've got a long way to go. She's learned too little so far, but she'll come around soon enough. She'll see the genius behind the gore.

I'm pleased that part of my plan is over. Breaking into morgues, dealing with the mangled remains of dead bodies, breaking into Tower 42 last night, all of it is making me as tired as Layla.

I will not be deterred by lack of press coverage nor the tenacious climb of WIT. There's a chink in every armour. I just have to keep chipping away until the bell tower falls. Layla will thank me one day, I know it. When WIT and everyone in charge of that fucking company is buried under the dirt, when IMAtech is consigned to history, Layla will see. She'll understand then my tactics were necessary.

A few days later, Harry messages to invite me out for dinner. His message sounds jovial, like he's on a luxury yacht and not a sinking ship. It's clear I need to find a way to be that damned iceberg. I catch up on the news and have an urge to punch a wall. The reports still have nothing but good words to say about WIT, not a column inch given to how bad IMAtech is or the stunt I pulled. How hard it is to tarnish the reputation of rich companies! One severed hand in Little London bar and the place would be shut forever and never get business again. WIT, however, with its shiny exterior and wealthy board members, seems invincible.

I, though, am more determined than ever. A mountain doesn't collapse overnight. One pebble falls, then a rock, a boulder, and finally a landslide. Layla needs to see that. All I'm doing is throwing the first stones.

The landslide is still to come.

I dress for dinner the next evening, an outfit far more conservative than what I wore to the CEO party. A fitted knee-length dress I found in a charity shop just down the road from Layla's work. The sort of place wealthy people drop off their excesses and where the paupers such as me can still smell their expensive perfume on the fabric, and only imagine the price tag it originally came with.

I meet Harry at his house before we leave for the restaurant. He pulls me close and grins as he gives me a kiss. 'Adam will be there,' he says, and I know what he means. His revenge plan is as incomplete as mine.

In the car, on our way to dinner, I look at his arms, at the places where I bit him so hard I drew blood and bruises. I lick my teeth, remembering the texture. Hidden under his shirt, no one will know of my sadistic pleasure. It's pain I can inflict without drawing attention. The feel of his skin between my teeth aroused me for more reasons than one. Perhaps one day, I'll bite with a molar, tear into that pretty-boy flesh like hyenas into a carcass.

No doubt Layla isn't a biter. She probably enjoys a kiss and cuddle, a lick when feeling the most adventurous. People like Layla take no pleasure in a bite. She doesn't understand the primal pleasure in the texture of skin. It's like a dried apricot, only a whole lot sweeter.

After I'd bitten Harry's biceps earlier, he leaned over and kissed my cheek, then smiled that pin-up boy smile of his. It's a shame to hate him this much. At least I get to play with my toy before I discard it.

The restaurant is as fancy as I assumed it would be. Fussing staff, too many pieces of cutlery and background music that sounds like something to help you sleep rather than enjoy yourself. I sit in my chair after the waiter pulls it out for me, and after he places my napkin on my lap, I scoot closer to the table and I listen. The voices all around are low volume, but I'm always listening. All plummy southern accents, noses in the air, the sort of conversations that make them sound like they haven't had a fuck in years. I look around the room at the buttoned-up shirts and frigid skirts. If I could see up those skirts, I bet I'll find cobwebs.

Despite the plush furnishings, I can't get comfortable. For maybe the first time ever, I have a sensation of being out of my depth, like a Swarovski collar on a pitbull. I fidget, uncross and recross my legs, and grit my teeth.

I take some deep breaths and look across the room at a man carving up his steak. The blood oozes out. That steak knife, with its bone handle and silver blade, cuts through the meat effortlessly. I lick my lips and sit straighter, then gaze around at all the necks on display. Fuck them and their fancy-pants furnishings. They're all people, made of the same stuff as me. I am not intimidated by them. Katarina McKenzie doesn't even know what it's like to be intimidated. I like to own a room, so no way am I going to let this room own me.

I turn to Harry and kiss him on the mouth, then flick my hair over my shoulder and hitch my skirt up a bit to reveal more thigh. I might as well look like the working-class gold digger they no doubt all think I am. I can sense eyes on me, sizing me up, judging me. When I pull away from Harry, he's smiling. He doesn't give a shit what any of those bumptious, Pims O'clock Gatsbys think of him, so why should I?

The rest of the board arrive a few minutes after us. Harry stands to greet them, but I remain sitting, doubting very much that they would stand for me if I arrived late. Fuck them.

Diego has his latest partner, Francesca, in tow. Francesca holds her posture in such a way that implies she does not feel at all out of place, but she's faking it. Her shiny forehead and fidgeting hands give it away. That and her darting eyes and pinched smile. She nods to say hello, but she doesn't speak. She keeps her working-class twang well hidden. It's been a while since I did my homework on the board members. I wonder if Diego's ex-husband is still trying to rinse him for all he's worth. The poor lamb might be quantified in the hundreds of millions soon instead of billions. Bless.

'Past your bedtime, isn't it, Harry?' Diego says.

'Brought your whore, I see,' Harry says as he looks at Francesca.

I glare at him. No doubt he pre-prepared that quip. He's stooping as low as the other playground bullies. The dickhead.

'As did you, I see,' Diego says, recoiling at the sight of me.

I smile back sweetly as I bristle. How like these people to opt for ridicule over defending their partners. I purse my lips, repeating *fuck them all* over and over in my head. I'm not above putting up with some lowlife comments. I work in a bar after all.

Parin arrives with a woman I don't recognise from any research—likely wifey is at home tending to the multiple offspring. This woman looks like she charges by the hour and not very much. The tight git.

Jan Novac arrives alone and greets them all with grunts. For someone who made his fortune in the media—well, added to his inherited fortune from fossil fuels—I would have assumed he'd be a tad more articulate. Instead, he speaks like he has a toothache. His sparse hair is unstyled, his face ruddy with rosacea, and his wifebeater visible through his shirt. He really doesn't give a flying fuck what people think of him, and what I think would get me a punch in the face if I were to say it out loud. Wifebeater isn't just an item of clothing for Jan, if I've sized him up correctly.

Adam Ward arrives last, also solo. He's casually dressed in such a way that men who don't have to answer to anyone do. Jeans and a polo shirt that make him look preppier than a Ralph Lauren advert. His aftershave habit is as suffocating as his dead dad's, and just as off-putting. He takes my hand and kisses it while maintaining eye contact in some old-fashioned way from decades ago. It sends chills up my arm for reasons that he likely doesn't intend.

Drinks come before anyone has ordered, the staff clearly well versed in tending to this lot. Alcohol-free, I note with a huff of disappointment. Instead, it's overpriced flavoured fizzy water that the staff afford the same theatre as they would to champagne. I hope it will at least serve as a placebo.

'So,' Adam says when he's sat and had a drink. 'Good news today. Excellent work by PR. I still can't believe the fucking savages.'

'There's always going to be people who hate progress,' Parin says, with an air of boredom that's mimicked by the look on his date's face. 'They just want to sit on their arse all day and not have their time accountable to their employer.'

'I think, actually, this helped us,' Diego says, or rather shouts. His voice is like nails down a chalkboard. 'It highlights just how work-shy people really are. You can't change the world without ruffling feathers.'

Jan raises his glass. 'With WardZone ahead of schedule, that's going to add a ton of value to WIT. We're set to have the biggest market share of any tech company in Europe.'

They all clink glasses to that, and I'm sure they all look crestfallen at the taste of fizzy juice. Adam's latest stint at sobriety is proving to be a lengthy one, probably partly due to him enforcing it on everyone else. I enjoyed a stronger drink with Harry beforehand, and I know he still has some of his own preferred poison in his breast pocket. Smuggled in like some naughty teenager.

'You think the staff would be happy to have a job,' Diego says. 'I swear they want us to hand their roles to AI.'

'But what would a workplace be without people, that's what my dad always said,' Adam says, with what I imagine is meant to be a cheeky grin but looks more like a sneer. 'You can't look up AI's skirt, you can't have chemistry.'

'Exactly,' Harry says. 'Imagine being in a bar and being served by AI instead of some sexy woman.' He squeezes my knee and I force a smile.

'The IMAtech data I have collected from my factories confirms what I said all along,' Parin says, in a bland tone, clearly unamused by Harry and Adam's words. 'The women are less productive a week a month. The hormone monitoring we have done at WIT also confirms this. At least ninety seconds a day lost. Hormone monitoring must make up part of IMAtech when it goes to market.'

'The ethics committee had something to say about that,' Adam says.

'They'll come around soon enough,' Pain says. 'A licence is inevitable once we pitch it correctly. If we make the productive seconds a monthly target, they have time to make it up. Monitoring hormones is a good thing. It shows we are invested in the welfare of the employees.'

Harry leans forward. 'The dispensary is going well in the office, I understand. Baxter Pharma can scale that up. Iron, hormones, whatever, to ensure such feminine issues are not disrupting the company.'

'AI doesn't have such issues,' Diego says. 'I don't see why any company should have to tolerate it. If they don't like it, get that *#behave* trending again. Companies shouldn't have to suffer such woke ideals.'

Parin nods along. 'The gender pay gap they always drone on about makes more sense when you look at such data. It's a wonder no one has studied this before.'

This verbal ping pong makes my heart pound and all my muscles tense. I'm sure my biceps are as hard as Harry's. It's impossible to portray an air of disinterest when it is taking all my resolve not to ram the cutlery down their throats.

'There will always be some woke idiots trying to stop advancing tech,' Jan says. 'We have the press releases all ready to deal with any fallout.'

'Even my wife made some complaint about it,' Parin says, and they all laugh at that.

I make eye contact with the woman he's with, and a silent conversation passes between us. Her face twitches as she forces a smile, the jerky movements of her neck and back as she tries not to cower under the table. She's playing her part as best she can, like we all are. There's barely a second where women can just be themselves. There's always an outfit required, concealer to be applied, an expression to wear. Show your tits but not too much, laugh at his jokes but not too loudly, suck his dick but not too hard. Our whole fucking existence is theatre, with some man as the director, pulling our puppet strings to make us move and act however is required.

Fuck this.

I slam my glass on the table, and they all stop their guffaw laughing to look at me. My lungs heave a breath and in a split second I remind myself, I'm my own puppet master and right now, I need to play along with this whole God-awful charade.

'Sorry,' I say. 'My hand slipped.'

They all return to their conversation and I count my inhales and exhales. I release my glass and caress the steak knife next to me, running my thumb over the serrated edge.

Adam's posture and movements show he's engaged in the men's conversation, but the subtleties of his gestures are easily missed by the men and their testosterone-fuelled bullshit. He looks my way more than the others, even though he's sitting next to me and has to crane his neck to do so. He glances down when I uncross and recross my legs, the quickest flitter of his eyes that's easily missed. Otherwise, his eyes flicker between my eyes and my breasts. It never ceases to amaze me how easy it is to control a man's mind. A mere whiff of tits and they can't help but look. Cleavage is more powerful than any rich man's authority.

Harry gives me a peck on the cheek before he goes to the bathroom, and Adam seizes the opportunity to lean in. He puts his hand on the back of my chair as he speaks, like some physical leverage to shoehorn himself into my personal space. It's hard to believe the man isn't drunk. He has way too much confidence.

'I can see why Harry's quite smitten with you. He's like that with all the girls though. Just so you know.'

I nod. 'Right.'

'You've probably noticed how busy he is. Hardly had time for his current women, let alone additional ones. I assume you've seen him in the media?'

I nod again, inwardly wondering how long I can play along with this. My steak knife is still so close, his neck even closer. I can count the pulse in his jugular.

'Well, if you ever want some more personal attention, from someone who isn't such a mumma's boy, let me give you my number.' He hands me a business card, which I accept, and attempt a smile back. 'We could go somewhere tonight, if you want? There's the fashion exhibit at the V and A. I can get us in after hours. They have some vintage for sale. Maybe I could buy you something nice. Harry's probably too stingy to buy you anything. His parents keep his finances under their control, you know.'

I take a sip of my disappointing drink, purse my lips and narrow my eyes, hoping I appear like I'm considering his offer. 'Interesting,' I say, elongating the word. 'Whereas your dad is dead, so that's okay for you and your parental handouts?' I'm meant to be wooing him, but there is only so much I can take.

Adam visibly bristles and leans away. He takes a mouthful of his drink and swills it around his mouth a moment before replying. 'Harry does always have a soft spot for the wild ones.'

He smirks and eyes me up and down. 'Well, I'm sure you'll call me soon.'

He retracts his arm as Harry returns and takes his seat. The food arrives, whatever it is, Harry ordered for me. It smells divine, but all I can think of is the steak knife and Adam's pulsing jugular.

Harry gives me another peck on the cheek and I squeeze his knee. Harry wanted me to be alluring, and from that brief encounter with Adam Ward, I have learned that the more like myself I am, the more alluring I seem to be.

Chapter Thirty-Five

Layla

The train to Portsmouth takes just over an hour. By some miracle, the trains are all working and on time. A rarity for that line, especially at the weekend. I take it as a sign I'm meant to be going home for a bit. The universe is on my side.

I didn't tell Katarina where I was going. Instead, I left a note in the kitchen that said I need some time away. My dad's the obvious choice. It's Katarina's hometown too, but the city is big enough that even if Katarina does turn up in Portsmouth, it's unlikely we'd bump into each other. Does Katarina even have any family still in Portsmouth? I realise I've never thought to ask. Katarina never speaks of her family. Her nose is always too stuck in my business to mention it.

When I get off the train, not too far from the coast, I take a deep breath and splay my fingers, letting the mix of city and sea air flow over my hands to blow away the London grime. The taxis pumping fumes beside me can't stop me feeling clean, can't stop the air being much more breathable than it has been in my flat.

I walk to my dad's house rather than get the bus, wanting to savour time outside that isn't London. It's a pleasant enough day, patchy cloud and a temperature cool enough to feel fresh. The dominant sounds are angry seagulls and screaming kids. The constant beeping horns and swearing cyclists in London are long gone.

I look over my shoulder intermittently, unable to shake the idea Katarina or the police are following me. 'You're as culpable as me,' Katarina said. And she's right. It's my flat, my freezer. I'm subletting to Katarina. Her name isn't even on the lease. If the police trace those hands to the flat, she can walk away. I, however, would be screwed.

Somewhere in the distance, a siren blares and I jump. My feet glue me to the spot a moment, my heart thumping in my throat. The vehicle with a siren whizzes past. Just an ambulance. There's no police following me, it's only an ambulance. My racing heart slows and I resume my walk, holding my head up, waiting for the cool air to take my sweat away, trying to not look as guilty as I feel.

However far away she is, Katarina still feels close, like she's reaching for me, crawling into my bones. A tingle inches up my spine and I shake it free, the residual itch making me wriggle my shoulders. I take my coat off, the day not warm enough to justify it, but I want to be cold, to shiver from that rather than a lingering dread. Or perhaps that makes me look more guilty? I should be trying to blend in with everyone else wearing coats.

I put it back on. As it presses against my top, I fidget as my skin is clammy against the fabric.

The school Katarina and I attended is on my left. Graffiti of curse words are sprayed on the pavement outside, litter lining the street. I pick some up, but it barely makes a dent. A gust of wind blows more crisp wrappers to replace what I binned. It was a shit school back then and by the looks of it, it's even shitter now. I've done all right for myself, considering. The good schools are all surrounded by expensive housing. My parents did their best, but when the better schools are ring fenced to those who could afford the price tag on the adjacent property, achieving in life is equally as ring fenced.

It was the assumption that drove me mad as a kid. My parents assumed I wanted all the wealth they didn't have. But I didn't give a toss about that. All I ever wanted was a friend.

The corner at the end is the shop where the popular kids would stand outside after school, daring each other to try to get served alcohol or cigarettes. I can still picture Katarina there, her arm around some popular boy, dressed in a way I would never dare, laughing, swearing, being loud and garnering all attention. Me, small and mousey, would sometimes have to walk past that crowd. They shouted things like freak, frigid, and even worse things. As a young girl I'd laugh it off, not dare to say anything back, then pick up my pace, hurry along to arrive home alone with not a single friend to stick up for me.

Did Katarina ever shout those things? It's hard to discern whose voice the shouts were. She was there though, and she certainly didn't jump to my defence. I justified it before as kids being kids. They never hit me; it was just words. Sticks and stones, my dad used to say.

Katarina is a grown woman now, and adults aren't bullies in that way. Katarina is head-strong, I've told myself so many times over recent months. Loyal. Not a bully.

I take out my key and let myself into my dad's place. The smell hits me instantly. The general lack of cleanliness, his catheter decanting into a bag next to his chair, combined with the stodgy microwaveable ready meals of pureed yuck that is all he can eat.

'Hi, Dad.'

'Sweetheart!' his slur comes through excitably from the living room where he's sitting on his adjustable chair, piles of old annuals and newspapers everywhere. I step around them, carefully, knowing if I knock a pile over, I'll be in for it.

I lean in and give him a kiss on the cheek. 'Thought I'd come visit. I see your collections have grown.'

'Don't make fun of your old man,' he sort-of says.

I clear a pile of clutter from the chair next to him, keeping it all in order. I note the look of worry on his face as I touch his things. No doubt he has everything exactly where he likes it. I go to reach for a biscuit, then think better of it when I see the state of the table. It makes my flat look sterile. In fairness, he didn't know I was coming, so he wouldn't have made any effort.

Dad was a hoarder when he was mobile. Now he's housebound and has nothing else to occupy him other than collecting mountains of crap. I know it's getting out of hand, as does he, but I'm not going to try to change him. If I clean it all out tomorrow, he'll only get upset, then will build it all up again.

'A bird flew in here through the window the other day,' he says.

'Oh?'

'A black bird. Had to call Scott 'round to get it out. You remember Scott? My neighbour?'

'Yeah, sure.'

'You always used to like the birds. Gone off them now you're in that concrete jungle, London?'

It's hard to recall being fussed about birds. I shrug. 'I guess so.'

We chat for a few minutes more, then laugh along at a game show for a while, Dad knowing far more of the answers than me. Curled up on the sofa, it's like I never left, like I am still living here in this house, never having been to London, never moved to the big city to try to find my way in the world. I'm at home where it's comfortable and familiar with my dad.

After a couple of hours, I excuse myself and make my way upstairs to dump my bag and freshen up. My old room is un-changed since the day I left. Dad hasn't been upstairs in about that long. Thick dust coats the skirting boards in the hallway, cobwebs hanging like ropes from the ceiling. I push open my bedroom door and a cloud of dust flits up as the door scrapes against the carpet. Pale pink, same since I was a kid.

An empty gerbil cage is in the corner that once housed my only friends, and even those bit my fingers and recoiled from my touch. I couldn't even tame a gerbil. What chance do I have with Katarina?

There's a bookcase that holds a few books on gerbil care and wildlife. Some old video games are still in their boxes, games that featured magic and talking animals and sorcerers. The console, complete with endless dust bunnies collecting is underneath. I used to spend hours playing those games, wasting so much time I'd be lost in the worlds they created. When I played, I could imagine I was one of those players. I became someone else. That gave me peace back then. It was my form of escapism. It took me away from the misery I felt. In those games, being those players, I could be anyone. I was strong. I was needed. A hero.

On the shelf is also my yearbook. The hardback volume from my final year at school. I almost didn't buy a copy. It seemed pointless to remember that time, but not having a copy somehow admitted defeat. It was something to look back on, Dad said. The bad times will be over soon. It's good to remember the bad old days when things get better.

When exactly things would get better is the question I still ask myself. I thought that was when I was with Isobel, for a fleeting moment, before that ended in my worst misery so far.

I open the book. The only picture of me is the group class photo. My shaggy hair fell forward, covering half my face. My smile looks more like a grimace, my shoulders hunched forwards like I'm ready to run away or cower. Never happy to be in any place, I was always a split second from running away or getting mad. Katarina wasn't in my class, so I turn the page to find her class photo. Katarina's hair was back, her whole face on show, her smile dazzling even on the faded old pages. How bright her lipstick was even back then.

Over the pages there are more and more pictures of Katarina. She has a double page spread dedicated just to her, with notes from other kids saying how much they adore her. I shiver, and my eyes burn green.

Me being friends with Katarina now is so odd, it's only right that it would all turn sour. No one growing up so adored would be a normal adult. Katarina's narcissism is conditioned into her from childhood. She can't see the problem in her actions. Everyone has always loved her, whatever, she can do no wrong. Whereas I question everything I do after a lifetime of ridicule. Every decision I make is fraught with doubt.

Is this just what popular people do? Dismember corpses?

Framed on the wall next to the bookshelf is my release paperwork from St Mary's psychiatric institution. My dad framed that, telling me what an achievement it was. I didn't want it on the wall, but didn't protest. It wasn't like anyone else was ever going to see it. Getting out of the loony bin wasn't an achievement, I didn't think. An achievement would have been never to be admitted in the first place. It wasn't just one meltdown too many. It was the kind of rage that made me rip my hair out and scream until I threw up. The kind of rage that only a sedative injection could quell.

When Katarina encourages me to let the anger in, she doesn't understand the beast that risks awakening.

I hardly remember those days. I learned to forget. That's what Dr Cottrell taught me in our sessions that I maintained after being discharged. To lock away the badness, to focus on what's in front, manage the things I can control, and not worry about what I can't. I developed my gift to compartmentalise, to push the bad memories so far to the back of my mind and lock them away, it was as if they never happened. The therapy taught me to move on. I learned to close a mental door as easily as a physical one.

***

'Tell me what's going on with you,' Dad says over dinner. Fish and chips from the place we used to go to when I was a kid. Dad said he hadn't had food from there in forever, so I walked down and picked up a couple of portions. It's too much salt and fat for someone with my dad's health, but the joy it gives him makes me care less about the health implications. I watch him struggle to chew and I wonder if I should have blended it, but he savours the flavour more than the sustenance. He sucks on a chip and some batter, his eyes rolling back in delight.

'Nothing really, Dad,' I say. 'Just busy with work.'

'Any special person?'

I swallow a mouthful before I answer. 'There was. Not now.'

His smile wanes, and he gives me a small nod. 'Well, no rush on these things. You're still young.'

The wrong side of thirty doesn't feel that young. Everyone I used to know has settled down by now. It's exponential, the rush I always feel. Ever since I was a kid and didn't want to be a kid. Now I'm an adult and I'm just as trapped. When will it all stop? Will there ever be a moment of tranquillity where I can just be myself and not continually be playing catch up or trying to move to the next phase of life? I don't respond to my dad, just carry on eating my dinner. Perhaps savouring a meal with my dad is the only tranquil moment I am likely to have.

'Dylan has met someone,' he says. 'They're all settled now. She seems nice. Very pretty.'

'Great.'

'What happened to my scatterbrained little girl, huh?' he asks. He's looking at me now, his fork on his lap. 'I thought you'd stopped growing ages ago, but you're still growing up, still changing.'

'Think that's just life, Dad.'

'Your mum would be proud. She always knew you'd be a highflyer at work. It was all she ever wanted. You were always so clever and she only wanted you to apply yourself. And look at you now.'

He glows as he says this, and I can only assume his cataracts are worsening. I'd told him about the bit of character graphics I am doing and he thinks it's some massive promotion. I didn't correct him. Looking at me now wouldn't make anyone proud. A picture of my mum hangs on the wall above the mantle. It needs dusting like everything. She was mousey like me. All she ever wanted was some protégé.

It wasn't fair, I would protest as a child. Why wasn't it okay to do things I enjoyed, why did I have to apply myself? What was wrong with being a scatterbrained daydreamer? Why did I always have to try to be someone else? Mum was never proud. She always wanted me to be like the other girls: popular, high achieving, straight. Life lessons came late to me. Too late to please my mum, anyway. But Dad's right. She'd prefer who I am now.

After the carer comes to put Dad to bed, I have an early night, and it's blissful to catch up on some sleep. In the sanctity of my old childhood bedroom, and for the first time since I arrived, I don't sense Katarina's presence. I'm a million miles away from her and her antics. For a night anyway, I can push all the craziness out of my mind.

Chapter Thirty-Six

Layla

Before heading back to London on Sunday, I stop by the cemetery to visit my mum's grave. It was Dad's request. I've never understood the point of such sentiment. Mum isn't there and won't know that I am. Dead means dead. But Dad wishes he could go, and his request is his way of living through me, I suppose. It's en route to the train station anyway.

Some nettles have grown over the face of the plaque, and a fox turd sits curled off to one corner. Obviously, my brother didn't bother stopping by when he was visiting Dad's the other day. No one else ever visits the grave since we have no other family. Besides my dad and Dylan, there's no one who'd miss her. Mum had worked in human resources for the university. Head of HR, she said if anyone ever asked, emphasis on the head. The job title was probably true, since Mum's insistence in using it spoke volumes about how she perceived value. Everyone was a title or a qualification. Letters after a name meant more to her than the name itself.

The pointlessness of it gnawed at me when I was a kid, and my father's life also. They worked so fucking hard for so little. A roof over their head and dinner on the table. There was a line that I could see back then. One side of that line, those simple staples were regarded as luxuries. On the other side, luxuries came in solid gold. There isn't a word for those basics to those sorts of people. It's just what they have without question. The sky is blue, they have air to breathe, there's food in the fridge. That's how the world works for them.

I understand Mum's ambitions more now that I've grown up, now that I have bills to pay. Working hard when I was young seemed like a bore. More recently though, I see it as necessary. To prove myself. To be worth something. I've never been good enough at anything, but perhaps I can be the Layla Daley I was meant to be. The good daughter my parents wanted me to be.

It's unlikely anyone from my mother's work shed a tear when she died. She was probably as much of a dragon mid-management boss as she was a mother. Unyielding and relentless. Her colleagues were likely more concerned about how the extra hours would be staffed. If I were to croak tomorrow, that same attitude would resound at my work. It's a place where everyone is only seen as seconds logged.

One colleague did attend the funeral. I supposed that was customary. I don't blame the university. It's a big establishment. No one there had a face or an identity even. Employees are seen as a box to tick, a name merely useful as an email sign off. Sounds familiar.

I sit and pull my sleeve over my hand to protect it as I clear away the nettles. I gaze upon my mum's name for a while, her date of birth and death. Fifty-six years old when she banged her head and died, her high blood pressure a contributory factor in the brain haemorrhage. She had plans that would never be completed, desires that amounted to nothing.

In the damp grass in front of the grave, a worm pokes its way through. It wriggles up towards the light, considers the world briefly, then burrows its way back down under. What had Katarina said? The worms appreciate you for longer than your employer.

Looking at the worm now, she has a point.

On the train on the way home, Katarina creeps her way back to the forefront of my mind. My mental break has gone, and London and my flat await. I can't run forever.

All I ever wanted was a friend, and now I have one who is so loyal, she dismembers corpses for me. Perhaps I should be flattered.

On the train journey, I realise my thoughts need realigning. Katarina means well. She's on my side. She hasn't hurt anyone, not really. She's someone who creates chaos, and chaos follows her. And Katarina would have been careful. It was unlikely the police have any idea it's she who broke into the morgues. My regimented way of living is out of sync with Katarina's, but that doesn't make her methods bad. I decide to give her another chance, to thank her for her efforts. As weird as her scheming is, they're ideas born of kindness.

I will only ask one small favour, and that is she clears the freezer out.

***

I don't wince at the dirty dishes when I get home. I expected nothing less. I have a rucksack of groceries and clean what I need to make dinner. Katarina arrives home just then, looking her usual glamorous self.

'Hey,' I say.

'Don't worry,' Katarina says, holding her hands up. 'I've not been breaking into any morgues. Just popped out for some fresh air.'

'I'm making dinner. Chicken stir fry. Want some?'

Katarina raises her eyebrows and takes a tentative step forward. 'Sure.'

I open a cupboard and note the way it closes: fully and hangs straight. I open another and it's the same.

'I called the lettings agency,' Katarina says. 'A handyman came and adjusted all the doors. Said he'd get a quote for some window vents too, to help with the damp. You should get an email about it all.'

My jaw hangs open. How many phone calls and emails have I sent about the damp, and they've done nothing? One word from Katarina and it's all sorted. For a moment, I forget what I'm doing, then I remember the bottle of wine on the counter.

I dry some glasses I just cleaned, then pour some wine, a better bottle than I'd usually buy, and serve up dinner. 'I want to thank you.'

Katarina almost chokes on her wine. 'Really?'

'Yeah.' I look at my lap, searching for my words for a while. 'I know you've got my back and everything you're doing is just to try to help. I mean, your methods are fucked up, but I guess that's okay. You're right. It rattles more cages than just writing bloody letters.'

Katarina smiles and raises her glass. 'Cheers,' she says. 'To friendship and getting shit done.' And we clink glasses.

I sip and allow the wine to linger on my tongue for a moment. One peaceful moment. The meal is fine. I'm not a great cook and the vegetables aren't the freshest, but it's flavoursome enough and we eat, enjoying every mouthful.

I refill our glasses. 'Care to tell me if you have anything else planned?'

Katarina's smile broadens. 'Nope. Not yet. I like surprises.'

My brow furrows. 'I don't.'

Katarina stands, taking my hand. 'I've got an idea. Come on.'

'What? Where?'

'It's payday weekend. The shops are still open for another hour.'

Payday weekend means nothing when I'm in the red to start with. 'I can't,' I say, and take my hand back. 'I don't need anything.'

Katarina scrunches her nose and gives me an exaggerated look up and down. 'Yes, you do. Trust me.'

Trust me. I repeat that in my head. It sounds like a hissing snake.

Chapter Thirty-Seven

Layla

I struggle to think of the last time I bought clothes. Months, probably. Maybe longer. I always look the same, like exactly how Layla Daley should look. Comfortable cuts and not too revealing, the sort of clothes I can sit for hours in and walk home in without getting a wedgie or an itch. The sort of clothes Adam Ward and his new dress code initiative disapproves of.

The thrift stores and charity shops closest to our house are mostly quiet, though the disorder and frantic tidying by the staff indicate what a busy day they've had. They have the dusty smell of neglected cupboards despite the clothes all looking pristine. Katarina walks in and makes a beeline straight for a rack housing little skirts and tops that would make me self-conscious.

'Try this,' Katarina says, handing me a bright red dress that would fit tightly enough to reveal every curve and bump.

I back away. 'Oh, no. That's not—'

'Just try it. Come on, I'm going to try this one.' Katarina holds up a similar outfit for herself, holding it against her body and standing in front of the mirror. She doesn't need to try it on. It will obviously look amazing on her.

She drags me to the changing room, and after a few minutes regretting leaving the flat, I strip down to my sensible underwear and stare at the outfit hanging on the hook. I eye it like it will bite me or burn my skin off if I wear it.

Katarina knocks. 'You got it on yet? Lemmie see.'

'Not yet.'

'Does it fit?'

'Hang on.'

I lift the dress off the hanger, swallow, then slide it on. Squeezing my modest curves into the bodycon cut.

'Okay, I'm coming in. You've been ages.' Katarina opens the door, her own red outfit fitting her perfectly, accentuating all she has to show, whereas I feel like an overstuffed potato sack. 'Wow!' Katarina says. 'You look amazing.'

My head hangs low and my cheeks are redder than the dress. 'I look awful.'

Katarina steps to the mirror and links arms with me, admiring the sight of the two of us. 'You need to see yourself as others see you. Honestly, you look fantastic.' She steps up to the mirror and kisses my reflection, leaving a deep crimson lipstick mark on the glass. 'It really suits you,' she says.

Katarina walks out, leaving me standing there alone, an alien in my own skin. Of course, Katarina said I look amazing. It's exactly the sort of outfit Katarina would wear. I side-step along the mirror and line up the reflection of my mouth with Katarina's lipstick print, the deep crimson sitting over my lips. Looking myself up and down, I don't see myself, not how I should look. I see how Katarina would look.

I hand the outfit back to the member of staff as I leave the changing room, my face so hot I'm sure I glow in the dark as I know the shop worker must be thinking I was ridiculous to try on such a thing. I can't buy it. I am not Katarina McKenzie. I don't wear such things. Leaving the shop, I run so fast like the clothes are going to come after me to taunt me and call me names like the other kids did when I was at school.

When we get home, I shower and wash the charity shop smell off me. I use my shower gel and shampoo, not Katarina's. I use my own fragrance-free neutral products. In my room, I dry, then put on my pyjamas, comfortable attire I can sit crossed-legged in on the sofa without worrying about flashing. So unlike Katarina's silkie nightie that looks like she's always expecting a lover to turn up.

Would Isobel have liked me more if I'd dressed like that? If I looked like someone other than myself. If I'd been more like Katarina? I pick up the hairbrush with Isobel's pink hair in it, needing to see that flash of colour, needing to feel close to the woman I miss so much, the woman who was the one person who loved me for who I am.

The pink hair has gone. Instead, some glossy dark ones knot the brush.

My grip tightens around the brush, and my nostrils flare. 'Kat!'

Too rigid to move for a second, I scream Katarina's name again before stomping through to the kitchen. She's sitting at the table, her face a picture of innocence.

'You used my hairbrush!'

'So?'

So? My whole body flushes with heat as I fight to control my temper. 'It was Isobel's. It had her hair in it.'

'Well, a hair was never going to stick around for long.'

'It was all I had of her. It meant something to me!'

'It was just a hair. Kind of gross, really.'

Sweat trickles down my back, and I beat the brush against the palm of my free hand. 'You took that. You've taken the last of her from this house. You've erased her!'

Katarina stands, stepping close, her sneering face only a couple of inches from mine. 'No. You're the one who erased her.'

Chapter Thirty-Eight

Katarina

Monday nights at the bar can go either way: mad busy or like a graveyard. Graveyard is the flavour of this evening, so I pace, polish, rearrange, and anything else I can do to pass the time. The bar is getting quieter in general, a lot quieter over recent weeks. Davina moans about margins and I wonder why she doesn't at least try to smile at the customers. Her permanently downturned face is enough to put anyone off their drink. Davina blames the several new places nearby that have opened up. Too much competition, she says.

Despite her bitchy face, I quite like Davina. She speaks her mind, even if nagging me is at the blunt end of that. I know where I stand at least. A far cry from Layla's changing moods and moping.

I kicked out a pair of customers earlier. It was obvious they were getting high in the toilets. They didn't even keep their voices down when they were planning their little twosome escapades. I confiscated their stash as I did so, and one grabbed my breast.

'You didn't say no,' the prick said. And as I screamed at him, he claimed he couldn't hear me. 'Music's too loud to hear you,' he said.

Funny, I heard him plain as day. When he reached a second time, I crushed his hand so hard he made a pathetic little whimper and threatened to sue for a broken finger if I didn't return their drugs.

I snarled, then kicked him in the bollocks before turning to his mate. They both ran, like pathetic little rats scurrying back to their hole. Their arrogance is nothing when up against a woman's scorn.

A little bottle of GHB and a bag of coke has joined the rest of the wares in the box under the till. GHB is the date-rape drug of choice these days since it can render women incapable of declining consent. I can only assume they were planning on spiking someone. No doubt they think it makes women *#behave*. Predatory men weaponizing themselves in that way makes me want to destroy more than just the men on the board at WIT. It makes me want to castrate every fucker that walks the earth. Perhaps I should keep some tongs and pliers at the bar and cut the bollocks off every prick I suspect is going to prey on women. By the time I'm done with them, the Taylor Foundation for Vulnerable Women would be a thing of the past and instead, eunuch support groups would be needed.

That would be a better way to pass the quiet time at work than polishing shelves.

Davina at least agrees to turn the music down after that. She would probably have let those men stay for the business. Maybe she would insist they buy a bottle of something overly expensive to stop her calling the police, or offer them something on the house to stop them suing me. There's a baddie and goodie in every scenario; it's a matter of perspective. I'll be the bad bitch every day in those guys' eyes. Fuck them. I hate such pricks and have no desire to pander to them. Perhaps, in hindsight, that's why the bar is quiet.

I haven't seen Layla since our row, but I know she just needs time to cool off. I probably should apologise, but it was an honest mistake. And coveting a hair is weird, like she's planning on cloning Isobel one day. That hair isn't what's stopping Layla from moving on. Layla can't move on while no justice has been served, and that's something I am helping with.

I lean against the bar and relish in the quiet for a moment. It gives me time to concentrate on pressing matters. Revenge. The Texi I took the other day funnelled my plan to a concise and workable model, and now I'm aligning the steps. I decided I'm definitely not going to cut off anymore hands. That part of my plan is done with. Harry's skin cells are lodged under my nails. Forensics would have a field day. And, well, I don't want to get Layla in trouble. I want to make Layla see sense, to help her, not stitch her up. I'm her friend, and as such, I can educate her and help her be a stronger version of herself. She'll understand that soon. There is more I can do. A lot more I am *going* to do.

Davina goes home early, leaving me alone except for the odd regular. I amuse myself by turning the music down, then finally reading the historical artwork information around the place. The building dates back to the sixteenth century, when the cellar was actually used as a dungeon. Thieves and murderers were chained up down there, starved and whipped for their crimes. No wonder the place always makes me shudder. It's more than just the cool temperature that chills my bones.

When it's nearly been an hour since I've served the last pint, I wipe down the surfaces and consider shutting up early due to lack of business, then Adam Ward comes in. I don't notice him at first, so light are his footsteps from his boyish frame.

He shouts my name from the doorway. 'Katarina.'

I look up, unable to hide my surprise. 'Oh, hi.'

'Fancy seeing you here,' he says in such an over-accentuated joking tone, it makes me cringe.

'At my place of work? Yeah, weird.' I don't remember telling him where I work. Maybe Harry did. Maybe he had me followed. That thought makes my body tense and a wave of heat spreads over me.

A Bentley is idling outside with a chauffeur sitting in the driver's seat. He probably said to park it there on purpose, to show me what a lovely car he bought with a fraction of his inheritance. I'd respect him more if he'd taken the tube or walked here. Adam Ward's dick swinging contest does nothing but make me scrunch my nose.

He steps forward. He has his chin tucked close to his chest, his lips twitching in a way that reminds me of some drunk sleaze I kicked out a few weeks ago. I know he's mentally undressing me, and I know he likes what his mind's eye sees. If I do the same to him, I'm sure I'll see ironed underwear covering up a needle dick. His mouth twists in a way that he probably thinks is a sexy smile, but looks more like a cat's arse.

'Why don't you call it a night and come out with me.' It's not a question.

Yeah, because we all work for our rich dad's companies and can take time off as we please. I bite the inside of my cheek and choose my words carefully. 'Can't. It's my late.'

'What a load of crap.' He comes forward another step, hands in his pockets, and shoulders rolled back. I thought I knew how to own a room, but I'm nothing on this guy. He looks around, inspecting the ceiling and the pictures on the walls, at the historical prints and the framed photos of London's modern skyline, views he likely has from every office and apartment he owns. 'How about I buy the place. That would get you out of work.'

Oh, how fucking suave. I recoil in response.

'Because I could do that, you know. I could buy this bar like that.' He takes his hand out of his pocket and clicks his fingers.

I fight off a flinch, yet the feeling of insects crawling over my skin remains. I pick up a glass to polish. It doesn't need it, but I want something in my hand in case the desire to throw something at him gets the better of me. 'You'll have to speak to

Davina about that. I'm sure such things take a while to complete.'

'Well, aren't you a bright one.'

I smile my most bitchy smile, my eyes screaming *fuck off.*

'You're a tough woman to impress,' he says. 'God only knows why you're dating Harry.'

I put the glass down, then reach for another. 'He tries harder, I guess.'

He laughs, then turns on his heel and walks back to the door. 'I'll bet he does. Well, we'll see. I'll show you.'

Chapter Thirty-Nine

Layla

I'm restless at home. My bed is uncomfortable, every noise jolts me awake. Losing that last essence of Isobel is like losing a part of myself, a part that knew peace, a part that at least knew how to sleep. All I have left are my nightmares.

I glance over at the empty side of the bed. I always stick to one side, not wanting to encroach on the space next to me, the space where Isobel should be. The sheets on that side are unwrinkled and cold. The pillow is fluffed up and unused. I run my hand over it and shiver.

I still can't shake the images of the hands from my mind. I'm not mad at Katarina anymore for doing. . .*that*, at least, I'm trying not to be mad about that, but I am still so grossed out by it. Whenever I close my eyes, I see Katarina tiptoeing around a morgue, a saw in her handbag, searching for the limbs she wants to slice off.

I haven't dared to check the freezer. I don't want to know if they're still there or not. Katarina says they won't bite, but as I toss and turn, I imagine them creeping out of their frosty prison and pinching me as I lie in bed.

I leave early for work the next morning and grab a sausage roll from Paul's Bakery. It's as warm as skin. Body temperature. Each bite has the consistency of flesh. On my way to work, I flinch at every sound, looking over my shoulder like one of those severed hands is about to creep over me. The cool and soft grasp of a dead hand snakes over me whenever I think about it, which is every time I so much as blink.

I keep the sausage roll down, along with a coffee. The chilly morning isn't cool enough, and I unbutton my coat as I walk. I regret taking the tube, as the smell of living bodies is like an aroma of the pre-deceased. A man opposite holds his copy of *the Metro* in his hand. His hand, pink and plump with life. There's a pulse in his wrist, his temple too. But for how long? The morgue is everyone's destination. That thought takes some of the stuffiness away. It's probably cold in a morgue. Almost as cold as my freezer. How many hands are there? Ten? Twenty? Five corpses? Or ten?

The sausage roll was a bad choice.

By the time I walk through the doors to the WIT office, the coffee is threatening to run straight through one end and the sausage roll the other. After a quick toilet break, I sit at my desk, compose myself, but feel no better.

The rest of the staff arrive in silence and sit after their visit to the dispensary. What started with a few colleagues dosing up is now over fifty per cent of the workforce. The popping sound of blister packets is louder than the keyboards first thing, made all the more obvious from the deafening lack of any conversation.

Underneath the collective seconds tally is a new light-up board, this one with a line, a green spot in the middle and red on either side. *Hormone levels,* it reads. Currently, the marker is hovering just a little outside the green into the red zone. Still too much of something, apparently. The sight of it makes me tense so much, I swear the marker dips farther into the red. My IMAtech buzzes with a popup message. *Supplement advised! Stay efficient! Support our research!*

I grit my teeth and load up my computer, then start working where I left off yesterday. My little hiatus at home has made the previous week seem like ages ago. Even the day before is lost in my brain fog and I struggle to remember what I was doing. I click on my workbook and remember I was finishing the characters for the new game. It beats typing code, and it allows my imagination to drift a little, to picture the faces I wish I could have. The goodies in the games are always so aesthetically pleasing. The ogres are the evil ones, as if being ugly makes you bad inside and out. So unlike real life. Just another lie concocted by the media to get into the pretty people's pants.

I have a sip of water as I load up the images, then spit it up when I see the work I've done so far. I wipe my mouth on my sleeve and stare at my screen, then look slowly side-to-side, hoping to God no one has seen what I've done. How had I not noticed? The characters I've been finishing are nothing like they were when I took over. Their faces are a likeness of the WIT board, only not exactly. They have wounds, deformities, blood oozing from injuries. The Adam Ward lookalike only has skin on half of his face, the other half is burned off. Diego Smith has eyes gouged out, but it's unmistakably him. Parin Shah is a zombie, all rotted flesh like those damned hands. It's as if my subconscious took over and made them look how I imagined after all my bad thoughts had been acted upon. In front of me is displayed the very darkest of my thoughts. My secret desires. What is *supposed* to be secret.

Before anyone can notice, I start deleting. A heavy pit lodges in my gut as I set about erasing all the work I'd done the week before. So many hours wasted, so much time going down the toilet. I sniff back my upset as I note my IMAtech tally going down. That damned bit of tech understands that I'm not progressing with my work. Deleting the work is like going backwards. I pause for a moment to think, and as I pause, the IMAtech tally continues to decline. My shoulders roll forwards as helplessness empties me of any strength. This isn't going to be considered productive work seconds, but what can I do?

For a moment, my hand hovers over the mouse and I ponder if perhaps the board will like it, think of it as a gimmick. But no, they won't. It's insulting, threatening even. My inner most evil thoughts are exposed, my nightmares illustrated. The only one that looks human and vaguely healthy is Harry Baxter, besides some dribble and a squint that makes him appear like he has the IQ of a vegetable.

I bite my lip, then subdue the sobbing I want to do by gritting my teeth. *Dammit!*

So much work I have to undo. And quickly. I don't look up from my screen all day, just erase and draw over and delete, all the while terrified of my thoughts. Petrified and confused that my mind can have such power over my hands, my darkest subconscious taking control. They are my thoughts, private, and I never discuss such thoughts with anyone.

Only now, they're bursting to get out.

Chapter Forty

Katarina

The bar is more upmarket than Little London, with only top brand spirits on offer and furnishings that are more comfortable than my lumpy sofa. Not as comfortable as Harry's bed, which is where I would prefer to be tonight. Spending my night off bar work in a bar is a tad tedious, and Harry's company only adds to that.

I have to admire the bar staff's manners though. The place is heaving and they keep their cool, not skipping any corners with the cocktails and making sure the presentation is perfect. I never have so much patience during a quiet night, let alone a busy one. Perhaps that's another reason why Little London's takings are down.

Harry, dressed in his typical jeans and collared shirt, takes my hand across the table. He leans in close, like he wants to be near me, like he actually enjoys my company when not between the sheets. We're only screwing. This isn't a serious relationship. I'm sure about that. He's probably posing for cameras, expecting there to be some paparazzi or fan somewhere. I keep my hair over my face since I've no desire to be the subject of gossip columns.

'Adam's going to be crazy for you, I know it,' he says. 'He can't handle not having something he wants.'

That being on Harry's mind explains the public affection towards me. The two of us pictured in the papers will make Adam more determined.

I smile back, try to maintain the eye contact he's delivering and hide my frustration. Having a conversation with Harry Baxter is like talking to a dog licking its own arse.

It worries me Harry thinks we're at that stage of a relationship where we don't need the physical gratification. Like getting to know each other is somehow as fun. I'm wearing my best underwear that's good for displaying and then dumping on the floor. Wearing it sitting does nothing but itch in places I can't publicly scratch.

'I hate having to use you like this,' he says with genuine concern in his tone. 'You're worth so much more than that.' The compliments have been coming thick and fast this evening, like he really is getting attached. I wonder if maybe he expects some compliment back, but I give him none.

'Once he confesses, I'm taking you away. Let's go on holiday somewhere. Where would you like to go?'

I sip my cocktail, a French martini. How do they get it so smooth? Mine always come out slightly separated. 'I always wanted to go to San Francisco,' I say, without really thinking about it.

Harry nods. 'Yeah? Done. Easy. First class the whole way.'

I smile back. Perhaps if Harry Baxter wants more from me, it won't be the worst thing in the world.

'You should quit the bar work too,' he says. 'Come work for my parents' company.'

I grimace at this. Big Pharma is not where I see myself. Sporting a lab coat and goggles? No thanks. 'You hate your parents and their company.'

'I'd like it a lot more if you were there. Think about it. We could see each other more often.'

My grimace remains and I fidget. We could hardly fuck at work for Baxter Pharmaceuticals, so there seems little point in seeing him more there. If my displeasure shows, Harry doesn't appear to notice.

'You've been such a support for me,' he says, and I'm relieved that at least he doesn't start crying. 'All your help. I just want you to know how much I appreciate it.'

I have been a support, and it's taken every ounce of my patience to not rip his head off every minute I've spent with the fuckable bore. I need his trust, and that has meant I haven't been behaving like myself at all. I've portrayed myself all wrong, giving the impression I'm somebody else. I've been lost in this game, forgetting I am Katarina McKenzie. Alluring, sexy, fun, impulsive, not the sort of person who makes plans and likes men who require compliments and who think crying is attractive. It's hard to play this role. I should have put a stop to the crying as soon as the first tear rolled down his cheek.

I finish off the last of my cocktail and Harry clicks his fingers to order another.

'What if he doesn't confess?' I ask.

'He will.'

It seems foolish Harry hasn't even considered the possibility Adam is innocent. Typical of a spoiled brat. Not a doubt in his mind he's right, despite him having the intelligence of a woodlouse. 'But if he doesn't?' I press. 'If it was someone else, Jan or Parin or someone?'

Harry shakes his head. 'I'm a hundred per cent certain it was him. And, well, if somehow it doesn't work and he doesn't confess, then he'll be back on the bandwagon and another stint in rehab awaits. No big deal. He's been there before.'

Our fresh drinks arrive, and I take a large sip before giving him the sort of nod and expression that conveys I admire him, that I think he's the smartest man in the world. This role really is becoming tricky. 'And what will it mean for you, for the board?'

He raises one eyebrow. 'Katarina McKenzie, are you worried about me?'

'Of course.' Yep, really tricky playing this role.

'Well. . .' He sits back and makes a loud exhale. 'I might take a higher position at WIT, I guess.'

'A promotion. How well deserved.' By some miracle, my sarcasm doesn't manifest in my tone.

'I know they all think I'm stupid, that I'm not capable of anything. But when I prove it was Adam, they'll think better of me then.'

God, the man is such a dumbass. 'I suppose,' I say, looking up at him through my eyelashes. 'You could do good things for the company. Like, you could stop IMAtech.'

Harry laughs. 'God, no. IMAtech is making WIT the biggest tech conglomerate in the world, not to mention the boost to Baxter Pharma with all the supplements.'

My smile tightens. It was worth a shot.

'You know,' he says, dipping his voice, 'and this is between you and me. They tweaked the timer on it recently. Work seconds count for less, rest seconds count for more. Only a tenth of a second for each, but multiply that over the company, and the efficiency of the workforce has improved twenty per cent!'

I can't feign admiration at that. I retort on impulse. 'That's sick, Harry. Seriously? As if the staff aren't burned out enough as it is.'

'AI doesn't burn out.'

'No, but people do.'

He reaches over and strokes my cheek. 'You're so caring.' I want to recoil from his touch, to bite that hand off. I opt for stone-cold glaring instead, and his eyes soften as he takes his hand back. 'This is the way of the world now. Once staff progress up the ranks, then the IMAtech is altered. But while they're just crawling around at the bottom, they need to prove themselves, to support the company.'

'The company will be nothing if the staff are all exhausted.'

'That's exactly what the supplements are for. When IMAtech rolls that out, it'll make Baxter Pharma even bigger. That's a win for everyone. Trust me. It's all going to be fine.'

He sounds so smarmy I want to smack him. 'I read about that woman. She crashed her car into a wall when she fell asleep at the wheel. She worked at WIT.'

'That was unfortunate.'

'I think the word you mean is tragedy.'

His shoulders sag at this, and he gives a small nod. 'You're right. I know you're right. Her autopsy showed she was anaemic and on some other meds. With the new blood work monitoring with IMAtech, we can be sure the correct levels of all hormones and minerals are optimised.'

'That's invasive.'

'I know, really, but it makes sense. It's a trial at WIT now, but it's a matter of time before it's the global norm. Especially for women. It's scientific. Unless we only employ men, women's issues need to be accounted for. So many women drop out of the workforce for ages when they have kids. It only makes sense they do their fair share while they can. Or else, it's more AI. And nobody wants that.'

A knife, a broken wine bottle, a fork, my fist. There are so many weapons in front of me I can use to ram through his throat. My jaw cramps from clenching my teeth and Harry notices my body's tremors. He grabs my hand.

'Hey, listen. When I have more power, there is more I can do. With the stock market doing so much better, there is more I *will* do. I guess it's easy to get lost in success and forget all about the little guys.'

Little guys. I put my drink down and push it away. Its sweetness has turned sour.

'See how good you are for me?' he says. 'You're my compass, guiding me through all of this.'

Yep, definitely sour.

'We're going to set things straight, you and me,' he continues. 'Adam will confess and when I have more power at WIT, I'll do what I can to help all the employees.'

I raise my eyebrows. 'You'll stop IMAtech?'

'No, but maybe I can make a difference, like stopping the time discrepancy or something. I suppose that is a little unfair.'

Oh, what a fucking hero. I pick up my drink again and wince through the sharpness of it. 'Great,' I say. 'Just great.'

Chapter Forty-One

Layla

I don't dare look at my IMAtech on the way to work. I'm so behind. I know it. Looking will be stress on stress. I spent an entire day erasing my previous work and my heart races just thinking about it. It makes me want to rip the heads off the board at WIT. I want to smash up my computer and stick the fragments in their eyes. I imagine them in real life looking a hell of a lot worse than I created for the game. Torn off flesh, choking on their own entrails. What does it feel like to burst an eyeball, I wonder. Would that even cause them enough pain?

I shake my head, squeezing my eyes closed for a second, and try to focus on the job at hand. I have to shut the bad thoughts away. Let Katarina take the lead, like she said. Leave Katarina to think the bad thoughts. She's stronger, more mentally equipped to deal with such darkness.

By some mercy, the board didn't show their faces yesterday, which helped to channel my mind away from peeling their skin off and dousing them in petrol. I arrive at work an hour early this morning, and as soon as I get in, I manage to shut the bad thoughts away, to close that door on the darkest parts of myself.

I have a flask of coffee and a box of snacks, and I type code. Reams and reams of it. Sometimes immersing myself in work isn't a bad thing. I don't look up, don't glance around the office, nothing distracts me. The only sound is keys tapping. It is, for once, hypnotic. I am so busy I have no time to think, to daydream. The brief moments when I have to look at my keyboard, my own hands are pixelated, like my mind is blurring them out, not wanting to see.

I had a dream the other night. Someone's hands on me, stroking me, squeezing, putting them in places to cause me pleasure. Now I doubt hands could ever cause me pleasure again.

I don't check the time on my watch, not wanting to look that way, but a glance at my IMAtech tells me I've been at it four hours without even noticing. I zoned everything else out for four solid hours.

'So, tonight—you'll come?'

How long has Joel been talking to me? I've been paying no attention to anything but my screen for so long, I hadn't heard his voice. I hadn't even noticed Joel sitting there or anything that was going on in the office. It's like I have tunnel vision. I look up from my screen to glance over at Joel. His hair hangs in lank tendrils over his forehead, his shirt is creased and mis-buttoned. He made an attempt a few days ago to wear a tie at some point, and by the looks of it, he's slept in it ever since.

As politely as I can, I reply, 'What did you say?'

'A drink? At a bar?'

'Oh. . .' I look back at my screen, hoping my blush only shows on one side. 'Sure, whatever.'

'Great.'

What have I just agreed to? A date? Was Joel asking me out on another date? I really emphasised the *friend* word last time. Did he not get the message? I continue to type for a moment as my mouth runs dry, then I sacrifice some valuable IMAtech seconds to look at my phone, trying to appear more interesting than I know I am. Perhaps I am busy, have a full social calendar I'm not aware of, other dates, plans, *anything*.

Katarina has linked her diary with mine. She probably thinks she's being helpful, but instead it seems like bragging. All that's in mine are Katarina's plans and her work shifts. A glimpse of what my life could be if I was that popular and interesting. The blanks tell me my future holds nights in alone, falling asleep on the sofa and watching crap TV, for that is how dull I really am.

I bristle, then wonder when life became such a grind. Isobel always had a busy schedule, with her passions, animal rights, and environmental stuff. I always have no plans, yet any offer is never enticing enough. It's not that I desire my own company, it's just the one person I desire is dead. I realise the part of me that died with Isobel is holding me back, that I am merely existing. Working and sleeping yet being tired and bored is the tedium that's my reality of day to day. I am in a slump I'm never going to get out of if I always say no to everything.

I look up at where Antonia is sitting. She hasn't even stood near my desk in days, hasn't even looked my way. It's like she's deliberately keeping her distance. I glance over at Joel instead. He isn't the worst looking. A shower and a different shirt and he could be passable. Sure, he's annoying, but that's probably more to do with my intolerance and tiredness than Joel. He is a man, which isn't my usual flavour, but perhaps underneath his unwashed exterior he's a barrel of laughs.

Sod it. I should go on a date. I deserve to be desired, to at least practise dating. It probably isn't even a date. I just misheard. But I certainly could do with having some sort of social life, to have something in my diary besides Katarina's plans, to have a friend besides Katarina.

I click through to my phone camera and look at myself for a moment. I have makeup on. When did I start wearing makeup? Likely, it's just the dregs from some time ago. I barely remember dressing this morning, let alone putting on mascara. My hair isn't frizzy like it used to be. I've been pinching the odd bit of Katarina's shampoo and it seems to be helping. It shines in silky waves, soft curls bouncing off my shoulders. I could never afford such shampoo, and as I recall my bank balance, suspect it's probably my shampoo anyway.

'You okay?' Joel asks. 'You look blank.'

Maybe he's attentive and caring. He's almost the only one who ever even asks if I'm okay. 'I'm fine. Just busy. All the code starts to blur into more code after a while.'

'Go to the dispensary. Trust me. It helps.'

'No. I really don't want to give in to that.'

'I've got some spare Texi if you need? Just take them. It'll help.'

I swallow and stiffen, pausing my typing for a couple of seconds. Katarina said not to, but Katarina also cuts human hands off corpses and leaves them in the freezer, so Katarina clearly doesn't have the best judgement. I bite my lip for a moment and think, why not? 'Sure,' I say. 'I'll take one, thanks.'

Joel takes a blister pack from his pocket. 'Here, take a strip. I've got loads.'

I take it and stare at the little yellow pills for a while. Sixteen in that strip. 'Is it one a day?'

'Yep. That's all you need.'

I nod, then press out a pill. I swallow it with some water, and it traces a bitter trail down my throat. A cloud of shame smothers me as every pill taken only bolsters up Baxter Pharmaceuticals. I don't doubt that nearly everyone in the office is on Texi, everyone is supporting Baxter Pharmaceuticals. That family lords over all the minions, drugging us into doing their bidding. It's so fucked up, but it's that or be replaced by AI. What choice do I have? I am simply not good enough as I am. I never have been.

I picture the smug grins of the Baxters. I rarely see Hugo and Malorie Baxter. Their son Harry is their posh little errand boy. One of Britain's most eligible bachelors, according to the glossy magazines who think having a ton of cash in the bank is all women look for. He has the sort of pin-up good looks that's probably maintained by a team of staff trimming every hair and rubbing cream into his skin for him. Imagine being one of those staff members, replacing those creams with acid, missing one of those hairs with the scissors, and ploughing it into his oesophagus instead.

Bad thoughts, Layla. Stop it!

Maybe there's something more practical I can do. No chance people that rich have clean hands. No one gets that rich and dodges the dirt. They're just better at covering up the stains.

I start to imagine the impact of a scandal on the Baxters. Perhaps some sexual assault scandal, something really bad to turn the public opinion. Harry Baxter is such a pretty boy. The media simply love him. His parents are often publicly photographed at various philanthropic events, donating money to popular charities. Probably to justify some misdeeds, to convince themselves they're good people while they drug the nation and work them to death.

I can't fantasise for long. Literally can't. The Texi kicks in and I'm engrossed in my work, my hands barely able to keep up with my brain. The lines of code on the screen are like fairy lights, a lure, drawing all my focus. Seconds and minutes fall away as I work tirelessly for the rest of the day, staying an hour later to catch up on some of the previous day's lost seconds. At seven p.m., I'm amazed at what I've achieved. Texi really does work. The annoyance of that takes away any sense of accomplishment. The damned Baxter drug actually works.

Chapter Forty-Two

Layla

I make my way to the bar with a pang of guilt knocking on my chest. Guilt for taking Texi, for still having fifteen of those little pills in my handbag and being pleased about it. Or is it guilt for going to the bar? Something inside tells me I shouldn't have a social life. Out of work hours are for sleeping, eating, practical things, and moping. Fun things aren't for the likes of me.

Isobel is gone. She'll never enjoy a social life again. She loved a bar, usually choosing a corner booth to giggle in. Perhaps that is what's niggling at me the most. Survivor's guilt. Really, I just want to wallow.

Isobel worked in a bar when she was at university, she'd said. Some grunge place with sticky floors and music so loud, it would ring in her ears when she went to bed. She spoke of it in a wistful way, all fondness and nostalgia. No one would ever say that about working for WIT. If I ever get out of that place, I'll speak of it with a taste of bile and backache.

The bar is only two minutes' walk, still I count the seconds all the way. The sound of a ticking clock is my constant companion these days. My life dripping away. My parents always told me: knuckle down, work hard, make the big man proud. Aspirations of grandeur being more important to them than fun times. Isobel would disagree and without Isobel's influence, I'm watching my life slip by. I thought working hard would bring contentment, a feeling of satisfaction. More and more it's leaving me agitated, like my skin doesn't fit anymore.

I stall in the doorway of the bar for a moment, frozen to the spot. It isn't just Joel in the bar, but several other office staff members, many of whom I've forgotten their names or never bothered to learn. My breath catches when my eyes land on Antonia. I haven't spoken to her in ages, but now she sits in front of me, glowing like a spotlight is on her and the rest of the bar just fades away.

'Nice of you to join us,' she says, and pulls up a chair beside her.

'I told you she'd support this,' Joel says.

My face flushes and with wobbly legs, I walk over and sit. I'm so close to Antonia, our knees brush each other. I swallow the lump in my throat. Isobel would want me to move on. Katarina would tell me it's about time. It's only me holding my life back.

I look around the group, all colleagues from WIT. Have they invited me before or just never bothered to include me? Joel passes me a pint as I wonder, support for what?

Antonia turns to me and gives my arm a squeeze, sending bolts of electricity through me. 'I'm really glad you're here,' she says.

'So,' Joel says. 'It seems the bloody share price is untouchable. Whoever did those hands was sick, but it at least gave us a glimmer of hope.'

'It's hardly the right strategy though,' a woman says, her face paling at the mention of the hands.

'What is the right strategy then?' Antonia asks. 'IMAtech simply can't be allowed to be rolled out worldwide.'

I stare wide-eyed at the group, the cold pint in my hand adding to the cooling relief that it isn't a date with Joel. It's much better. They are all here to bad-mouth IMAtech, like a support group. They're all as sick as I am with it.

'If we can't match AI productivity, we're out. That's just the way it is,' Joel says, folding his arms.

'I don't know about you, but I'm fed up with having to rely on Texi to get me through work,' a middle-aged man with badly repaired glasses says. 'That stuff is making me twitchy, I'm sure of it. It's impossible to wind down afterwards.' He looks twitchy. His drink wobbles in his glass.

'The evening pill from the dispensary helps. I go there every two hours or so throughout the day and my levels are near-on perfect.' One woman says this without a hint of intonation in her voice.

Antonia tuts. 'It's just more money in the bank for Baxter Pharma.'

They all murmur in agreement and drink to that. I say nothing but listen, mouth hanging open, my chest inflating. I've been so alone, with no idea there were others wanting to plot and avenge too. I never speak to anyone at work, really. I assumed they were all just putting up with it. But here they all are, upset, angry, my own turmoil reflected in them. Even Antonia, who plays along with the bullshit from the board more than anyone. They're working together to find better solutions than Katarina and her gore.

'I wrote a letter,' I say, boldly projecting my voice, 'to the council and the papers. They didn't publish it or write back, or anything though.'

'We've all written letters,' Antonia says, shaking her head.

'Yeah, they don't do anything with them.' Joel gives me a pained smile.

The twitchy man speaks up. 'It needs something more drastic. I mean, they injected us.' He points towards the red lump on his collarbone, the lump we all have where the chip was injected. 'They mutilated us. They monitor our insides. They killed one of our own with exhaustion.'

I flinch at that. Antonia rubs my shoulder, and I loosen under her touch.

'We're all in agreement that something needs to be done,' Joel says. 'More letters, maybe?'

'I don't think that will help,' Antonia says. 'But we need a plan. All of us together, we have a voice. We need to do something once and for all.'

Chapter Forty-Three

Layla

I arrive home a little tipsy from the few drinks I had, my mind reeling with any possibility that could result from the meeting with my colleagues. We hadn't come up with anything credible, but there is a support network and a common goal—stop IMAtech or at least make it ease up a bit. I was tempted to stay out later, having no desire to go home and share my living space with the hands, but I am still so tired. Perhaps Katarina has moved them by now, although that seems unlikely. Katarina never does anything I ask.

'Where the hell have you been?' Katarina asks as I walk through the door. 'I'm late for work.'

I startle at her curt tone, then shrug. 'So don't wait for me.'

'You should have told me you'd be late. I was worried.'

I hang up my coat and scowl at her. 'Oh, for God's sake. It's hardly as if I'm going to be traipsing around some morgue cutting off limbs.'

She holds her finger to her mouth. 'Quiet. And I'm allowed to worry.'

I slouch, and only then do I check the time. I really am late. Katarina's my friend, so of course she'd worry. I should be more considerate. But I'm sick of being a pushover. Emboldened by my drink, I think, why should I have to answer to Katarina?

'Why?' I ask. 'Just because you have such a busy social life—thanks for putting all that in my diary by the way—you think you're the only one allowed to have plans? And excuse me if I'm in no hurry to get back to my morgue flat.'

Katarina makes some grunt of disapproval, then stomps off to her room to get ready, and I sit heavily at the kitchen table. I am mad at WIT, not Katarina. It's the beer making me short-tempered, that's all. I'll apologise to her later.

On the table, Katarina's phone pings. On autopilot, I reach for it. When it's in my hand, it pings again. I try to avert my eyes, but it's like a tug on a string. I shouldn't look, I know I shouldn't. I really, really shouldn't.

Hey babe, sorry can't do tonight, got to meet Adam at the Ivy. Still OK for tomorrow?

I yawn when I read it. It's just the guy Katarina's dating. I go to put the phone back down, then do a double-take as I clock the name. Harry Baxter.

It can't be. . .

I blink a few times, disbelief slowing my brain to a snail's pace, then load up previous messages. My heart rate spikes as I read multiple mentions of board meetings, of Adam, of WIT, preceded by dick pics and then, a picture that almost makes me hurl the phone out a window. A selfie of the two of them.

I stand up, my whole body rigid. Katarina and Harry Baxter. THE Harry Baxter.

My breath shudders in my lungs, my blood chills in my veins. Harry Baxter. How could she? My head throbs with such pain, I bend double and drop the phone on the floor.

I scream for her. 'Kat! Katarina!'

The clang of hangers from the bedroom is all that replies.

I scream again. 'Harry fucking Baxter!'

Katarina comes from her bedroom and snatches her phone back from the floor. 'What the hell are you doing snooping through my phone?'

'Harry Baxter! That fucker, Harry Baxter!'

'What?' Katarina raises her eyebrows and leans against the door frame. So relaxed, so unruffled. 'He's hot and great in bed.'

My fists go to my temples, and I squeeze my eyes shut. This can't be happening. My friend is not fucking my enemy. My friend isn't fucking my enemy! I open my eyes and Katarina's face is the same. All gorgeous and traitorous and so damned nonchalant.

'How could you? Harry Baxter!' I keep saying his name, trying to force it to sink in. Harry Baxter! 'You told me not to take Texi because it would be disloyal, and you're screwing him.'

Katarina smiles. 'One of us should have scruples. I vote you.'

'You two-faced bitch.'

'Ha! Don't you know it! Anyway, relax. It's all part of my revenge plan for Isobel.'

I bristle at the mention of her name. How fucking dare she say her name? 'Don't give me that. This isn't about Isobel. This is about you getting your kicks. Why do you even miss her so much? You didn't even like Isobel. . .you didn't even. . .' The obvious fact is like a punch in the gut. It halts my lungs and stings all over. I take a moment to process, to put the well-fitting jigsaw pieces together. How had I not seen it before? I'm so bloody stupid it makes me want to heave. My palm goes to my forehead as reality slaps me in the face. 'Oh, my God. You had a thing for her, didn't you?'

Katarina strokes her hair, holding her chin high. 'How could I not? She was gorgeous, fun, passionate. . .'

'Did you. . .' I swallow. My eyes are already streaming before I utter my next words. 'Did you sleep with her?'

'So what if I did? You dated her for like, five minutes.'

Tears drip from my cheeks, my insides hollow out and my back bows. I grab a chair and slouch forward, the beer churning in my stomach. 'She was mine. Not for five minutes. We were meant to be together. She was the one thing that was just mine.' I sit on the chair, my knees not strong enough to keep me standing, and my hands cover my mouth. 'How could you?'

Katarina stands taller, long, elegant, in control. 'She preferred me. And she's dead because of you, so excuse me if I don't cry a fucking river for you.'

Every bit of air is gone from my lungs, and I curl over like I've been winded. 'I don't even know who you are anymore.' From the edge of my vision, I see Katarina fold her arms, her face wearing a smug grin. 'You need to leave,' I say, barely a whisper. 'I want you out of my house.'

Katarina steps forward and leans down so close, I hear her mouth move with her words. 'Except it's *our* house. And no. I'm not going anywhere.'

Chapter Forty-Four

Katarina

It was maybe a couple of months before the accident. I came home from work, a little drunk and stumbling through the front door, just as Isobel was in the kitchen getting a drink. She smelled of overly sweet cocktails. She and Layla were sharing a bed, Isobel explained to me, and over a glass of water she revealed that they hadn't been intimate yet. Lying side-by-side, cuddling and kissing was as far as they'd gone. Layla had wanted to wait, to savour every moment of their relationship, to unwrap Isobel one layer at a time.

Isobel's hair was purple then, dry and coarse, but the wildness of it suited her. She looked free. When I saw her, I was filled with a longing I'd never experienced before. I wanted to be on her, all over her, inside her. I wanted to know what she tasted like.

And I'm a woman who gets what I want.

It was impossible to tell who made the first move—our two souls collided with perfect choreography. We were so quiet, muting our groans and softly pressing our bodies against each other propped up on furniture, the door, a wall. I would have liked it to be fiercer, to reflect my hunger. Isobel's frustrations came to fruition as I held my hand over her mouth to muffle her groans. Her teeth clamping down on my knuckle was the tipping point for my own climax. When we were both finished, Isobel pulled away, looked deeply into my eyes for a moment, then, without a word, retreated back to the bedroom to lay with Layla.

The next morning after our encounter, Isobel sat at the table next to Layla as I got up to fetch a drink. I didn't speak, only a quick nod as acknowledgement, then I took my glass back to my room. We never touched each other again.

I still fantasise often about that illicit night, longing for another taste, with the freedom to make the noises I so desperately wanted, to hear Isobel's groans. No one excites me like Isobel did that night. Harry Baxter isn't a patch on her. When Isobel was gone for good, an eternity of never being with her again was crushing. My support for Layla during her grief was a show to cover up my own.

I would quietly watch the couple from the sidelines and think about that night, hot with yearning and wanting nothing more than to join them, but I kept my distance, biding my time. Only, I left it too late. A sense of heaviness weighs down on me every time I think of that.

I will not make the same mistake with revenge.

Layla can be mad all she wants, but that's only because she's scared and regretful. I know her so well. I know all that she keeps locked away. Through Isobel, we share a bond that runs so much deeper than just housemates.

Layla is like a snowdrop that bloomed too early; a little frost will make her wither. The coldness of reality has to be revealed to her bit by bit. Peeling off one layer of truth at a time.

Chapter Forty-Five

Katarina

I change a barrel in the cellar, brushing past the place I had been fucking Harry a few nights ago. The memory makes me bite down a smile as I hum distractedly while I work. Perhaps he'll invite me around later this evening, or he'll turn up. After thinking so much about Isobel earlier, I could do with a release.

As always, I check the barrel is propped against the door so it won't close on me. I reattach the gas, stumbling on my heels as I do, almost knocking over one of the bottles of spirits. There's too much stock for a bar doing so badly.

I know I'll have to look for another job soon. Being in such a quiet bar is boring, and as much as I hate the customers, I miss the admiration from them. The dullness of night after night in Little London leaves me too much time to dwell.

A screech comes from upstairs, and I end my daydream to run. Taking two steps at a time, heart pounding, dreading the worst. I find Davina standing with her hand over her mouth, a misty shine of tears in her eyes.

'What?' I say through panted breaths. 'Shit, you okay?'

'I can't believe it. I just can't,' Davina says, with a tremulous voice, her tears flowing freely now.

'What?'

'You heard of Adam Ward, CEO of WIT?'

I put my hands in my pockets and shift my weight. 'Yeah, of course. Who hasn't?'

She turns the paper around so I can see it. 'He's put a formal offer in to buy the bar.'

I snatch the paper and read it. My eyes bulge. It's an offer Davina would be a fool to refuse. *Fucking show off.*

I tense my jaw and hand the letter back, sounding as breezy as I can. 'I guess the bar is his then?'

'I can't understand it. This place has been tanking lately. Why offer so much for a failing bar?'

I rock on my heels and give a one-shoulder shrug. 'Beats me.'

Davina's face is pure joy, eyes glinting, and it's perhaps the first time I've ever seen her properly smile. I have to feel happy for her. If one good thing comes out of my fraternising with the enemy, at least this is it.

'Go home,' Davina says. 'Take the night off. Full pay. I'm going to close up. No point in trying to make money when the bar is as good as sold.'

I don't need telling twice. I grab my coat and make for the door. At least if Adam Ward comes in, I won't be there. It makes me hate him all the more, that he thinks I can be so easily bought.

Nice try, dickhead.

Chapter Forty-Six

Layla

I scrub my whole body in the shower until I am raw. My hair hangs in wet tendrils. Katarina, the traitor, has gone to work, thank God. I can't bear to look at her. Any image of her I conjure makes my toes curl and my skin crawl.

How could she?

I drink gin, avoiding the ice tainted with dead hands in the freezer. Not that I care about the hands anymore. I care about Isobel. We may have only been dating for a few months, but she was the love of my life, or at least she was *meant* to be the love of my life, and Katarina took her for herself.

I drink another gin, neat, no tonic to take the sharpness away. It's good, the eye-watering strength of it. It makes me gag, but that only makes it hit the spot more.

Fucking Katarina.

I go to Katarina's room and look through her clothes, flicking through the disorderly hangers, and I mentally label each item: whore, traitor, slut. Anyone could sleep with whoever they want if they dress like that. It wasn't Isobel's fault. Katarina handed herself to her like some overripe fruit, *eat me now or I'll spoil!*

I had wanted to wait, too scared of rushing things, too scared our relationship would fizzle out quickly. Perhaps if I hadn't waited, perhaps if Isobel was satisfied. . .

No. I can't think like that. This is all that slut's fault, not mine. I wanted to savour Isobel. Katarina wanted to steal her.

I pick out a short, fitted skirt, a pair of too-high heels, and help myself to her curling tongs and make up. I do my face, all smoky eyes and deep red lipstick. After another few gins, I put on one of Katarina's low-cut tops that shows more boob than I ever have on display. I look in the mirror. This is what Katarina sees every day. Made up, presented, on show, and ready to take whatever she wants. What is the world like for Katarina, who does what she likes without sparing a thought for anyone else?

Wobbling in the heels, the amount of gin not helping my balance, I stagger out of the house. I grab some pre-mixed cocktails at the shop and take the tube to Tower Hill Station, sitting on the tube next to some discarded takeaway packets that stink of fried meat. I try to keep my head up, but I sway with the motion and my stomach heaves, downing the cans of drink, adding to the spin. Across the vestibule, some letchy guy grins at me. What would Katarina do? I sit upright and give him the finger.

At the station, I walk, zigzagging the street all the way to the Ivy where Harry said he was meeting Adam. Harry fucking Baxter and Adam Ward in the same restaurant. I should have brought some kind of explosives with me to blow the place up.

But revenge for Isobel isn't on my mind right now. Angering Katarina is.

Harry Baxter is outside the restaurant and I stop dead in my tracks. He's so recognisable from all the articles about him. That smirking grin, leaning against the wall, he looks straight out of a catalogue. Half in shadow, he glances up at me and we clock eye contact. God, he is hot. *No, he can't be.* That's the booze talking. He's a monster. A big, sex pest monster. He says not a word but smiles and looks me up and down, his face glowing with approval.

I approach him, attempting the sort of swishing hips that Antonia does so well, hand on my hip and roll my shoulders back in some confident swagger like Katarina. I stop a foot or so in front of him. 'How about we go somewhere private?'

He cocks his head and raises one eyebrow. 'Sure,' he says, before waving for his driver.

His Bentley arrives, and he steps around, then opens the door, standing to one side. I hold my head high, walking in Katarina's shoes, and get in.

***

I wake, or at least, my eyes open. Being awake seems a long way off. My head is fuzzy, the sound of my own breathing muffled like I'm underwater. It's early, I think. The sun is only just peeking through the blinds. Blinds? My bedroom has curtains, not blinds.

Where the hell am I?

The bed is so much nicer than mine, smells better. My limbs glide over the sheets, crisp and cool that cover the lump-free mattress. My tongue sticks in my mouth like my spit is made of paste and my head throbs. I roll over and gasp. There he is, still asleep, next to me. Naked.

I peek under the covers. I am also naked.

Shit.

My eyes adjust to the light, squinting through my headache, and I take in the room as he groans and stretches himself awake. My stomach churns as I slide over and I grab my clothes, not my clothes, but Katarina's clothes, feeling like some whore as I pull them on.

'Hey, beautiful,' he says, his voice husky with sleep. 'What're you doing?'

'I. . .' I fight to speak. My mouth is too dry. The only liquid in the room is a mostly empty bottle of champagne. The sight of the used condom on the floor next to that makes my stomach lurch even more. 'I need to go.'

'Nonsense. Stay.' He reaches for me.

'No,' I flinch and pull the skirt on, not that it covers much.

'You weren't so shy last night. Come on, let's have another round.'

I stand and lean away from his reach. 'I have to go. Bye.'

I run for the door before he has time to say another word, past a picture of Peter Ward hanging on the wall that makes my need to throw up even more urgent.

Outside, the rising sun is too bright, shining on me like a spotlight and I throw up as soon as I feel its warmth. The concierge at the door doesn't give me a second look. No doubt Harry has taken back worse states before. They must think I'm a prostitute. My face burns with embarrassment.

The walk of shame feels exactly that. Eyes are on me everywhere. My secrets spilled. What have I done? I betrayed Katarina. Sure, I was betrayed first, but that doesn't make it okay. That is something Katarina would do, not me. Not Layla Daley. And to fuck him, *him*, of all people? I have betrayed myself too. Was it even good? My memory is a blur, an impression of a memory, like Monet painted it.

When I get home, I drink some water, leaving spills on the side, and then eat half a piece of bread with no plate, a trail of crumbs following me. I kick my shoes off in the general direction of the front door, leaving them haphazardly scattered before collapsing into bed.

Chapter Forty-Seven

Layla

I've never called in sick before. I'm just not the type. Isobel did. I remember one Monday when Isobel said she needed some time off, and she tried to encourage me to do a sickie too. I steadfastly refused, citing my desire to prove myself, to make up some lost time.

Working today would have been impossible. I'm way too hungover, wracked with guilt and a feeling of filth. I don't even email my sick note until an hour after I am meant to have started work. My IMAtech has been buzzing incessantly to tell me I'm late, that my levels are off. *No shit.* No doubt it knows my blood alcohol content is enough to knock out a horse.

I'll have to make up the hours, and I'm down already. My colleagues will be playing catchup on my seconds lost and that will make them hate me. I've no energy to cry out my shame. I hold onto the bed frame when any emotion hits, causing the room to spin, then try to sleep some more.

A full day and night's sleep isn't enough to cleanse my mind. I can justify my actions in so many ways, but that's kidding myself. I am Layla Daley, and I don't do such things. I thought Katarina was my friend, but she's taken everything from me, even my own sense of self-worth and her influence has led me astray.

I hate Katarina, yet I stooped as low.

She's turning me into her.

***

The next day, I arrive early for work. There were moments the day before when I thought my hangover would never go away, but after a day in bed avoiding Katarina and eating nothing but dry toast, I'm ready to face the world again, and refreshed enough to make up some lost seconds.

Antonia approaches me bang on 9 o'clock. I can't read her face: upset, appalled, some sort of general disdain towards me. It's like she knows, and she can smell him on me. I want the ground to swallow me up. 'I need to fill in your absence form,' she says.

I don't take my eyes off my screen. My fingers are flying over the keys, my usual knuckle aches mostly abated after a day off. 'I was throwing up all night after seeing a load of severed hands fall down. I'm still having nightmares about them and felt too ill to come to work after the trauma. If we were allowed to work from home still, I would have made up the hours.'

From the edge of my vision, Antonia gives me a small nod, then loads up something on her laptop. 'The company response is to advise you to go to the dispensary. There are tailor-made supplements available to get you through any time of difficulty. Hardships outside of work needn't affect your ability to be efficient. With IMAtech, you can be at your best, always.'

I don't need to watch her speak to know she's reading. She drones on as if she's reciting the shipping forecast.

As she walks away, I bite my tongue and clamp my mouth shut. I should have apologised to her, or said something nice at least. I was too honest, too brash. Antonia hates the company too. I can almost see Katarina in the corner of my eye, smiling, giving me a thumbs up, hearing her whispers in my ear, making me say what she would say. My typing gets harder, my fingers slamming on the keys.

'Things okay with you two?' Joel asks.

'What?' I snap. 'Sure. Same as ever.'

'Reckon she'll pass that on to the board?'

'No, of course not. And if she does, they won't change any-thing. Like she said, if I'm upset, I should visit the dispensary.'

Again, too outspoken. I should keep my head down and concentrate on my work. They'll be pinning me down and ramming pills down my throat soon or sacking me. I'm being rash and stupid. Impulsive.

Like Katarina.

'Well done for saying it though,' Joel says. 'Antonia can write that down. They might read it.'

I look up for a second and see a glint of admiration in his eye. Of course I did. I'm sounding less like Layla and more like Katarina. And everyone admires Katarina.

'We're meeting again after work,' Joel says. 'Just a quick one. To talk, you know? Come?'

I nod. Diplomacy, teamwork, the right sort of action is exactly what I should be doing. 'Sure. It'll be good to try to put a plan together. To really get something done.'

And to stay away from Katarina, of course.

Chapter Forty-Eight

Layla

Everyone is so tired at the bar after work, they all agree to stay for only one drink. I sit at the table that has an ashtray on it, despite smoking being banned in bars for about twenty years. From the looks of the table, that was probably the last time it was cleaned. I stare into my pint, struggling with every sip. A day ago, I swore I'd never drink again, and my stomach isn't ready to accept alcohol just yet, even the smell of the bar is reminding me of what I threw up outside Harry Baxter's building, which reminds me that I fucked Harry Baxter, which turns my stomach even more.

I should have ordered a coke or lemonade. I'm so mentally drained that even trying to be sociable is exhausting me more and I hunch over. The musty-scented chair is uncomfortable, while the table is littered with crumbs and spills, it makes me worry what sort of state my apartment is in.

I don't sit next to Antonia. I'm still riddled with wanting to cower away, racked with shame for what I did, for calling in sick. She looks my way and I avoid eye contact, sure she can read my mind and is as ashamed of me as I am. She tries to get a dialogue going but is met with yawns and irritability.

Even Joel struggles to summon any enthusiasm. Twitchy guy is absent, off sick apparently. Signed off now with stress, even the Texi wasn't enough to keep anxieties at bay and his refusal to visit the dispensary for anything else has left a black mark next to his name in his HR file, according to Antonia. His seconds will have to be made up by the rest of the team. This hasn't been stated by WIT, but they all know and they all consider him selfish, not a team player for causing more work for everyone. He should have done his bit and dosed up. My day off the day before is met with similar disdain and guilt makes me heavy and drawn, weighed down with uselessness, wishing to be anywhere else, to be anyone else.

No progress is made in plotting tactics, and I feel no better for it. Passion for the cause seems to have waned under a thick blanket of fatigue. The drastic action that Katarina had taken disgusted people, but at least it spurred some fervour. Now, momentum stalls and everyone is sleepwalking into their fate like zombies. The inevitable awaits us all.

I arrive home on autopilot. I can't even remember leaving the pub or the journey home, such is the monotony. The same walk to the tube, the same overcrowded train smelling of feet and squashed bodies, the heat stifling even on a cold day, the same sluggish walk back to the tedium of my apartment from the tube after staring at the same screen at work all day.

The one pint has gone to my head and I go straight to my room, then lie down to sleep. Just to catch up on a little bit more sleep will make me feel better again, will give me some inspiration and help me get through the next same old day.

I wake hours before work, aching and clammy from a nightmare. I shiver and rub my eyes until my vision has black dots.

My nightmare was too real. Katarina and Harry were fucking. I was there, watching. I knew what his body looked like, knew how it felt to have him inside me. The thought makes my gut heave. There was death in the dream, cries of pain and panic. All fuzzy edges, like it was in soft focus, some old movie with a grainy picture. More sepia than colour. Faceless people and echoing voices. I couldn't make out words, only the scent of fear. In the haze, the image of her was pin-sharp, as real as my own reflection. Katarina held a weapon, and her eyes were darker than ever.

I tiptoe around the flat to get a drink, not wanting to wake Katarina. She's home, her shoes have been left strewn across the hallway as always, a half-drunk glass of water on the side.

After I have some water, I return to bed to stare up at the ceiling and dread what Katarina's been up to.

Chapter Forty-Nine

Katarina

Harry looks like shit and struggles to come. He's clearly high on something. He tried to talk to me as soon as I arrived at his house, but I made a move for some more physical company instead. I'm not in the mood for talking. I need to fuck my worries away and his leather, wipeable sofa serves nicely as a platter to serve up my desires.

Layla hasn't spoken to me since our fight, since she tried to kick me out. She was trying to shut me away, and the thought that she might succeed makes me grip Harry tighter, my fingers biting into his back.

I shouldn't be thinking about Layla while Harry is so deep inside me. Yet my mind is mulling over how to phrase things to her, to make her see that what I'm doing is for the best, that my feelings for Isobel shouldn't upset her. It should enhance her own feelings. It at least shows she has good taste. As my thoughts wander to Isobel, I groan, arching my back, and Harry fucks me harder.

'You like that?' he asks as he adjusts his angle.

'Yeah,' I say, thinking of Isobel, with her wild hair and passion like no other, her daydreaming and her wicked laugh. 'So much.'

That Isobel had feelings and desires for Layla too means that Layla is my equal, and I know that's what she desires to be. In this horrible world, it's best to seize every ounce of pleasure you can get. That's what I've been trying to explain to Layla, to let the bad shit go away, to take the good stuff for her own. I wrap my legs around Harry, latching on to every bit of gratification I can get.

When we're done, he pulls his jeans back up and says, 'There's this woman who works at WIT. They found a complaint she was going to submit about Peter. Can you believe it? The man is dead, and she wants to drag his name through the mud.'

I dress and smooth out my hair. 'Well, at least you found out first.'

He's twitchy, with dilated pupils and sweatier than he should be. 'Yeah, it's good. I'm going to find out about everyone who tried to cross him. Starting with Adam. He's been sober for what, a year? He's always such a blabbermouth when pissed or high. I'll spike him. A little GHB in his juice should get him going, and he'll spill everything. The board needs to be there too to witness it.'

I know the drug well. I've confiscated enough of it in Little London before. The drug that's not only used for date-rape but gets you more drunk, looser, makes inhibitions melt away. I've seen men pass it to women who they want to take home, and I have intervened when drinks were spiked. Could I be that evil that I'd spike someone to get them high against their will?

Yeah. If that person is Adam Ward, easily.

'He's bought the bar,' I say. I wasn't sure if Harry knew. If Adam would have boasted already.

Harry's jaw drops, then a smile spreads across his face. 'Seriously?'

'Yep. Trying to buy me, I think.'

'Good move, Adam.' He nods, clearly impressed.

I give him a punch on the arm. 'Hey! He's a dickhead, remember?'

'Yeah, course. Definitely.' He pulls his T-shirt on. Shame. His torso is the only bit of him that doesn't look like crap today. 'You must have really gotten under his skin. Not tempted, are you?'

I grimace as I put my own clothes on. 'Ew, no way. But this could be helpful. I could host a party there, just for the board, a little congratulations on buying the place.'

Harry's eyes sparkle. 'That would be perfect.'

I'm well aware it would be perfect. I've played it over in my head enough times. I'm fully dressed now, my lacy skirt pulled down and my top more modest than usual. When Adam visited the bar and looked at me like that, he made me feel cheap, that I should hide myself from view. Bile stings my throat as I think of him mentally undressing me. Far better I'm the one doing the imagining. Imagining what he looks like with his skin peeled back.

'So,' I say. 'Friday?'

Harry startles and pauses before he answers. 'God, that soon.'

My eyebrows raise. 'Second thoughts?'

'No. No, definitely not.' He leans in and gives me another kiss. 'Everyone is still thinking it was suicide. No. This needs to come out. He needs to confess, then Adam will be out of my way. Then that shit will be finished, and they'll appreciate me for once.'

'This Friday then.' I smile. 'I can put whatever in his drink. Easy.'

Chapter Fifty

Layla

First thing in the morning, I look at Katarina's phone. Instinct drives me, that dream feeling like a premonition. Her phone is clean, wiped almost. Nothing incriminating at all, save for a few dick pics from Harry Baxter. I recoil at the sight of it. I had touched that thing. I wish I'd snapped it off, or at least ripped his banjo string. It was another opportunity missed.

I shake away the thought. It's one influenced by Katarina. I need to clear my head of her, to cleanse that bitch out of my mind and rid myself of her words and her image. I have to shut away the badness she's imprinted on me.

Doctor Cottrell, my therapist from years ago, taught me how to do that. 'Lock the door,' he'd say. 'Shut it all away and move on. Leave the bad memories in that mind safe.' I close my eyes and visualise it, taking out a key and turning it. All the evil thoughts, the awful memories can stay in there.

That door doesn't want to stay locked anymore. Its hinges creak when it reopens, the last things I put in the safe falling out with a bump.

I walk to work rather than break up the journey with the tube. The dirty streets are lined with rubbish, too much to pick up, but I retrieve a few cans and bottles and relocate them to the bin to save it from harming the birds. Even pigeons need looking after, Isobel always said.

The weather suits my mood: dark and brooding, not raining yet, but the threat is there. Static laces the air and makes my scalp tickle. Chills creep over me like there's someone watching. As cold as that makes my veins, my skin flushes with shame for feeding Katarina's lust for revenge. If I hadn't moaned about IMAtech so much, maybe Katarina wouldn't care. If I had made more of an effort to get over Isobel, maybe she wouldn't have cut up corpses and bolstered Harry Baxter's ego even more by fucking him, then I wouldn't have ended up fucking him.

My tears might as well be made of petrol, as each one I cry stokes her fire.

Katarina didn't love Isobel like I did. They may have been intimate, but their bond wasn't the same. There was nothing there beyond physical attraction. I am sure of it. Whereas we had a connection, the first stirs of love that would have blossomed if we'd had more time.

We'd seen each other the day before. Stayed up late, made love, chatted, had fun. Neither of us had the sleep we so desperately needed. I should have let her sleep, should have kissed her goodnight instead of indulging in time with her. Katarina was right when she said I erased her.

I can't think about that now. I can't start crying at work again. The misty vision of tears will stop me working efficiently, and I am still hours down on the week.

I arrive at work and sit, turn my computer on and take a deep breath, mentally preparing myself for another day of the monotony. Joel is already here, though he says nothing. His usual pleasantries are absent, his posture more slumped than usual. His phone is in his hand, his face fallen and blotchy.

I don't want to ask. I can't afford the distraction, but he always asks me, so I have to. 'Hey.' And then I eventually say, 'You okay?'

He looks up and tears fall. 'You haven't heard?'

'What?'

He holds up his phone, and I read the local news article. My hands go to my mouth and my vision clouds with tears. The headline sucks the breath from me, and my lungs stagnate in shock. She's smiling in the picture. Warm and beautiful. Tears trace my cheeks as I read the article. Antonia is dead. Found in the street near her home, passed out, unresponsive, she was pronounced dead at the scene.

'Oh, my God. No.' My voice quivers as my hands shake. I read on and the cause of death makes me choke. Texi overdose. 'Oh, my God. No!'

'They're saying accidental overdose,' Joel says through his own sobs. 'I can't believe it. She was so careful. One a day. Everyone knows that. Just one a day.'

'Not Antonia.' My voice catches in my throat and comes out as just a whisper. 'No. . . I. . .excuse me.' I run to the bathroom, racing the chunks climbing up my throat. I bend over the basin and heave up my breakfast, crying as I do.

I sob and sob into the toilet until my body is too exhausted to sob anymore. Convulsions of dry heaving pulse through me, but they stop when my body has no strength left even for that. I stand on weak legs and wobble when I open the door, dropping my handbag. It opens as it hits the floor, spilling its contents. I crouch down, pick up my phone, a lipstick that Katarina would wear and I never would, my purse, and some litter I picked up and didn't bin. Among the mess is the blister pack of Texi Joel had given me. I pick it up, then drop it again, my hands shaking too much to hold it. I back away, leaning against the sink and stare at it, too afraid to touch it again.

The pack is supposed to have fifteen pills.

It is empty.

Chapter Fifty-One

Layla

I get no work done. How can I? There's an emptiness to the office. Antonia's footsteps are absent and her chair cold. We aren't sent home out of respect like when Peter Ward died. The board members don't even come into the office today. There's no condolence memo from them. Not a word. It's as if Antonia didn't matter. An email arrives to remind everyone to visit the dispensary, and like a flock of sheep, they do.

Happy pills, motivating pills, vitamins, iron, endorphin boosters, and cortisol suppressants. IMAtech pings every two hours and they get up, shuffle along to the dispensary, hiding their tears and worries behind the guise of WIT-approved, Baxter Pharma-supplied supplements.

Stay efficient! Support our research! With IMAtech you can be at your best, always.

How can we be at our best when one of our best has died? There's the occasional whisper among the staff.

'She self-administered. If she'd stuck with the advice from the dispensary—'

'IMAtech would have told her when she was due a dose. She obviously ignored it.'

I rub my temples, then push my palms into my closed eyes. It doesn't stop the tears. A headache pierces my skull. Even empty, my stomach churns.

The empty pack is still in my bag. I consider throwing it in the sanitary bin or an ordinary bin. It screams at me from my handbag. In my mind's eye it's glowing through the leather, as if everyone can see it like some flashing beacon.

How it's empty is what I keep asking myself. Fifteen pills to none. As I half-heartedly attempt to programme this awful game, all manner of scenarios go through my mind. Antonia had taken them, that pack isn't mine, I had taken the pills myself, someone else took them.

Someone else. It's that scenario that eats away at me.

I've bitten several nails down to the skin, my denial needing something to chew on. I didn't give those pills to Antonia. It wasn't me. I would never do such a thing.

Katarina's lipstick is in my bag. Is that my clue? Had Katarina planted it when she emptied the blister pack?

I play the night over and over in my head. I didn't keep an eye on my bag. It was under my chair, or I thought so anyway. Antonia had maybe two pints to my one. Less than one. I didn't even finish it. I wasn't even in the pub that long.

Poor Antonia. I cry intermittently throughout the day, adding to the percussion of sobs through the office. I never even had the chance to tell her how I feel. I never even figured it out myself.

On my way home, I scroll through the news. A statement from Baxter Pharmaceuticals has been released. It's only one death from Texi. *Only one*, they actually say that. They express their regret, but the dosage is clearly stated, and they can't be responsible if people take too much.

My tears soak my phone, my shaking arms making it hard to read the words. They speak about Antonia as if she was a junkie. But she wasn't. I know she wasn't.

The statement goes on from the Baxters, not mentioning Antonia, only their own products.

This sad case shows the need for IMAtech's next stage of licensing. IMAtech is more than just motivating employees at work. It has the capability of monitoring hormone levels and to detect depression before it gets too bad. We can tailor-make supplement doses daily, even hourly. No one need suffer silently when Baxter Pharmaceuticals and IMAtech are given the green light to blend the two major industries of tech and pharma. To make this an essential tactic in the workforce, this level of control is necessary in today's climate. This case highlights the need to bridge that gap, and rest assured, WIT and Baxter Pharmaceuticals intend on doing exactly that. An employee's biochemistry should not be some guarded secret. Instead, it should be as open as their name or eye colour. It is simply data that we at Baxter Pharmaceuticals can use for the betterment of all. Because, at Baxter Pharmaceuticals, we get you, inside and out.

I put my fist in my mouth and bite, my eyes staring at the screen until they blur. Someone walks into me and curses, shoving me out of their way. I've forgotten I am walking home. The busy street disappeared for a moment, now it bombards me, invading my senses, letting me know this is real and not some awful nightmare. That statement rattled me so much, reality tries to slip away. They're using Antonia's death as a fucking sales pitch. Something like this should be soiling their reputation, but instead they're twisting it. That's what a multimillion-pound PR team gets you.

I put my phone in my pocket, then march the rest of my way home, upright, my previously bowed back straight as all my muscles tense. Rage heats me as I eat up the pavement and I arrive outside my building in record time.

I pause in the street, catch my breath, and my trembling body stills. Is Katarina home? I can't be sure. But if she is, what do I say to her?

I didn't spike Antonia. I wouldn't. Never. Was Katarina there, following me? Spiking Antonia seems far-fetched even for her, but there's a maliciousness to her I've seen, a tunnel vision in her desire to create chaos without sparing a thought for anyone else. She cut hands off corpses. She's capable of anything.

I can't shake the thought away. Katarina could be a killer. A murderer. And she's living in my house. She's taking things too far—she's implied as much. I shiver, fear chilling my insides. Katarina has to leave. I have to be rid of her.

Or else it was WIT. The board wanted Antonia quiet, for whatever shitty thing Peter Ward did to her to be silenced. They're seeking their revenge. And that means they could find out about what Katarina's been doing and seek revenge there too.

I walk through my front door as quietly as I can and listen for a moment. It's silent inside. She must be out. I bundle up all of Katarina's things into bin liners. Clothes, makeup, the shoes that are always haphazardly left across the doorway. Where will Katarina go? Harry's, probably. She could go to Portsmouth, as I'm sure she still has some family there. I hate myself for caring. I shouldn't give a toss. My priority is to get Katarina out of my life. She's a liability, and being near her is dangerous, even if she's not causing the danger herself. I'm in self-preservation mode. What happens to her isn't my responsibility. I Sellotape a note to the bin bag saying, *You have to leave today. Sorry.*

I clench my jaw at the note. Why should I apologise? This is my house. The only thing I'm really sorry about is that I ever let Katarina in.

I rip that note off and write another. *You're out. I don't want you in my house anymore.*

By the time I'm taping that note on, Katarina arrives home. She opens the door, letting a cool breeze in, then slams it behind her. She looks down at what I'm doing, her deep red lips forming a dark smile before shoving me out the way and taking the bags, walking through to her bedroom and tipping them out onto her bed.

I have no proof. I can't accuse her of spiking Antonia, nor can I be sure WIT did it. I know nothing except that being near Katarina is too risky. 'You're going too far,' I say. 'I don't trust you. I can't live like this. You have to go.' My voice doesn't sound as hard as I want. I sound more like a pleading child, weak and nagging.

Katarina arranges her cosmetics back on the shelf, then hangs her clothes up in the wardrobe as if I didn't say anything. I stand in the doorway watching, waiting to be noticed, for Katarina to at least acknowledge I've spoken.

When all of her things are put away, she turns and faces me. 'Sweet Layla. Don't be silly. I'm doing something about the injustice. You should be pleased.' There isn't a hint of shame or anger in her voice. Her words ripple with her usual self-assured-ness, and my whole body trembles.

I shake my head, but don't dare step closer. I swallow, finding some courage hidden within me. 'No,' I say, as firmly as I can manage. 'You're going about it all wrong. I'm in a group with the other staff. We're all seeking a solution. A non-violent way, a proper way.'

Katarina laughs. 'I know about your little group,' she says, and my breath catches. It's almost like she's admitting she was there. 'And your letters and meetings won't change anything. What I am doing is effective.'

'No.' I beg, my courage being torn from me. I hate how pathetic I sound. 'No, it'll work. It's the best way. No one getting hurt is what's important. Please, just leave. I don't want you around anymore.'

Katarina steps closer, then right past me and to the kitchen. She opens the fridge and takes out what little food there is and eats it, chewing slowly, locking her eyes on me. 'Nice try,' she says with her mouth full. 'But you'll never get rid of me. You'll see soon, I'm good for you. I'm the best thing in your life.'

Chapter Fifty-Two

Layla

I lie in bed awake all night, hugging my knees, staring at the door. Sure any minute Katarina is going to come in, or the police, or WIT, someone labelling me a killer. When I close my eyes, it's Antonia's face I see. Her stern face at work, how she flustered around the board members when they came in, keeping her disdain so well hidden. She always tried. Whatever she did, she gave it her all. She didn't deserve to die.

My grief for Antonia sends shockwaves through me. I understand grief. I've been here before. Fresh and new and raw, though, is fear for myself. As selfish as I know that is, fear lodges in my gut and stops my eyes from giving in to sleep. The darkness offers no subterfuge for my wretched shame. I'm culpable, since the pills were mine, whether it was Katarina or WIT. I try to think of some explanation, of anything as to why the pills are gone. If Joel asks, I'll say I binned them, that I was too scared to take them after what happened to Antonia.

Does the bar have CCTV? Will anyone think to check it? What will that even show? A skulking Katarina stealing from my bag, or some hitman hired by WIT. In that case, maybe CCTV will be a good thing. It will prove my innocence. It's not my fault, I repeat to myself time and time again. I am Layla Daley, a good person. Not a killer.

The real killer might be the other person who lives here, who leaves her hair tongs on the dresser, her shoes by the front door. She paints her nails red and is due home any minute.

Why would they take my pills? That's what baffles me. They're so easy to buy anywhere. Why bother pinching mine?

They're trying to set me up. That's the only justification I can think of. Whoever wanted Antonia dead wanted me to take the blame. Is it because I told Katarina I'd go to the police? Is it because of the letter I wrote to the press? Or because that video was made on my computer? That damned viral video. Or those graphics I made? Someone has seen my evil thoughts depicted. Someone knows what the depths of my sick mind is thinking.

Oh, God. They know. Someone is on to me.

I sweat through my nightclothes, and when I'm too sticky to get comfortable, I shower in the night, creeping on tiptoes, an imposter in my own home. It doesn't matter how many times I wash, those hands are still on me. Spongy, dismembered hands, cold with death, squelching as they finger their way over my body. In my own hands, I feel what it must have been like to saw through bone, my teeth chattering with the vibrations. When I look at the shower water pooling around my feet, I'm sure it's tinged red. How could Katarina have done that? She's capable of anything.

I dry myself, then crawl back into bed, still eluded by sleep. I put on my glasses, then look at my phone instead. I read the news, looking at the picture of Antonia's lovely face. I so wanted to get to know her more. We had a common enemy, that was all. Antonia's only crime was knowing me.

I flush with guilt when a part of me, a deep-rooted part I can't rid myself of entirely, whispers maybe this is a good thing. That this is the scandal Baxter Pharmaceuticals needs. Their sales pitch statement might be seen as just that, and people will understand the real danger of IMAtech. If it was Katarina, then that would have been her aim, to tarnish the reputation of the company. Such news may hit their share price. They will know that without Texi, IMAtech is ineffective. The circle of life is broken.

I laugh at that thought, a hysterical, hopeless laugh at my own stupidity. Of course Baxter Pharmaceuticals won't be affected by this. They are another massive company, the biggest of Big Pharma. Baxter Pharmaceuticals still makes opioids, benzos, and all manner of other drugs people have died from, that have ruined lives. One more death isn't going to hurt them. One more overdose is like swatting a fly to them. They'll brush it off as no more than a speck of dust rather than the tarnish they deserve.

A bigger scandal is needed. A bigger drama. The realisation of that makes me run cold, and sends pain shooting across my temples, for Katarina will know that too. And how much further will she go?

I leave for work early, just to get out of the house, away from Katarina. I must have slept at some point last night, as I didn't hear her come in. Perhaps she stayed at Harry's. I don't dare peek and see.

Somehow, I'm still running late. I walk too slowly, not bothering with the tube again, wanting the cool morning air to blow away my bad thoughts. My feet hurt from walking. They always hurt these days. My functional flats are not functional enough. I probably need an insole, a massage. That chiropractor appointment still hasn't happened. IMAtech tells me I'm late, tells me I didn't sleep enough, my hormone levels are off, and that I should visit the dispensary. IMAtech tells me everything about my body I already damned well know, only it tells me it can solve all of this if only I buy into Baxter Pharmaceuticals therapies.

I can't be medicated again. I just can't.

I must try harder to succeed without it. I walk slower, steady my breaths, yet still it pings and buzzes.

There's a crowd outside the office, all of my colleagues standing like emotionless shells, just waiting to start their day. It's then I notice the police tape cornering off the entrance. By the looks of the gathering, none of my colleagues have been inside yet. Dread creeps up my spine, sweat seeping through my top, and I push my glasses up my nose. Where was Katarina last night? What has she done?

'What's going on?' I ask some colleagues, somehow keeping my voice light and quiver-free.

'Look inside, see?' A woman points to the entrance.

I shove myself in front of some taller bystanders, closer to the entrance, to the yellow police tape that's flapping in the light wind. Through the tall glass windows, I can make out words painted across the wall inside. Huge, bright red words. The smell of raw steak tells me. I don't need to ask if it's written in blood.

IMAtech KILLS. WIT WANT BLOOD

My breath stalls in my lungs and I step back, passing through the crowd, away from the throng, away from the coppery aroma that lingers in my nose. I force an exhale, again and again, pushing all the air out with my diaphragm, but still the smell won't go. I am smelling the contents of my own arteries, my fear spilling from them. I shoulder-barge my way back farther, into some clear space where I can move and breathe.

Katarina. It must have been her.

I get my phone out and dial Katarina's number. She doesn't answer, so I call again and again, until her sleepy voice greets me.

'Hello?' she rasps.

I speak down my phone in an angry whisper. 'Kat, what the hell have you done? Was this you?'

I sit at a bus stop and wait for her reply. There's a long pause. My IMAtech buzzes to say I should have started work already.

'Katarina?'

'What? It's early. Stop shouting.'

I look around, sure I'm out of earshot, but in case I put my hand over my mouth to funnel my voice. 'Is it human? That blood?'

Katarina chuckles. 'You like it? Good, isn't it?'

'Fuck's sake Kat. Is it human?'

'What if it is?'

I bend and clutch my stomach as it cramps. 'Oh, my God. Human blood.'

'Did it make the news?'

I whimper. Is that all Katarina cares about? 'That's not the point. You're going too far, you hear me? You have to stop this. Please. Just stop.'

'I'll stop when they do. Now leave me alone. I want to sleep.'

Katarina hangs up, and I'm left staring at my phone.

The app buzzes again. I'm a minute down today already. My phone pings with an email from HR. All staff are to work from home, since the office is shut for a police investigation.

I stand, my legs like dead weights, then drag my body home before Joel or anyone has a chance to talk to me. I can't face them and can't form words. Denial is all I have: Katarina can't have done that. This can't be happening.

I stare into the mid-distance, eyes unfocussed on anything. I fear what's ahead of me, what lurks around the next corner, of what's waiting for me when I get to my flat. My flat is supposed to be my home, but it's the place where I feel the least safe of all.

I detour on my way, delaying the inevitable. I walk past shops, cafes, and businesses where people are congregating, chatting, laughing, showing what it is to be normal, to have normal friends. A glimpse at a life that I never seem to have. A life that I have never grasped.

Denial is useless. I have to be practical, to free myself from the situation. I need to get away from Katarina, to get her out of my life in order to have the life I deserve. But I have no idea how. I hope Katarina will sleep all day. Working from home, we'll be breathing the same air. Katarina might wake and fill my mind with bad thoughts, with justifications, to try to make me more and more like her.

I walk past a coffee shop and stop outside, the decision taking no more than a split second. I go in, get my laptop out, then order a coffee.

If I can avoid going home, I will. Somehow, I just have to stay away from Katarina forever.

Chapter Fifty-Three

Katarina

When the news comes on and plays the story about the blood, my entire body tingles with delight. It's a featured story on local London news, which is the most important news. Who gives a shit about what happens outside of London? Certainly no one in the tech world. My lips curve into a smile and my eyes sparkle as I watch, engrossed.

Further upset aimed at the launch of IMAtech as a message was sent loud and clear to WIT...

To me, it sounds like poetry. It makes breaking into the blood bank worthwhile. It makes the even later than usual late night bearable to think I have their attention. My only regret is that it wasn't Adam Ward's blood. With every letter I painted, I imagined it was his blood pebble-dashing the wall, spraying like a geyser from his jugular, his face ashen and frozen in fright.

Soon. Not much longer now.

I smile all the way to Harry's place. I messaged him while the news was playing, my success getting me in the mood for some physical exertion. He sent his car to save me from getting on the tube. Worried about my safety, he said. Since there's someone with a vendetta against WIT. The driver held the door open for me and stood to attention as I got in, like I'm somebody really important. The car is so huge, I can stretch out fully. There's a compartment with champagne and crystal glasses, but I refrain for now. No doubt there will be something nice to drink at Harry's, and I don't feel like celebrating on my own. I'm meeting him at his apartment again, his 'city place', so he calls it. His countryside manor is his favourite abode, though I have yet to see it. The luxury apartment in Chelsea is perfectly adequate, I think. Why would I ever want to go to Surrey anyway? Nothing ever happens in Surrey.

I haven't seen Layla all day. I worry so much about her and spent ages today pacing the apartment and scratching my head as to why she's still cross. My little deed should have put me back in her good books. It is exactly the sort of action that's needed. The press are on our side now, reporting on the upset. There is only so much that media heavyweight Jan Novac will be able to sway to his cause.

It's all baby steps, a few acts before the grand finale. The tide is turning on public opinion. I can feel it. Surely Layla will soon too.

***

'Stupid bloody kids, or eco warriors or something. People that don't want to do a hard day's work.'

Harry hasn't stopped ranting since I arrived. Maybe I should have had a drink in the car on the way over to take the edge off hearing it all. I sit on the sofa, listening for a while before getting up and fetching a drink, since he's too preoccupied to play host. As I sip my wine, I do my best not to grin from ear to ear. He looks hot when he's angry, his brow all furrowed and his muscles taut. I wonder when it will be the right time to start taking his clothes off. We both have some energy that needs to be burned off.

'They'll find them. I'm sure,' he says. 'And when they do, I'll sue them for everything they're worth and then some. That bloody Texi-death was bad enough. This as well is giving me a headache.'

I wince at how he refers to the Texi-death, not even mentioning her by name. Life is cheap to him. Human beings count as nothing but speed-bumps. If he thinks people are so disposable, I'll make sure his life is treated just the same.

'Maybe we should concentrate on the matter at hand,' I say.

He stops pacing, then walks up and pulls me in close, cocking his head. 'Oh, yeah?'

I open my legs for him, the heat of his anger permeating through. I start to unbutton his shirt. 'Friday is only two days away,' I say, as he hikes up my skirt.

He presses against me and kisses me. 'You are my little anarchist, aren't you?'

I remove my top, then his. 'Anarchy still needs preparation.'

'Well, first things first,' he says.

I keep my mind on him, his body, relishing in my own pleasure, enjoying the perk of this relationship while it lasts. Two days and this will all be over. Two days and I will never fuck Harry Baxter again.

A pity for him more than me. In two days, he'll never be able to fuck anyone again.

Chapter Fifty-Four

Layla

The office is open the next day, business as usual, the memo says. Business as usual, as if no one has died, as if blood hadn't stained the furniture. The mess was cleaned up, forensics have taken samples, and that's all us minions are permitted to know. The board will be in the office all week. With the IMAtech launch being so huge, it's to be all hands on deck, the memo says. I grimace at their poor choice of wording. I don't want to visualise the metaphor.

I slow my pace when I approach the office, dreading what I'll find. More blood, some carcass, Adam Ward's corpse strung up outside? Relief washes over me when there's nothing of note. No police tape, no screams or dismembered body parts. Perhaps the news story was enough, and Katarina's achieved what she was hoping to. The news report sounded on our side, that was progress. Maybe she'll stop now. Maybe my nightmare will be over. Katarina has chinked away at the WIT armour enough.

The office smells of a potent mix of bleach and wet paint. What couldn't be cleaned off has been painted over, covering up the gore as if it were never there.

The atmosphere at work is different. There's no queue at the dispensary. The white coat-wearing staff member behind slouches over the desk. My colleagues' usual emotionless faces are now animated. A day away from whatever that desk is dishing out seems to have left them refuelled with vigour. Instead of the silence, except for the tapping of keyboards, there's a restlessness. I worked tirelessly in the cafe yesterday, made up a lot of lost time, but the seconds tally in the office tells a different story. The collective IMAtech tally has nosedived, like the staff aren't even trying. The hormone level chart is deep in the red.

I sit at my desk, not too far from where the presents and flowers had once piled up when Peter Ward died. The flowers that were put up around the office have long gone. There's nothing for Antonia. At her usual desk, someone has placed a bunch of carnations.

I walk over, and the card reads, *This should never have happened.*

I carefully place the card back, open so the words are visible, then sit again and start working.

Someone walks to the dispensary, and a chorus of tuts follows them. They turn around before they get there, then go back to their desk.

'You're actually working?' Joel says when he arrives.

I continue to type, affording him only the briefest glance. 'Of course.'

'Well, no one else is. Not until there is justice for Antonia.'

Justice for a WIT related death is a useless cause, I know this too well. And if justice is to be doled out, the punishment would come my way or Katarina's. I keep typing. 'Well,' I say. 'Not working won't help. It'll just get you the sack.'

'Antonia only took Texi because of the workload they demand from us. That dispensary is only necessary because of the workload. They want this game ready. They want to prove IMAtech works. Striking will stop all of that.'

I pause my typing for a second and watch my IMAtech tally sink lower. If productive seconds are what's needed, if we all stop working, maybe that will get someone's attention. It's a huge risk though, and I can't afford to lose my job.

'Come on,' Joel says. 'It'll only work if we're all together. All of us versus a few of them. You heard the news yesterday. The press are reporting how everyone hates IMAtech. We've got to keep the momentum up.'

I sip some water, then chew the inside of my cheek before replying. 'What are our demands?'

'Exactly what Antonia wanted. To stop IMAtech. To cut it out.'

I snort a laugh. 'Yeah, right. They've invested billions in IMAtech. No way will they cancel it.'

'It's what we've been aiming for this whole time.' He sits on my desk, creating a barrier between my eyes and the screen. 'We have to try. This is our chance. We owe it to Antonia.'

My vision glazes. I owe it to Antonia more than anyone. My mind goes to the hands, the blood, to poor Antonia. Joel's method is far more sensible, far more diplomatic. He's right. Keeping up some momentum is our only chance. Could I be brave enough and risk my job to take it? Katarina would say blood deserves blood. But a strike, a simple strike, that's what Isobel would do. And perhaps, if it works, it will stop whatever Katarina has planned.

I turn away from my computer and look Joel in the eye. 'Okay. Let's strike.'

***

Banners have been prepared. It's clear what people spent their day working from home doing. No wonder the seconds nose-dived. Outside the office door, I hold up my sign. It's not the most imaginative there, but it is concise: *Stop IMAtech!*

Around a hundred people work in the office, the so-called Powerhouse of Productivity now being anything but as we all stand outside the office, chanting *IMAtech unfair*! We stamp our feet and hold up our signs and wait for the board to arrive.

Rain threatens but it stays away, the dark clouds making the air stuffy and uninspiring. Passersby give us all a cheer, cars honk, and the atmosphere grows into something euphoric, something alive. I fizz with anticipation, that we're finally doing something, that we're going to make a change for the good. Together, maybe we stand a chance.

Cars pull up, chauffeur-driven Bentleys with blacked-out windows that we all know belong to the board. We face the cars, still chanting, pointing our signs in their direction.

Stop IMAtech! IMAtech unfair!

The cars drive on, no board member dares show their face. I film the cars driving away, ready to show Katarina later. This will prove to her a protest can work, that blood isn't needed.

Despite the noise, my usual headache dissipates into nothing as all the tension leaves me. My back isn't hunched, my feet don't hurt. I accept colleagues' hugs and my lungs inflate more than they have in so long.

We're doing this. We are going to make a difference.

Chapter Fifty-Five

Katarina

I laugh so hard when I see Layla's video message. Bless her for thinking that little demo will do anything besides get her the sack. Isobel paid with her life. An eye for an eye is all that can be done.

Stopping IMAtech would be great. Making those who impose it suffer will be the icing on the cake. I lick my lips. I have a sweet tooth and that icing is all that can satisfy me.

I haven't bothered opening the bar. Half the lights are off, and the only sound comes from the gentle hum of the fridges. The sale is going through, and my wind-down jobs consist of stock-takes and cleaning up, ready to hand the keys over. The bar across the road looks a lot more fun and I decide to apply for a job there instead. No way am I going to work under Adam Ward's rule.

A knock on the front door grabs my attention. I look up to see Adam Ward smiling at me. The sort of smug smile that makes me want to throw up.

I walk over. 'What?' I say through the window.

He leans in so close his breath fogs the glass. At least that covers up his face a bit.

'Well,' he says, 'it's a couple of days until I get the keys, but I thought I could have another look around the place.'

'We're closed.'

'Oh, come on. It's basically mine anyway.'

I hesitate, then think, why not? I still need him on my side until Friday. I can string him along. It's easy to play the bitch and the hard-to-get attitude is clearly something the spoiled brat gets off on. I open the door and give him a wide berth as he enters, taking overly large strides, walking like he's a foot taller than he is.

'Nice,' he says. 'Getting the place all ready for the handover.'

'Yep,' I say, and get back to work counting the bottles of spirits.

'I'm thinking of leaving it closed all week, then doing a big opening night, inviting loads of important people. No alcohol. I'm envisioning a health bar, all high vitamin, visually appealing drinks and snacks. Not just another bar serving the same old booze. This will be a new direction for social lives. What do you think?'

'It's your bar. Do what you want.'

'Oh, come on, sweetheart—'

I recoil at the pet name.

'—I want you to be involved here. There's a promotion in it for you.'

The big picture, I remind myself. My plan could be ruined now if Adam's mad at me. I stand a little straighter and meet his gaze. 'A promotion, you say?'

'Of course. Manager. I wouldn't trust anyone else. A pay rise too, of course.'

I allow one side of my lips to lift up, hinting at a smile. 'I suppose you'll be celebrating here Friday when you get the keys.'

'That would be a good idea. I'll get some food sent over. You can make some of those mocktails,' he says, looking at the drinks menu on the wall.

I wonder how long Adam's sobriety will really last now that he owns a bar, then remember I don't need to wonder. I can count the hours.

'Sure,' I say. 'Mocktails it is.'

His smile looks more like a sneer. For every step closer he makes, I take one back. The guy is a weed. I have no fear of him making an advance. I could beat him off as easily as I could a kitten, but that doesn't mean I want to be anywhere near the leech. He takes a stool, then sits at the bar as I make him one of the mocktails, an alcohol-free cosmopolitan, complete with umbrella garnish and fruit.

'I know you think I'm buying this bar just to win you over,' he says. 'But I want to build something without my dad's help. No one will ever respect me for taking over WIT. I didn't even want it. I always wanted my own company, that I started, you know, off my own back. That's what this bar represents to me. My own challenge.'

Bought with the money your dad handed to you. I don't say this. I need him to trust me a bit. I pick up a glass to polish and I listen. Always listening.

Adam rambles on like he's pissed, though he's articulate enough to prove he's sober. There's just something men find when sitting at a bar, a member of staff idling away on the other side. It's almost equivalent to a therapist's couch. He doesn't stop talking. He goes on and on about his relationship with his father, his desire to prove himself, how hard his dad was on him.

All of what Adam says, I already know. I've only met the guy a handful of times and researched him, but everything I've found out about him is the truth. His relationship with Peter was strained, but he didn't hate him. There's no relief that he's dead. Adam is never going to confess to killing his father because he didn't do it. And it dawns on me that if I know this, Harry does too. He must. Even someone with the intelligence of a marrow can tell that Adam didn't kill Peter.

'Sometimes I even doubt it was suicide,' he says. 'People hated him. I'll bet it was that woman at WIT. She wanted to screw him, but then kicked off when he tried. At least she's out the picture now before she can try to cause trouble. That's karma for you.'

A glass cracks in my hand, and I place it back down, slowly, fighting the tension brewing inside. I pick up another, needing to fiddle with something, to busy my hands with something, or else I'll wring his neck.

It dawns on me, bit by bit, as Adam continues to talk, clearly liking the sound of his own voice. Harry's motivation has nothing to do with Peter's death. Harry just wants Adam out of the way. In the same way Adam tries to claim whatever Harry has for his own, Harry is doing just that. An old best friend rivalry that's being taken one big step further.

Chapter Fifty-Six

Layla

I'm buzzing after the first strike-day, energised and the most
alive I've been in ages. All the staff too, without their tailor-made
supplements, have some energy for activities other than just
sitting at a desk. Finally, I'm part of something bigger than
myself. Such action is greater than the sum of its parts. My voice
is hoarse from chanting and my legs sore from standing all day,
but I don't care. I pick up a takeaway on my walk home, eating
it on the tube, then when I get home, I go to bed straight away
and sleep more soundly than I have in weeks.

The next day, I'm on the picket line again. Through the
window, the collective seconds tally nosedives further. The hormone levels are off the charts. IMAtech is failing. There's no way
we can make up that time.

There has been no email or even a visit from the board. The
strike, as far as I can tell, has been completely ignored. Concerns
about money and my job niggle at me. I chant less loudly than
I did the day before, shying away from my colleagues' contact
and hold my sign a little lower.

'Maybe we should have some Texi to help with our focus on the strike?' one man says.

There's temptation in the eyes of some, but the resounding vote is no. We will not give in to Baxter Pharma.

My arms ache, my feet hurt again. Could WIT sack all of their employees? I still have so much to do, programming, I never even finished off one of the characters after I had to delete everything. WardZone's release date has already been announced. What will WIT do to counter this action? They can't have an AI designed and ready to take over straight away.

I check my phone. My work email inbox remains ominously empty.

Joel called the press yesterday and told them about the strike. Our chants continue as we await reporters. I imagine Jan Novac panicking and phoning around all his contacts, threatening them with that gruff voice of his, sweat glistening on his broad forehead as he yells and voices his demands, making sure they don't come.

Maybe he has done that, as no press arrives.

The staff shrug it off, although the euphoria we all felt the day before simmers down. Heads hang lower, hands are in pockets more than air-punching and clapping.

'No matter,' Joel says. 'We've all got phone video footage. We'll post everywhere on social media. That's more powerful than the news these days anyway. One viral video, that's all we need.'

I recall the last viral video and admire his optimism. 'Sure,' I say. 'We can all post something.'

The day ends with no press turning up, no article even in the free papers. Our videos circulate but no viral reaction.

Katarina will say, I told you so, that a strike won't avenge or help anything. I hate it that she may be right, but even more, I hate the unease that inches over me.

Katarina will still want action, and since the strike hasn't delivered any sort of result yet, my throat tightens as I try to imagine what sort of action she will take.

When I get home, she's out, thankfully, I can't face her now. I can't see her smug *I told you so* face. She'll hint at her next move. She'll no doubt let me know she intends to do more. She'll fill my stomach with twists and knots and dread as she plots and I worry.

I sit at the table, pick through what little food I have and try to shut her away, her intentions, her past actions, her voice that gets under my skin. I try to lock all of it in my mental cupboard of bad memories as if they never happened, as if Katarina never existed. And then, for a moment, I can imagine I really am rid of her.

Chapter Fifty-Seven

Katarina

I've spent an hour prepping alcohol-free cocktails for Adam and the board. The sickly-sweet smell of fruit is giving me a headache, and I recoil my nose more than I usually do from the stench of spirits and Red Bull. The caterers deliver hors d'oeuvres that I lay on the tables after snacking on a few myself. There are no spirit bottles in sight. I've taken every bit of alcohol downstairs to the cellar, adding to the horde of overstock.

The buyout happened so quickly, I barely even said goodbye to Davina. She pretty much skipped out the door with a big smile on her face. *Good for her.*

Tonight, Harry, Adam, and the others are to come in and celebrate his buying of the bar. Just a private party for those few board members. A way for Adam to show off. Perfect.

The GHB is hot in my pocket. One pipette is enough to knock out a horse, according to what I read online. I have five. One for each board member, minus Harry's parents, since they're sure not to come. And with the syrupy flavour of the drinks I serve, they'll never know.

Diego arrives first and tilts his chin up to look down his stupidly small nose at me. Whoever did his rhinoplasty should give him a refund. It makes him look like a pug. He hands me his coat and parades around the place with his squashed face in a mixture of disgust and confusion. We don't exchange pleasantries. Diego makes no effort, and I certainly can't be bothered. I'm saving all of my false charm for when Adam arrives.

I crank the music up a little louder, an old trance playlist, just to drown out Diego's silent disdain. I laugh to myself at how much I despise Diego and all of them. Stretching out my fingers, I imagine I'm a spider and this is my web.

Harry arrives shortly after, to my relief. Being alone with Diego for too long comes with the risk of knife injury or strangulation. I'm already cracking my knuckles when Harry, all smiles, comes through the door. He wraps his arms around me and gives me a kiss. Perhaps it's sweet he isn't as snobby as Diego. Besides saying I should take a job at his parents' company, he's never even hinted at bar work being too low on the pecking order for the likes of him up there on his throne of familial wealth. He probably enjoys how much it likely annoys his parents. I'm the one way he's able to rebel.

Parin and Jan arrive next, and I'm pleased I have so much of the drug. Jan looks like he'll need the full horse's dose and then some. Parin, not so much. He'll probably pass out if he so much as stubs his toe.

Then Adam enters, face plastered with that weasel grin of his, and I'm relieved I saved all of my glib welcomes for him. If I hadn't, I'd likely smash one of the glasses over his horrible face.

They all shake hands, then partake in the usual banter towards Harry and his overbearing parents. They each help themselves to some hors d'oeuvres and I pour drinks into the fanciest glasses I have, topping them off with overly showy garnishes before adding a generous splash of the secret ingredient in my pocket.

A little ping on a glass and Adam asks them to raise their glasses. 'To future endeavours,' he says, and they all drink.

Their tight-lipped smiles give no hint they can taste anything besides the fruit and soda. They continue conversing for a while as my heart pauses. For a moment, I wonder if I got something wrong. Maybe too small of a dose, or maybe the fruit counteracts the effects. They laugh haughtily, then drink some more.

'And to Peter,' Parin says. 'A great man who clearly produced a great son. Peter was a man who said what he thought, what everyone else is too scared to say. That's a tough legacy, Adam.'

'One I hope to live up to,' Adam replies and gives me a nod.

'Here, here,' they all say and drink again, and I grit my teeth.

'Fucking quotas for women on boards, rights for queers, for people who went to shit schools,' Jan says. It's the most I've ever heard him say, and my heart races as I worry again I've gotten the doses all wrong. 'Peter was the one voice of reason in the madness that is the modern world.'

'Exactly,' Diego says. 'This fucking country wants to abolish tried-and-tested methods to pander to the minority. We owe it to Peter to do our bit to ensure the country doesn't tank because of this stupidity. IMAtech is this country's saving grace. Making sure that whatever stupid quotas they come up with next, the workforce gets the job done.'

'With Baxter Pharma helping anyway we can,' Harry says, and for once, the others don't even mock him.

As I listen, my hatred for all of them soars, and there isn't a doubt in my mind I'm doing the right thing.

Five minutes drag on forever, and my chest tightens, while my hands go clammy. I check the time and it's been ten minutes. My body temperature escalates and I fan myself with my top, busy preparing more drinks with shaky hands, trying to look innocent and attentive.

I catch the moment Adam goes cross-eyed, his words ejecting in a spittle-laced slur. Parin puts his arm out to ask if he's all right but misses and topples over instead. Harry's eyebrows knit together. Half his face slopes down as he tries to turn to look at me, hitting the deck before he's turned ninety degrees, landing right on top of Diego, who's already unconscious and dribbling.

Jan stays standing for one terrifying minute. I eyeball him, willing him to go down. He takes a step closer, his mouth moves, but only a grunt comes out—no change there—and he bares his teeth, then reaches for me. His reddening face turns purple, and his body follows his arm forward, then down with a loud thump.

Ouch. I wince.

I stare at all of them for a second, my heart buzzing with excitement, then remember that I can't waste any time. I lock the front door, then crouch next to each of them and squirt a bit more of the drug into their mouths for good measure. Jan's nose is gushing blood, while Harry's head must have clipped the skirting board. There's a gash down his forehead, creating a red puddle on the floor.

I take them each by their ankles, dragging them, their already injured heads thumping on every step as I pull them down the stairs, leaving a trail of blood behind.

I dose Jan again, sure he's the only one likely to rouse prematurely. Once they're all piled in the cellar, I catch my breath, stretch out my arms that are shaking from exertion, then allow myself a moment to appreciate the beautiful sight of it. Several hundred billion in net worth, all piled up like rag dolls in the cellar. I wet my lips.

Harry's lying in an awkward position, one arm twisted beneath him, his legs bent. I run my hands through his hair, his head wound mixing blood in with his hair product. Such a shame. He really is a stunner.

From my pocket, I retrieve all the cocaine I have collected during my time working in Little London and I blow a large bump up Adam's nose, then leave the rest on the freezer along with a straw. Just in case the rest of them fancy some.

After, I take their phones and chuck them towards the stairs, move the barrel away, then shut the door, locking them all in.

Chapter Fifty-Eight

Layla

I'm sitting at the kitchen table when Katarina arrives home. I haven't seen her in a few days, and I jump as she opens the door, then stare as she walks through to wash her bloodied hands in the kitchen sink.

'Are you going to explain?' I ask.

A dark smile forms across Katarina's lips, and her eyes shine even darker. It's like the dream I had, the one where Katarina's pin-sharp with black holes for eyes.

'I'd rather show you,' Katarina says. 'You'll be pleased this time.'

My face falls. I turn my head away from her and towards the window. My reflection is as pale as a ghost, any hint of colour drained. I wipe my clammy hands on my trousers as I stand and follow. There's no fight in me to resist, and not knowing would be even worse. At least she's telling me rather than waiting until I find out for myself. That's a small mercy. Katarina leads the way, as she always seems to, with me a mere shadow trailing behind.

We walk in silence. I have no ability to speak. Katarina's taken so much from me, why not my voice too? The dark grin she wears remains steadfast for the entire walk. Her strides are confident, not the slightest wobble in her killer heels. The evening is cold, and she doesn't even wear a coat, preferring to show off her skin instead. Yet she doesn't shiver. Her icy exterior has a volcano of heat underneath, ready to erupt.

My mind mulls over a thousand possibilities. Perhaps by the time we get to wherever we're going, whatever mess Katarina has created will have cleaned itself up. Perhaps it really won't be that bad.

I can kid myself sometimes.

I should go home, ignore her, run away from whatever carnage she's created, but my legs follow as if I'm a puppet. She has me on a string and is pulling me all the way there, the gravity of her an inescapable force.

We arrive at the bar, its windows blackened and a closed sign on the door.

'Why are we at the bar, Kat? It's closed.'

'I'll open up.'

'I don't fancy a drink right now.' That's a lie. I fancy a bucket full, but I need a clear head.

Katarina's keys jingle, some cheery sound as she unlocks the doors, then relocks them once we're inside.

The place smells clean, like bleach, similar to how work smelled the day after she painted those big words in blood on the walls. Plates of barely touched snacks lay on the counter.

Pitchers of juice beside them. Five half-drunk glasses stand on a table.

We walk down the stairs and I note little blood spots on each, a smear where a cloth had rubbed over the step down the middle. A half-arsed attempt at cleaning, which means it was probably Katarina who did the cleaning.

At the bottom of the stairs is the cellar, cool and damp, a door with a barred window shutting off one end.

'Go ahead, take a look,' Katarina says.

My eyes are wide, but I'm stuck to the spot. My body shakes as a trickle of sweat traces its way from my neck down my spine.

'Go on,' she says.

I step forward, swallow in my gravelly throat and wish I'd helped myself to a glass of whatever's in the jugs upstairs. I jump a foot backwards as a face appears in the window, then bangs against the door.

'Fuck's sake, Kat. What the fuck are you doing? Let us out right now!' Harry Baxter, wild with rage, is at the window. Blood smears one side of his face. His words come out slurred like he's had too much to drink, his eyes unfocused. 'Look.' He's closer to the window now. There's no glass, just metal bars. I can smell his syrupy breath. 'I got the confession. It's all done! Adam's going mental back here. There's bottles of spirits he's necking. He's totally lost it. I've never seen him like this.'

I want to look away, but my gaze stays fixed. Harry's there, injured, locked away. The sound of his voice is deafening in the space, the echo hammers at my ears.

'It's probably the four Texi I put in his drink,' Katarina says. Her voice is so calm and reserved. 'That and the cocaine is a pretty messy combination. It'll keep him awake though. I want him conscious for all of this.'

'What? Four!' Harry's voice shoots up a few octaves and I jolt back again. 'That's way too many. Why would you do that?'

'You're saying he confessed? To killing Peter?' Katarina asks, her voice cool and monotone.

'Yeah. Yeah, he did. Now let us out. I hate small spaces.'

Katarina steps closer, her nose only inches away from the bars. Harry's hand reaches but the holes are too tight, and he can only fit a couple of fingers through. Stepping on tiptoes and keeping a hand's width away, she peers in. 'Weird. Because why would he confess when he didn't do it? I killed Peter.'

My chest tightens and the room spins. Did she just say that?

Harry's head jerks back, his unfocussed eyes now looking straight at her. 'What? Shut up. No you didn't.'

Katarina doesn't flinch or waver. She folds her arms, and her pursed lips twitch up into a sneer. I look at her, and a chill inches up my spine. It's a chill of fear and disgust, but not of surprise. Katarina's capable of anything, and in my bones, I know she's telling the truth.

Chapter Fifty-Nine

Katarina

It was the reason Harry came to the bar that first time. I'm sure of it. Peter recommended the place, since I had been so nice to him when he showed up. It was a quiet night. Peter Ward was a few decades older than the usual customers, and even stranger, he was alone. I recognised him from the media articles, though I didn't let on. He was even weedier than his son, a slight frame for someone so overbearing. He dressed like he'd been dropped in from the 90s. His suit was the kind of cut that's obsolete these days, his aftershave too, usually consigned to the past.

Traditional. That was how I profiled him.

And traditionally, men thought they owned the world.

I poured him an Old Fashioned, a cocktail choice that made me laugh with the irony, and Peter shared in my amusement.

'What can I say,' he said. 'I like what I like.'

I know that look in a man's eyes. What he liked was me.

Gold diggers. I've seen so many during my time working in Little London. I know how to play the part. Flattery, make this old git think he was someone I idolised, despite his seventy-year-old arse and drooping jawline. I could tell he wasn't bad looking once, many years ago. Stress and time had etched their course through his hairline and hung off him, tugging heavily on his skin.

Still, I could see past all of that. A plan was forming. I leaned against the bar and listened to his gripes, moaning about his son, how useless he was, how he wanted Adam to stand on his own two feet instead of relying on taking over Peter's role in the company. I kept quiet for a while, listening, the occasional nod to let him know I hung off his every word.

'Talk to your son,' I eventually said. 'You're obviously a good father.'

'I should. Soon. I will.'

I diverted the conversation towards more light-hearted topics to make him smile and relax. His shoulders dipped, his face brightened, and a spark of desire glinted through his eyes. My giggles were so girlish and flirty, I hated myself. I touched the nape of my neck when I laughed, and bent forwards so he could see down my top. I stroked his arm and complimented him. 'Oh, what a great man you are, how smart you are,' blah blah blah until I had to hide my retching behind a bottle of beer.

Testosterone is a predictable hormone, and every flutter of my eyelashes and every lick of my lips had him becoming putty in my hands. I just had to make him wait.

'Come home with me,' he said. 'I'd like to show you my home. There're some artworks there I think you'd like.'

I didn't mention his wife, his age, or anything that might put him off. I played the coy, hard-to-get role, to keep him begging.

'I just couldn't. I am not that sort of girl.'

He left his number. 'I think you're the exact kind of girl I like. Call me when you change your mind.'

The arrogance of him made my toes curl.

It was a few days later when I called him, after Harry and Adam came into the bar. Despite the hour, Peter answered my call immediately and sent a car to collect me. He was up late, some work stress I had to listen to and nod along to for an unpalatable amount of time.

'Sorry,' he said. 'You didn't come here to listen to me moan. I know why you came.'

I flicked my hair over my shoulder and pushed my bosom forward. 'You need to get this off your mind first. Maybe write him a note. You don't have to give it to him. It's a good way to cleanse the mind though.'

'Aren't you a clever girl.'

I bit my bottom lip. 'I'll wait for you on the balcony.'

Desire tore through his features as I walked away. Such desire makes the most powerful men weak. From the balcony doors, I watched as the pen sat idle in his hand for a moment, then he began to write. Just three words were enough before I banged on the glass and blew a kiss.

He dropped the pen and came outside to join me. I pushed him against the wall, pressing my toned body up against his feeble one. His mouth on mine was akin to off whisky. I held him close, before tossing him over the balcony like he was a bag of rubbish. He clawed for me, and there was a millisecond where I thought he might latch on and take me too. But I freed my arm and shoved him harder. His legs clipped the guttering and hurtled him around. He didn't even have time to scream. The slightest gurgle was his last word before I heard the glorious sound of his head smashing into the patio.

Chapter Sixty

Layla

From behind the door is the sound of smashing glass, a raging Adam Ward cursing and swearing, mingled with the occasional loud inhales of snorting lines.

'I left some extra cocaine in there for him,' Katarina says to me with a wink. 'Just to be nice.'

There's a groan, what sounds like a wall being thumped. My eyes bulge, but I don't dare step closer. I flinch at every sound. Every hair on my body stands on end as my heart races.

Katarina killed Peter Ward. My housemate, my one friend, really is a killer.

Harry's still at the window, tears cutting rivers through the blood smearing his face. Every now and then, he goes cross-eyed, as if lost in disbelief, then his coordination comes back, and he glares with eyes like daggers at Katarina.

'Why, Kat?' he eventually says. 'Why'd you kill Peter?' His voice lacks the coolness of his eyes. Each syllable is punctuated with him swallowing back tears.

'For what he did to Antonia. The old pervert. Not to mention the shitshow that's WIT. His support of the Clarity Directive. Do I need to go on? The man is better off dead.'

'Antonia?' I say. 'You knew Antonia?'

Katarina doesn't answer. She turns her head and smiles at me, and of course I know why. It seems we have the same taste in women. It shouldn't surprise me that she got in there first, just like with Isobel.

I look over at Harry and startle because he's eyeballing me. Those now sharply focused eyes are staring straight at me. I step back. He can't get to me. I know the door must be locked. Katarina would've made sure. But he glares at me as if he's about to eat me alive. He must recognise me from the night I spent at his.

'Talk to me, Kat,' he says without breaking eye contact. 'Tell me what the fuck is going on. Just let us out and we can talk.'

'I'm. . . I'm sorry,' I say. 'I'm sorry Katarina killed Peter. She shouldn't have done that.'

From the corner of my vision, Katarina smirks all the more.

'What?' Harry says, still staring straight at me. 'What do you mean? Why the fuck did you kill Peter? Just let us out.'

In the window, Adam appears, equally bloodied, his whole face almost as red, his eyes wide and savage. 'You killed my dad. You fucking whore! I'm going to kill you!'

Again, he's looking right at me.

'It. . .it was Katarina,' I say, 'there.' I point to her in the corner, where she stands very still, with the same relentless smirk spread across her picture-perfect face.

'What are you pointing at?' Harry says. He lifts his hand to rub some blood from his eye. 'Look at me, Kat. What the fuck?'

I stare at Katarina. 'Well?' I say. 'Talk to him. This is your mess.'

Harry slams his fist against the bars. 'Who the fuck are you talking to?'

I jump, the sound of the bars ringing in my ears. 'I'm talking to Katarina.'

'What the fuck?' He slams his fist against the bars again.

'What?' My head is woozy as I struggle to understand. I knit my brows and glare at Katarina, at the image of her. It flickers, *she* flickers, as if on some old, dodgy television. I pull my head back. 'Kat?'

Katarina raises her eyebrows and shrugs. She flickers again. Streaked and grainy.

I blink and press the heel of my hands into my eyes. There are a few spots in my vision from the pressure afterwards and I sway on the spot. I turn and look at Harry, who still eyes me. Diego's face shares the window now, baring his teeth.

'This is why I fuck men,' Diego says, slurring more than the other two. 'See what women and their hormones do? Christ, Harry. Your parents need to pull some more strings and make those pills essential. No doubt this woman is all jacked-up on oestrogen or something. It's like *#behave* meant nothing! After all the good that did, these women are still fucking feral.' He narrows his eyes at me. 'Time of the month, is it love? I remember you now. You spilled coffee on me. You work in the office at WIT. Did you not tell Harry that?'

I blink again, slow and purposefully, then run my hands through my hair, tugging on the ends. 'Why would I tell Harry? I don't even know Harry, not really.' What did Katarina give them? They're all high, hallucinating, and confused.

Harry punches the bars again, then screams as his knuckles crack, the sound of jingling bottles coming from behind. 'What the fuck, Kat? We've been dating for weeks.'

'Layla,' Diego says. 'That's what you said your name was. Layla.'

'Yes,' I shout and nod. 'Thank you. I'm Layla. That's Kat.' I point to Katarina, where Katarina was, and I look that way. But now there's just a blank wall. I snap my hand back, my head and eyes jerk from side-to-side, searching the room. 'Kat?'

Her voice comes from behind and I whip my head around. There's no one there, just a haze, as if in a fog. I can't see her face. 'I never lied to you,' Katarina's voice says. 'You just refused to see. You shut the truth away.'

My breath shudders, my eyes still searching for the source of the voice. 'Kat, where are you? What truth?'

'Who are you talking to?' Harry shouts.

'Fuck's sake, Harry,' Adam says and cackles. 'Your girlfriend's a nut job.'

'You needed me,' Katarina says, from somewhere in the room, only not from anywhere—from inside my head. 'You imagined me because you needed me and everything I could do for you.'

'No. No.' I spin around, my hands go to my temples. 'That's ridiculous. You're real. I know you're real.'

'I'm what you needed. Everything you did, you needed me to take charge.'

Everything *I* did? I didn't do anything. The hands, the blood, Peter. No. No. I wouldn't do that. I am Layla Daley, a good person, a hard worker. I would never do such things. Katarina is the reckless one, the impulsive one. It was all Katarina.

'I was your scapegoat,' Katarina says, as if she can hear my thoughts and my denial. Her tone is so confident, so self-assured. So Katarina. 'Now it's time for you to take control.'

I look to the barred window, tilting my body away from it, away from the chaos that Katarina has made. I shake my head and my stomach twists with nausea. The faces in the window are all looking at me, at only me.

Because there's no one else in the room.

'You know what's going to happen,' Katarina says. 'You know because you planned it all.'

My skin prickles all over, every hair standing on end. My mouth moves, but no words come.

'You've shut those memories away, Layla. It's time to let it all out.'

Frozen to the spot, the room around me blurs as I search my memories, the ones I locked away. Behind the barrier I keep closed. There are bottles of spirits piled up in the cellar, locked up with the board members of WIT. The gas pipe that feeds the heating traces the ceiling, and it's leaking ever so slightly. I know this because Katarina planned it all. I can feel the coolness of the bottles in my hands from when they were placed there, can hear the clang of metal as I made a leak in the gas pipe, can feel the heaviness of the barrel I moved out of the way to make sure the door closed. I hear their heads thumping on the stairs as I dragged their unconscious bodies down to the cellar. I even feel the vibrations in my feet. I've experienced it all because Katarina had.

'No.' I whimper. 'No, please.'

'It's too late,' Katarina says. 'You know it's too late. It's how you wanted it. Remember, Layla. Feel your anger.'

I smell it then. Above the metallic tang of blood from their wounds and the bleach smell from the poor clean-up job. It mingles with the damp dungeon aroma of the cellar. Gas. The small leak Katarina created is condensing in the cellar. Any moment it will catch. The alcohol will add to it. They'll all burn alive.

'This is how you stop IMAtech,' Katarina says. 'This is how you get revenge. An eye for an eye.'

'Let us out of here now, you crazy bitch.' Jan's massive head takes up the entire window. A loud thump as he throws his weight against the door.

An eye for an eye. But there are ten eyes in there. Ten eyes belonging to five people. And none of them are worth a fraction of what Isobel was.

My vision clouds over, and my head throbs. My shallow breaths can't stop the room from spinning. I step back, stagger away from the anger in their faces, away from the flammable gas, away from the carnage, then turn and walk back up the stairs. There are eighteen steps up to the bar from the cellar. I know this because I have walked these steps so many times before.

I stare at the front door a moment as I consider leaving and saving myself. But then, there seems little point. I can't run from the repercussions. I sit at a table, the one nearest the door, and wait.

Chapter Sixty-One

Katarina

It's so obvious now you know.

I don't say this out loud. There's no need. I think it, pushing the thought into her mind too. I can feel it, her hatred, the reluctance in her acceptance. She knows this is the right thing to do, she's just having a hard time processing it all. I wanted to peel off one layer at a time, but this is a whole bunch at once.

Her pale face has been staring at the table for a while. I know she hears me. I know she can see me. I know because I can see and feel her.

Five of the wealthiest men in the country wiped out with one explosion. How can she not be delighted about that?

She's sitting so still and stiff. She's trying to hide from me, like she doesn't fully understand yet. I need her to acknowledge me. She has to accept this is the right thing to do.

I lean in close and speak out loud this time. 'This is what you wanted, Layla. In the deepest part of yourself. This is what you most desire. Remember all your thoughts, all that you wanted to see happen. All your dreams have come true.'

She sniffs. 'Is it? If you are me, that must be true.' She looks up now, her eyes searching my face. 'You're so clear. Not grainy anymore.'

'Good. I'm glad.' I take her hand. Her skin is cold. 'I'm so glad we're here together.' I sense her discomfort. She's rigid and knotted. 'They had this coming. All of them. If Adam Ward had looked at you properly, just once, he would have seen we're the same person. We are nothing to him. So he is nothing to us.'

She fidgets and swallows. 'So,' she says. 'You and Antonia?'

'Well, it was you and Antonia, really. She wanted to keep things out of work. Professional. She really liked you.'

'No. She really liked *you*.' She squeezes my hand a little tighter. 'You didn't kill her?'

'Of course not.'

'But the Texi. . .'

'Look in your bag.'

She does, her eyes widening as she removes the full pack of Texi, one tablet missing, just as it should be. 'I don't understand. . .'

'The empty one was just some rubbish you picked up. You're not a killer, Layla.'

Her eyes shine, a spark of relief. She gives a small nod. She's telling me she trusts me, and she's thanking me, I'm sure. 'And that viral video, the dodgy character art?'

'Yep. All us. It was good, wasn't it?'

She reaches for the jug of mocktail, then pours a glass. She stares into it for a while before looking up at me. As we make eye contact, her tears fall. 'Will it hurt?' she asks.

'Them? Probably not. It'll be quick.'

'And us?' Her glassy eyes are pleading, and I sense her acceptance.

I shrug and smile. 'Nothing we can't handle together.'

The blast comes moments later, sending us soaring into the air. For a brief and beautiful moment, we're flying, weightless, with not a worry in the world. When the flames shoot up from the cellar, I delight in their glow. For I know I'll see Isobel again soon.

Chapter Sixty-Two

Layla

The garish white light of the hospital dazzles me when I open my eyes. The pain doesn't hit until a moment later, then it comes in droves, like I am still on fire, like my flesh is still burning. I cry out.

A nurse comes to calm me. 'It's okay. You're safe,' the nurse says. 'You can have more for the pain.'

'No!' I say as I try to sit up. I'm hooked up to a drip from my non-bandaged arm. 'No drugs, please.' I don't want any. I want to think clearly. I need to know what's happening, even if that means pain.

'Your dad's here. Shall I send him in?'

I relax back down and my panic eases. 'Dad? How? Yes, please.'

The nurse leaves when I'm lying more comfortably, then my dad comes in, being pushed in a wheelchair by his neighbour, the great ogre of a man I know from my childhood. Their faces are both pale, radiating concern.

'Oh, darling,' Dad says as he reaches for me. He stands for a second, one arm hugging me, the other supporting himself on the bed frame. We stay like that for a second. My dad weeps, but my tears won't come, like the fire extinguished them all.

'My neighbour, Scott. You remember Scott? He drove me here. I had to come. Oh, thank God you're okay.'

I look at Scott and nod. Dad sits back in his wheelchair and holds my unbandaged hand. His warm and soft hand is so real, I know I must be alive.

'Are you in any pain, sweetheart?' he asks. 'Can we get the doctor to give you anything?'

'No. I can handle the pain.' It's hard to get my words out. I let go of his hand to take a cup of water from the side instead, then have a sip, holding it in my mouth before I swallow. It stings all the way down my scorched throat.

'They say you'll have some scars,' he continues. 'But that doesn't matter. You're as beautiful as you've always been.'

As beautiful as Katarina? The thought of her, of all that happened, hits me like another wave of pain. My face twists with confusion. I look around the room.

Katarina is nowhere.

'Sweetie, what's wrong?' Dad reaches for my hand again, squeezing it tighter. 'You understand where you are?'

I continue to scan the room, my eyes darting from corner to corner. 'I don't know, Dad. It was so awful. I'm so confused.' Where is she? Has she gone? I don't feel any different. I don't feel that I have her darkness in me.

'It was just an accident, sweetie,' he says. 'A gas leak. Nothing you could have done.'

A gas leak. Was that really it? My tears arrive then, streaming down my cheeks and my stomach convulses as I try to fight my sobs. Nothing I could have done? Is that what my dad really thinks?

'I just don't understand,' I say between sobs. 'I don't understand anything. I don't even know who I am anymore.'

'Oh, darling.' He strokes my wet cheek. 'Sure you do. You're my baby girl. You're my Isobel.'

Chapter Sixty-Three

Isobel

Isobel. That name hits me like a punch, winding me, halting my lungs. How can I be her?

'Sleep, Isobel. Get some rest,' he says, noting my pallor and quietness.

My dad's words hang in the air long after he's gone.

You're my baby girl. You're my Isobel.

I close my eyes, squeezing them tight. My memories are locked away in my mind safe. I visualise the key and unlock it.

I was down three hours on my IMAtech. I'd been taking Texi, but it still wasn't enough. My mind wandered too easily, whatever was going on away from my desk was more interesting than my work. I found conversations hard to follow, like a kid on sugar.

'How do you do it, Layla?' I asked as we lay in bed and I was already looking for something else to play with. I took a stress ball from the shelf and fiddled with it, then a scarf that I wrapped around my fingers, then fanned myself with the duvet. We were hot and sticky from our antics moments earlier. 'Your timekeeping,' I continued. 'My dad has forever moaned about mine. My mum, when she was alive, was always, "apply yourself, Isobel, concentrate, Isobel, get your head out the clouds, Isobel".'

'Well, forget that,' Layla said. Her voice was so soft and so kind. Always so kind. 'You're perfect as you are.'

I snuggled up to her then. 'I just wish I could be more like you.'

Layla stretched and yawned. 'On that note, I need to go. I do need some sleep tonight.'

I tightened my hug, wrapping my legs around her too and kissed her neck. 'Stay here. Join me for the anti-hunt march tomorrow.'

She looked at me with those eyes that were always so serious and warm. 'I really shouldn't.'

'Come on. You know you want to.' Every part of my skin that touched hers tingled, alive and sensitive.

'I find it hard to sleep here.' She fidgeted on the mattress, like she so often did.

'One more chance,' I pleaded. 'And if you don't have a good night's sleep, I'll never hassle you to stay again. We'll always go to yours.'

Layla smiled and kissed my forehead. 'Okay. I'll stay over. But I won't come on the march. I have time on IMAtech to make up as well.'

I gasped. 'You! You have minutes to make up?'

'Not many. You're clearly a bad influence though.'

I grinned, then kissed her on the mouth. I got up, walking to the kitchen to make hot chocolate. Layla just needed one good night's sleep, then she'd be used to staying over. Layla's place was so much farther away, worse bars and noisier. It would be better for us both if she got used to staying at mine.

I fetched a couple of mugs and put some milk on the stove. In Layla's mug, I put a sleeping pill. A mild one. One easy to buy without a prescription. Just to help her relax. For good measure, just to be sure, I added another one.

The next morning, we said groggy goodbyes, Layla saying her head felt foggy, but she needed to get home and catch up her IMAtech minutes. I forgot she'd driven, usually preferring to take the tube, but there were so many engineering works on the line, she'd taken her car.

I waved her off as she left early. Only, she never made it home.

After the anti-hunt march, I got the train home to my London flat. Katarina was, as always, there to hear all the gossip, keen to know how her influence had secured me the relationship of my dreams.

When the news story played, and Layla's face filled the screen, I tore in half. My heart ripped from my chest, shattered, and the world closed in around me as if I were dead and buried.

It should have been me.

The world was a better place with Layla Daley in it. All I did was make things messy and worse. My grief was instant, I already missed Layla more than I could ever comprehend.

The only thing that seemed natural was to become her.

Chapter Sixty-Four

Isobel

Katarina sits on the end of my bed. There's no dip that comes from her weight on the mattress. Did it used to be like that on the sofa at home too? I would hear her footsteps, feel her take my hand when she got close, her breath warming my face. She's the girl I admired from afar at school. I should have known she'd never really be my friend. That should have been more of a giveaway than the lack of indent on the furniture.

I can't free my brain of the image of her, here and now. She's pin-sharp, in hyperreal focus. That dark look of hers has been replaced with something all the more caring. Her hair shines in bouncy waves, never a strand out of place. A picture of perfection as always.

'It's so obvious now, you know,' she says. But it isn't. Not at all. 'You've always been Isobel. You just wanted to be someone else. You didn't think you were good enough, but you are. You always were.'

Like I wanted to be Katarina. But it's not the same. I can see Katarina, clear as day. Isobel is gone. 'I can't be Isobel,' I say. 'I don't know how. I don't remember.'

Katarina reaches for my hand. The touch is warm and soft, as real as my dad's. 'Sure you do. You've just shut her away. You tried to erase her, to punish her, to punish yourself. You just need to tune in to those memories.'

I squeeze my eyes shut. My watery vision when I open them again gives me no more clarity. 'I can't. I can't be her.'

'You'd claim that about being Katarina too, but there you go.'

But I am not Katarina. I mean, she may be a projection of me, but she's not me. She's the part I isolated. She's what I stripped away. She is separate from me.

My bandaged arm throbs like it's being prodded by a hot poker. The pain shoots all the way to my shoulder, my neck, and around my head. My vision fogs as every new reality dawns on me. The worst one hits just then. 'If I am not Layla, that means she's the one who's really dead.'

Katarina nods, then shrugs. 'Yeah. That really happened. Physically, she may be gone, but you've kept her alive.'

'If I am Isobel, if I accept that, then Layla will be really gone. There will be no more Layla Daley in the world.' Grief hits me like a tsunami and I choke on my tears. 'I can't. I can't be Isobel. I have to keep her away so Layla lives.'

'You don't have to choose, you know. No one is just one personality, not really. We're all a mix, all mongrels. Just accept that they're both part of you. We're all a part of you. Visualise Isobel and Layla, like you do me.'

I shake my head and wipe my eyes on the blanket. The riddles are too much. My head is too muzzy to accept any of this. 'I'm crazy. That's what this all means. I'm actually crazy.'

Katarina scoffs. 'Why? Because you adapt? Because you act differently with different people? Everyone does that. Everyone is faking it. Cosmetics, clothes, padded bras, bullshit job applications and laughing at jokes that aren't funny. Women have to change their appearance, their personality, and everything to suit partners and families and the general public. Women are always too much of something and not enough of something else. You're no different. Remember? You're incredibly ordinary.'

Ordinary people don't blow up buildings. Katarina's life lesson isn't working this time. She's not getting under my skin, probably because she is my skin. I glance out of the window at the night inching closer. I woke up yesterday as Layla Daley, a good worker, not a killer. Yet I'm going to bed a murderer.

Katarina eyeballs me with such sincerity I recoil. 'Revenge isn't murder.'

Katarina looks just like she did when she was sixteen. I remember her at school, popular, laughing, confident. She has the same haircut now, wears the same clothes, luckily fashion has swung back around. Her makeup is done in the same way. That lipstick, some colour they don't even make anymore. Heather Shimmer, I think it's called. Somehow, Katarina appears more mature. Her skin has lost its plumpness a little, and her eyes have hardened. My subconscious has added enough time to make the image plausible.

She looks just like I remember her. Just how Isobel remembers her.

But I don't feel like Isobel. Isobel had a contagious laugh, a way of not caring if she was late or behind. She cared about wildlife, knew what all the birds were, she could even identify a bird by its song.

As I lie in hospital now, I'm already worrying about my absence at work, if I locked the front door to my flat, and whether the police will want to talk to me. Isobel would have a hundred excuses already lined up. She'd forget her part in it. She'd shut that door.

How can something imaginary look so real? There's an opaqueness to Katarina, like she's in front of a green screen, a darker outline as if she's been coloured in. She has a presence like she's layered in front of everything else, like she's at the forefront of my mind.

I squint my eyes, rub them, but Katarina is still here.

'I wanted to be her,' I say, my chest burning with jealousy like I'm still fifteen years old. 'You, I mean, to be your friend. I just wanted a friend.'

'Well, now you have one.'

I almost chuckle at the irony. Katarina puts her hand over her mouth, fighting back her own laugh—because I want her to. I'm some psycho puppet master, and Katarina is my dysfunctional toy.

'A friend doesn't make their friend do such bad things,' I say, more solemn now. 'But then, you didn't make me a killer. I guess I just am one.'

Katarina arches backwards and stretches her arms out as if in a yawn. 'Meh. Never mind,' she says, so relaxed, she may as well be talking about a parking ticket, not murder. 'Those guys deserved it.'

The TV is playing the news in the corner. Adam Ward's face catches my attention, and the headline underneath reads: *Adam Ward, WIT CEO, dies in blast.* Adam's face is then replaced with Parin Shah, Diego Smith, and Jan Novac. Four people I killed.

I don't want to hear the news article, but Katarina does, and she reaches for the remote to turn the sound up. I see her hand hold the remote, my own appearing and feeling empty. I still can't believe it. I still don't believe Katarina isn't really here.

The sound of the TV fills the room.

Police are investigating possible insurance fraud gone wrong, since Adam Ward had recently purchased the bar for an inflated price. High levels of narcotics and alcohol were in his system. Adam Ward was known to be an addict, and he was likely a victim of his misadventure. Another member of staff at the bar, Isobel Harrison, was harmed in the blast. Her injuries are not thought to be serious. Harry Baxter, of Baxter Pharmaceuticals, survived but remains in a serious condition.

'Harry's alive,' I say, my jaw dropping.

'Well, that can't be good,' Katarina says, her tone laced with mischief.

'Don't,' I snap. 'Don't even think about it. Let me talk to him. He might not remember anything. Please, let's just give him a chance.'

Katarina studies my face for a moment, narrows her eyes, then huffs. 'Fine. But if there's any doubt, I'm going to shut him up.'

Chapter Sixty-Five

Isobel

Standing is hard. I'm attached to a drip. My left arm and left leg are wrapped in layers of bandages, and some of the skin up my neck has what looks like cling film stuck to it. There are wounds across my face, doused in some white cream. My hair is a mess; no surprises there. I wonder if Harry will even recognise me.

I drag my IV around and walk out of my room, down a ward, then towards the intensive care unit. Peering through the windows, I search the beds for Harry. He isn't there. That leaves me with both dread and relief. He's either dead or not critical or somewhere else. My heart rate picks up. I have to find him before Katarina. Before Katarina does something else bad.

Walking back down the ward, past some private rooms, I do a double-take as I realise it's him. His entire body is wrapped in bandages, half of his face too.

I step into the room, slowly, as if I'm approaching something dangerous. 'Harry?'

He can't turn his face, only his eyes move to me, and I step around.

'Harry? Oh, my God.'

A tear falls and adds to the wet streak down that side of his face.

'Come to finish me off, have you? Be my guest.' His voice rasps and he coughs.

'No,' I plead. 'No, please. I would never, I didn't—'

'Oh,' the word comes out like an attempt at a laugh. 'You're not her then. You're the other one. It's funny how you can look like her, but there isn't the slightest resemblance. I should have spotted it that night you turned up at the Ivy. I knew there was something weird about you. Like a twin. You're so different.'

I swallow, my face heating as I look at the floor.

'He deserved it anyway,' he says. 'Tell yourself that if you feel guilty. He may not have killed Peter, but he was evil. I'm sure he was trying to tank my family's company so he could buy it cheap. That's why he was trying to turn people against Texi.'

'Texi? Antonia?'

'That woman at WIT. Yeah, I'm sure that was him. Can't prove it, but I'm sure.'

Just like he was sure about Adam killing Peter. Somehow, this time, his theory makes more sense. My body arches forward. I want to shrivel away and disappear. My own worthlessness making me hollow. Antonia and Layla were both far better people than me. They should be here.

'I voted against it, just so you know. Only after Katarina told me IMAtech sucked.'

'Against what?'

He wheezes and coughs some more. 'The drugs, to control everything. A pill for every feeling and emotion for every hour of the day, according to what IMAtech demands. To roll that out with IMAtech, not just at WIT. Maybe with Adam dead, it'll stop now. Maybe it won't. I don't know.'

Some movement in the edge of my vision alerts me to Katarina. She's in the doorway, hovering just a few steps away.

'You still need me,' she says.

I don't dare say a word back, aware of Harry being so close. My jaw tenses and I bite my lip.

Katarina continues. 'We need to be sure. We need to take down every board member of every company who wants IMAtech. You know someone needs to stop these corporate giants from controlling the world. And we need to stop the Clarity Directive for Antonia. For everyone.'

'I really liked her, you know,' Harry says with a sniff. 'She was different. Fun. Not pretentious. She was just, I don't know. . .exciting. I thought she was a good person.'

I still keep quiet, yet Katarina steps closer. She's right next to his bed now, but see-through, like a ghost. I'm resisting her. I can stop letting her in.

'Is she gone forever?' he asks.

I glimpse upwards then and see the sadness in his face. 'I. . .I don't know.'

He looks me up and down. 'You're as pretty as her, you know. I don't know how it works in your mind. But if that was the reason she appeared, then she didn't have to.'

My lips twitch, not quite a smile, but almost. 'Thanks.'

'I know you're not her. I don't blame you.'

My shoulders hunch and my insides hollow out. It's the kindest thing he could've said. I look at his drip bag and wonder how much morphine is in there.

'I don't blame her either. Not really. I guess she did what she felt she had to do.'

He's high, talking nonsense. He must be.

'I'm still on the board at WIT,' Harry says. 'IMAtech is wrong. Katarina tried to tell me. I should have listened. I'll do what I can to stop it.'

An ally. From the inside. That's what I've needed all along.

'You don't have time for this bullshit,' Katarina says. 'He's talking crap. He's high on painkillers. Of course he blames you. We need to put an end to this now.'

Do we? Katarina's ways are fast, explosive, literally. Everyone is always in such a rush. Harry says he wants to help. I, *we,* owe him that chance.

The window on the other side of his bed has a view of the gardens outside the hospital. A patch of lawn, a few trees. Outside, blackbirds sing. I know their call. The starlings too.

I can try to stop WIT, and to protest against the Clarity Directive. I don't have to behave in the way those men want, but I don't have to misbehave like Katarina. I can do this my way. One step at a time. It may be slower, but it's the right way.

The image of Katarina flickers slightly, then fades. I take a deep breath, my skin tingling all over, the pain from my burns barely registering. That rip I felt when I heard about the accident has been there ever since, but now it's gone, healed over. My headache has finally eased. I stand a little straighter and smile, knowing I'm good enough. That I am capable. I don't need to be anyone else to achieve my goals. I can stop IMAtech. Because I fight for what is right.

I am Isobel.

A note from Emma

Thank you so much for reading Be Her. If you enjoyed it, please leave a review on Amazon or Goodreads. The QR code above will take you to the amazon page to leave a review. For small authors like myself, reviews are our bread and butter, and they allow other readers to discover books they'll love.

The sequel, Free Her, is out now. With all three personalities sharing one body, are Layla and Isobel strong enough to keep Katarina under control? With the Clarity Directive still in force, do they even want to control her?

Maybe they think the best way to fix this broken world is to set Katarina free.

Find out in the sequel, Free Her.

A short story prequel, See Her, is featured in the thriller anthology, The Secrets of Lilypond Lane. See Her explores Katarina's character and we see how she was when Layla admired her at school. You can check it out on Amazon now!

You can find me on all the main socials and feel free to get in touch. I love hearing from readers!

I am a British author, splitting my time between the UK and Italy. I love the snow, mountains, dogs, and all things outdoors. This book was written while I was living in a converted cow shed in the middle of nowhere. As amazing as peace and quiet can be, there is a part of me that misses the hustle and bustle of city life.

Emma's other works

Degrees of Freedom. When Harriet takes a job looking after Oliver, an android who looks just like a six-year-old boy, her aim is to earn enough money to leave her wealthy and abusive husband and start a fresh. But she wasn't aware Oliver would be so lifelike, and didn't expect him to fill the void in her traumatic life.. They develop such a close bond that Oliver isn't merely a robot to her. She sees him as a real boy — one she's grown to love as her own son.

As the job contract comes to an end, Harriet is faced with a difficult decision: return Oliver to the company that developed him, or risk everything to keep him while fleeing her husband's wrath.

Harriet is forced to fight for a love that society insists isn't real, questioning not only her humanity, but what it means to be a mother.

The Eyes Forward Series. This best-selling series is set in a near-future Britain. The global population has risen too high, and each book in the trilogy sees the government use sinister methods to reduce it.

If you are in the mood for some more twisted dystopian, my first series, The Raft Series, is also available now. In this world, the entire country has been sterilised and all non-human life made extinct. But poison comes in many forms and Savannah Selbourne must discover the truth.

Acknowledgements

Be Her would not be in print without the help of my wonderful betas and critique partners. Thank you to Maggie, Mitra, Allison, Danica, Emily, Tara . . . and I am sure I have forgotten someone! Their time and honest feedback made this book what it is today. Thank you also to my editor Shannon K. O'Brien, for being so incredibly thorough, and Natasja Smith for her proofreading skills.

Thanks especially to my partner, John, for giving me the space and time I need to write, for his support, patience, and encouragement.

And thank you for reading it.